LAST GLEAMING

Love and Death in the Age of Pandemic

Books by Ray Dan Parker

The Tom Williams Saga
Unfinished Business: Retribution and Reconciliation
Fly Away: The Metamorphosis of Dina Savage
Pronounced Ponce: The Midtown Murders
Last Gleaming: Love and Death in the Age of Pandemic

**For more information
visit:** www.SpeakingVolumes.us

LAST GLEAMING

Love and Death in the Age of Pandemic

Ray Dan Parker

SPEAKING VOLUMES, LLC
NAPLES, FLORIDA
2024

Last Gleaming: Love and Death in the Age of Pandemic

Copyright © 2024 by Ray Dan Parker

All rights reserved. No part of this book may be reproduced or transmitted in any form or by any means without written permission.

The characters in this novel, the events, and the settings are all fictional, except for limited references to historical characters and events whose sole purpose is to establish a background for this story. Any other resemblance to real persons, alive or dead, are purely coincidental and unintended by this author.

ISBN 979-8-89022-230-5

I dedicate this in memory of a great author and wonderful friend, Will Ottinger. Without his patience and advice, I would never have had the success I've enjoyed as a writer.

Acknowledgments

I want to thank my agent, Nancy Rosenfeld, for her untiring efforts on my behalf and to my friends Jim, Cole, Jerry, Judy, Bill, Mel, Arthur and William, who have contributed so much to this process.

Prologue

West Midtown

Atlanta
September 18, 2019

Garth Braithwaite pulled his SUV into the driveway of his West Midtown home and pressed the garage door opener, revealing a wall of boxes. He'd brought them with him from California two years earlier. *I've got to unpack this shit or get rid of it,* he thought. Leaving his car out front would only give his pissy neighbors something else to complain about.

Living so close to Georgia Tech allowed Braithwaite the convenience of coming home for lunch, an occasional break from long hours of biomedical research. He retrieved his book bag from the back seat, thinking he might get a little stress relief from the latest online game he'd discovered . . . or perhaps from some porn.

The biochip design had proved challenging. Braithwaite's colleague, Sean O'Meara, had the patience of a monk, but his funding sources had deadlines. Braithwaite's offshore clients worried him the most.

His mind drifted back to his days at Cal Tech and the beautiful co-eds strolling the campus. How he would've loved to have recruited them to assist in his current work, but a single mistake had cost him that opportunity. Now, he would have to settle for research subjects who made a professional virtue of discretion.

As he stepped into his newly furnished living room, he froze, thinking he'd heard a soft noise. *Probably just the air conditioner.*

Then he turned. The stranger beside the bookcase stood motionless, his expression impassive, almost apologetic. Then Braithwaite saw the gun, his own gun.

"Oh shit!" would be his final words.

* * *

A point of pride for Steven Saldano had been that never, in his brief but lucrative career, had he killed anyone . . . *that is, until now*. He'd been *so* smart, he thought, casing his targets, determining when they'd be away, showing up in an unmarked van disguised as a repair man, never taking anything his victims could later trace. What he did get, cash, electronics, jewelry, silver, he sold through a single fence, Simon Wilhoite. *Why did I take Braithwaite's goddamned laptop and phone? What could have possessed me?*

Saldano closed his eyes for a moment, thankful he'd worn latex gloves. He knew the police could trace DNA from a single strand of hair. *But with all the cum stains in that place I needn't worry about that.* For good measure, he removed the batteries from the laptop and phone, not sure if the cops could trace them.

He crouched in the corner of his fifteenth-floor apartment and ran a hand through his shock of black hair, staring for the last time at the luxurious furniture and paintings, rented for the sole purpose of impressing the young women he brought home from local bars. His leased Porsche sat parked downstairs in his assigned spot. Now he'd have to leave it all behind. *How do I do that without arousing attention?*

When Wilhoite hired him for the Braithwaite job he mentioned a client and a list of items the man wanted. Saldano had intended to camouflage his mission by stealing a few nondescript items.

Last Gleaming

How did I know the man would come home in the middle of the day? I should never have accepted this referral. It stunk from the beginning.

Unable to locate the items Wilhoite's customer requested, Saldano instead grabbed the first objects of value he saw. *How could I be so stupid? These are easily the most identifiable things I could have taken. What do I do with them now?*

Snapping out of it, Saldano sat at his antique desk and fired off an email to his landlord saying he'd be out of town for several weeks and would pay the next month's rent in advance. The Porsche could remain in the parking deck until a repo man came to get it.

By the time anyone missed him, Saldano would be long gone and living under a new name. A second missive, addressed to his latest girlfriend, informed her, as gently as he could manage, that he'd found someone else and wished her a happy life.

Saldano would have to wait a long time before returning to the only profession he'd ever known. He needed a while to think. He couldn't risk getting caught. Before going underground, he'd collect the money Wilhoite owed him . . . and maybe a little extra for his trouble.

In the meantime, he needed another place to stay. He'd find a cheap apartment in a rough neighborhood and pay for it in cash. He couldn't risk getting a car yet. He'd have to use public transportation, when he could, and take a cab when necessary. From his safe he removed his remaining cash and a stack of Krugerrands he could sell once he settled in somewhere else. He stashed them in the hidden compartment of a battered suitcase and threw in a few old clothes.

Before leaving, he stared out at the downtown skyline and southeastward toward the Atlanta Federal Penitentiary, where his old man spent his final years. Saldano shuddered at the memory of his visits there as a child. *Whatever happens, I am not going to end up there. Once I clear up a few loose ends I'll head out west, LA perhaps.*

The visit to Wilhoite would wait. *No sense being hasty.* Saldano donned some old clothes and caught a bus in search of a cheap motel.

Chapter One

Last Gleaming

Smyrna, Ga.
SunTrust Park
September 18, 2019

Oh say, can you see by the dawn's early light . . .

Fighter jets from Dobbins Air Force Base raked the sky, momentarily drowning the voices of forty thousand people belting out the *National Anthem*. Standing behind William Wakefield, a drunk redneck bellowed, off key, "Jose, can you see . . ." The aroma of beer and hotdogs rode on the air so thick and humid William could taste it.

He turned to his date, Misty Sax, smiled and caressed her hand. Since he'd first laid eyes on her in his freshman math class he'd thought of little else. It had taken him two weeks to work up the courage to ask her out.

Above them the evening sky darkened to a purple velvet as Venus materialized in the west.

"This is the first time I've been to the new stadium," Misty said. "Your brother was *so* sweet to give up his ticket."

"Hmm. I'm trying to remember the last time anyone described Henry as 'sweet.' Besides, it's a school night, and he has a test tomorrow."

"I love baseball," she said, "not the game so much as . . . just . . . being here."

"It breaks your heart. It is designed to break your heart."

"What?"

"My favorite essay. Bart Giamatti's *Green Fields of the Mind*."

"Oh yeah! I read that in high school. I suppose Giamatti was right. When we lived here my parents would take me to Turner Field. It seems the Braves *always* broke our hearts."

"Well, they're doing a lot better now. I'm glad you decided to come back to Atlanta. Maybe you brought us some luck."

She shrugged as her gaze focused somewhere beyond left field. "Somebody had to take care of my grandma, now that she's all alone."

"What took your parents to Charleston?"

William could see from her sullen expression that he'd touched on a sore subject.

"They'd gone through a rough time. My dad travelled a lot. Then one day, he sold his company and retired. I guess sweeping us off to the *IOP* was his way of making up for not being around when my mom and I needed him."

"The IOP?"

"The Isle of Palms, near Charleston."

"You mentioned in class that you're planning to major in Agronomy. What made you choose an ag major?"

She gave him a sly smile. "If you're about to say that it's a profession for men, you might want to rethink that."

"No. Not at all. It's just that you're the first agronomy major I've ever met."

"Well . . . It's just that I just get so much *shit* from my mom. You should hear her." Misty rolled her eyes, lowered her voice an octave, and gave a perfect nasal imitation of an older woman. "My daughter . . . the farmer."

He laughed. "What do you plan to do with an ag major?"

She leaned away from him, studying his face. "You sure ask a lot of questions."

"I guess it's an occupational hazard. I'm studying journalism. And I'm naturally curious as to how people make important decisions, like their careers and who they marry."

She shrugged. "I want to help fight food insecurity, what with the world's population expanding, and all. If people don't have enough to eat, then . . . nothing else matters."

"But KSU doesn't offer agronomy."

"I know. Right now, I'm getting my gen ed out of the way and trying to pull up my GPA while I take care of my grandma. Eventually . . . I'll transfer to Georgia to finish my degree."

William suppressed the urge to ask when that might be. "What do you want to do after you graduate?"

"I want to go to Israel and live on a kibbutz. It'll be a great experience."

Unsure how he should respond, William changed the subject. "Tell me about your grandmother."

Misty brightened. "My grandma! What a character! You'll have to meet her." She sighed, and her smile faded as quickly as it appeared. "I'm afraid when she's gone *so many* memories will pass with her, *so much history*."

"Like what?"

"Well . . . she thinks she was born in 1937. She has no memories of her biological parents. She became separated from them at Auschwitz. An older woman hid her away and cared for her. When the Russians liberated the camp, she came to the United States with a group of orphans . . . And there she met Myron Sax. You should see their old photos. They were such a handsome couple."

"Oh my God! What a story. I'm dying to meet her."

"Yeah. I'd like to record that story, maybe write it down. But I don't know where to start."

The crowd erupted as Josh Donaldson parked a low fastball over the left field fence. Before William had time to think, he found himself on his feet, hugging Misty, jumping up and down, screaming. Her luxuriant red curls tickled his nose, and the fragrance of honeysuckle made him momentarily forget the game.

He caught himself and stared into her pale blue eyes. She gave him a coy smile, as a blush warmed his face. He wanted to say something to her but couldn't put it into words.

Instead, he flagged down a beer vendor, and they settled back into their seats.

"So, how about you?" Misty asked. "What's your story?"

"Well, Henry and I moved here from Virginia with my mom a couple of years ago. We lived with my grandad in Midtown for a while. He's a retired newspaper writer named Tom Williams. Later on, we moved out here to Smyrna."

"So, you could have jogged over here from your house."

"More like a healthy bike ride."

"Why did you move to Atlanta?"

"My mom left my dad. She became a partner at a law firm in Vinings where *her* mom practiced before she died."

"That must have been rough. What does she think of you pursuing journalism?"

William laughed. "She is *not* happy. She thinks I should major in Business or Pre-law. That's about only thing she and my dad have agreed on in years."

"What does he do?"

"He's an Assistant Secretary of State."

"Whoa! I'm impressed."

"Don't be. He's impressed enough for both of us."

"What's his name? I'll have to Google him."

"William Harmon Wakefield, Jr. He answers to *Bill*."

"So, you're William Harmon III?" she laughed. "It sounds so . . . *patrician*."

"Give me a break, will you?"

"Do you think your dad has ambitions beyond the State Department?"

"Oh, I'm sure he does. Every time he looks in the mirror he sees a future president."

"Seriously?"

"Maybe a *slight* exaggeration."

"Do you think he'd have a chance of getting elected?"

William shrugged. "Who knows? He could count on the support of my Grandpa Harmon, even though they don't agree on most things."

"Tell me about your Grandpa Harmon."

"He's a former U.S. senator. Now he acts as a power broker, raising money for his favorite candidates and landing government contracts for his companies."

"What kind of companies?"

"Mostly defense contractors and tech startups."

"Your grandpa must have a lot of money."

"Whatever money he has . . . he married. My grandma, Evelyn Cabot Wakefield, comes from money."

The vendor returned and William ordered two more beers.

"So, what kind of reporting do you want to do?" she asked.

"Science and technology mostly. I've been interviewing my Uncle Sean. Tomorrow, I'm meeting with Dr. Braithwaite, his research partner. They're developing an implant that'll monitor your vital signs and notify your doctor when you have cancer."

"Sounds like science fiction."

"It's the next big thing in medicine. Schools all over are testing these things. Someday, these devices will direct nanobots that'll treat diseases and remove dead tissue. That's *way* into the future. The real money won't be in the device. It'll be in the software that runs it."

"Where will this *implant* get the materials to build the nanobots?"

"It'll assemble the molecules from nutrients in your body. It'll even tell you what food supplements it needs."

"Tell you?"

"Yeah, through a phone app."

Misty gave him a skeptical look. "So, where do you plan to publish these interviews?"

"Someday I hope to see them in *Scientific American.* Right now, I'm posting them on my blog site."

"Okay. I'll have to check that out."

By the seventh inning stretch, William's mind had begun to wander. Suddenly he felt a disturbance in the force. People around him began pointing at something. The drunk behind him tapped him on the shoulder. "Hey, dude. Y'all are on the Kiss Cam."

Such rare opportunities arrive like little gifts from God. Misty shrugged, and William kissed her to the cheers of a packed stadium. Again, it occurred to him that he needed to say something profound, but he couldn't quite grasp it.

He glanced back as the Kiss Cam as the image shifted to a middle-aged couple. This time the applause became louder.

"Where have I seen that man before?" asked Misty.

William stared at him. Blonde, tanned and handsome, he looked to be fifty, but could have passed for forty. "That's Bram Dennis. He's a state senator who's been in the news a lot lately. I believe he's running for the U.S. Senate."

"Isn't he like some . . . right-wing evangelical?"

"Yeah." William watched as the man tucked a curl behind his ear, preening for the crowd. *Where have I seen that gesture before?*

"He seems so . . . smarmy," Misty said.

"Yeah . . . well, he *is* a politician."

The game ended, leaving the Braves two wins away from clinching the NL East. As William and Misty made their way toward the Galleria parking lot, he pondered how he might score another date for tomorrow night.

"Hey," he said. "I have an idea. You said you wanted to record your grandmother's story, right?"

"I'm not sure she'll agree to it."

"If you introduce me to her, maybe *I* can get her to agree. I'll tell her I'm doing it for a writing class."

"That's a wonderful idea!" She gave him a playful poke in the ribs. "William Wakefield, cub reporter!"

She wrapped her arm inside his and leaned her head on his shoulder. "Thanks for a wonderful time. I loved it."

They stopped on the pedestrian bridge and kissed. Fans veered around them as though fleeing a burning building. A passerby yelled, "Hey, get a room."

When they arrived at Misty's grandmother's, William walked her to the door.

"We'll have to be quiet," she said, reaching for the knob. "My grandma sleeps at the other end of the house, but she could still hear us."

He held her close and gazed into her eyes. "I enjoyed tonight. I was thinking if you're not busy tomorrow . . ."

"You know, for an aspiring reporter, you're not very perceptive." She took his shirt in both hands and quietly pulled him over the threshold.

* * *

All the way home, William kept picturing Misty and wondering how he might spend more time with her. He had no delusions that having sex with her meant she wanted a long-term relationship. Though she'd never said as much, her transfer to UGA would probably happen as soon as Esther passed away. Such plans obviously would *not* include him . . . unless . . .

As he pulled in behind his mom's car, the words he wanted to tell Misty finally came to him.

Someday, hopefully decades hence, when I draw my last breath, I want the memory of tonight to be my last thought. Then I'll know I've had a happy life.

* * *

He stopped at the refrigerator thinking he might find a late-night snack. The house lay in total darkness but for a thin light leaking out beneath Henry's bedroom door. As he started down the hall, he spied a glowing ember on the patio. It made a smooth arc against the night sky.

Opening the sliding glass door, he found his mother, Marie, seated in a chaise lounge. The harsh scent of burning tobacco assaulted his nostrils.

"Mom, you said you were going to quit. What about that prescription Aunt Kathy gave you?"

"William, don't even start."

From her hoarse response he could tell she'd been crying.

"What's the matter?"

"It's your *brother*. We had an argument. He still wants to move back to D.C. I explained to him that your dad can't take him in. *Hell, he's never even there*. Henry seems to think he's grown now. Things escalated, and . . . he ended up calling me a *bitch*.

William spun on his heels. Throwing his brother's door open, he yelled, "*Dude, what is your fucking problem?*"

Seated at his desk, Henry stared up from his calculus text in surprise. "What are you talking about?"

"Your latest fight with Mom."

Henry closed the book and let out a sigh. "I *hate* it here. It's not like I have any friends."

"Maybe that's because you have a chip on your shoulder. You ever thought of that?"

"You sound like Mom."

"Yeah. Well, maybe she's right. I know she can be a pain in the ass, but, like it or not, she's the only parent we have. You're *not* moving back to D.C. to live with Dad. So, get used to being here because *here's* where you are."

William moved closer, towering over his younger brother. Bringing his face down until their noses almost touched, he said, "And if you ever call her a bitch again or disrespect her in way, I will kick your ass into the middle of next week. Am I clear?"

Not waiting for a response, he slammed the door and retreated to his room, where he lay awake for the next hour wondering whose voice had just come out of his mouth. *I've gotta get out of this house.* He opened his laptop and began searching for an apartment near Kennesaw.

Chapter Two

Garth Braithwaite

Atlanta, GA
September 19, 2019

Atlanta Police Sergeant Beth Long typed the last sentence of a homicide report and closed her laptop. Her cell phone buzzed. Late-afternoon sunlight, filtered through nearby blinds, cast striped shadows across her desk. Dust motes danced about like moths.

She pressed the receive button. "Long."

She listened and when the call finished, exclaimed, "Ah shit!"

Murder cases rarely came at convenient times, and Long hated asking her mother, Nancy, to pick up two-year-old Grafton from daycare. Rubbing her aching eyes, she reminded herself that she had chosen the role of an unwed mom with a demanding and thankless career.

Beth and Nancy had reconciled only recently after more than five years. They stopped speaking the day Beth dropped out of Georgia State and enrolled in the Atlanta Police Academy . . . the day after her dad's funeral.

Sergeant Leonard Long, gunned down in the line of duty, had been the center of his daughter's life. To Nancy's dismay, Beth kept his badge and clipped it to a picture of him in his dress uniform. A small hole in the center bore witness to the .22 slug that had taken his life. It stood as a reminder of why she had become a cop.

* * *

Last Gleaming

Long arrived at Bungalow Lane in the cozy neighborhood of Westparc Village to find two uniformed officers, David Meacham and Mark White, waiting for her. Gazing up and down the quiet, tree-lined street, she tried to imagine what a detached home in Atlanta's tony West Midtown neighborhood must cost.

David Meacham, the older of her two associates, dozed on a porch swing, his double chin folded against his collar. His partner, Mark White leered at the young women jogging past. He reminded Long of a dog who chased cars, never knowing what he'd do if he caught one.

"Okay, what do we have?" Long asked.

White glanced at his partner to see if he should answer.

Startled awake, Meacham replied, "Garth Braithwaite, sole occupant, worked at Georgia Tech. Crime scene specialists got here a few minutes ago." He pointed toward the sidewalk. "That gentleman over there says he found Braithwaite and called 911. His name's Sean O'Meara."

Fifteen feet away, a middle-aged man paced and fidgeted. Medium height and build, he had thinning sandy-colored hair and wore gold-rimmed glasses, a burgundy sweater and khaki slacks. To Long, his whole persona screamed "college professor."

She pulled a small notebook and pen from the inner pocket of her uniform. "Dr. O'Meara?"

"Yes?"

"I'm Sergeant Long, APD." She handed him her card. "How did you know Mr. Braithwaite?"

"Dr. Braithwaite and I were colleagues," he choked, "partners on a research project."

"How long had you known him?"

"About two years. Before that I was at Emory, and he was at Cal Tech."

"What can you tell me about him?"

"I didn't really know him outside of work."

"What prompted you to come by?"

"We had a meeting scheduled for this afternoon. When he didn't show up I became concerned. He never missed appointments without letting someone know. I tried calling but got his voicemail."

"What did you find when you got here?"

"I knocked and he didn't answer. I tried the front door and found it unlocked. He was lying on the floor inside. I called 911 right away."

"And you saw no one coming or going?"

"No."

"How would you describe Dr. Braithwaite?"

O'Meara stammered. "He . . . he was a very competent engineering professor, published in all the major journals. He specialized in the biologic uses of microchips . . . We . . . didn't socialize if that's what you mean. I don't know anything about his private life."

Long studied the man for a moment, searching for any sign of dissembling. "And you have no idea who would want him dead?"

"None."

"What sort of research were you and Dr. Braithwaite doing?"

Relaxing a bit, he said, "We were developing a microscopic device that, implanted in the body, will scan for viral diseases and certain types of cancer. Eventually we hoped to have the implants manufacture nanobots . . . molecular robots, that could repair or remove damaged tissue, get rid of harmful waste prod . . ."

"I see." Long had no idea what the man was talking about and didn't care. "Do you think Dr. Braithwaite's murder might have anything to do with your research?"

"I don't see how it could."

"Would any aspect of your project make other technologies obsolete, perhaps put companies out of business?"

O'Meara forced a smile. "I suppose so. Our intent . . . *my* long-term goal . . . is to make medicine, as we know it, obsolete."

"I can see how that might make some folks unhappy. Perhaps create a motive for murder." She paused, grasping for something else to ask. "Dr. O'Meara do you have a phone number where I can reach you later?"

He handed her his card. As he started to leave, Long asked, "Tell me, did Dr. Braithwaite ever mention any family?"

"He had a sister in California. I think her name was Debra. The University's Human Resources department will have his emergency contact information."

"Thank you. That should be all."

A low murmur of conversation flowed from inside the house. Long walked in and found two crime scene techs leaning over a body. She obliged them by suiting up and donning gloves before entering, as did Meacham and White. The coppery odor of blood and the stench of excrement overwhelmed her. Meacham paused to apply Vicks VapoRub beneath his nostrils.

"When we got here," Meacham explained, "we found Professor O'Meara sitting on the front porch looking like somebody ran over his dog."

"And . . ."

"The front door was open. We called for backup, came in and cleared the place, no sign of the perp."

The victim lay face up on an oriental rug, eyes staring into eternity. He wore his shoulder-length brown hair swept back in a pompadour. Trim and fit, he appeared to be in his mid-forties and wore a ring in one ear. A small round hole in the middle of his forehead oozed blood into a crusted pool beside his head.

Meacham stepped back as a crime scene tech snapped photos of the body. "The apparent time of death was somewhere between noon and two p.m. yesterday."

"So, what else do we know?" Long asked. She stared into the dead man's lifeless countenance as though expecting him to answer. She'd long ago lost count of the murders she'd investigated but could never get past the thought that, but a short time earlier, this had been a living, breathing human being.

"The next-door neighbor tells us Braithwaite lived alone," said Meacham. "He had guests coming and going at all hours."

"What kind of guests?"

"He says a white limo would pull up out back and deliver several young ladies."

"How young?"

"Teenagers, from what he tells me, though he didn't sound sure. Men would show up, and they'd party until dawn. And then the limo would come back and pick up the girls. The neighbor complained a couple of times about the noise, but when the cops got here, the guests quieted down and they left."

Long made a note to check with Special Victims about prostitutes working the area in a white limo. "Did the neighbor mention any other visitors?"

"Nope."

The upstairs bedrooms resembled the aftermath of a frat party. In the larger one, sex toys and lubricants littered the gold velour cover of a waterbed. Another crime scene tech sprayed it with luminol and shined a UV lamp, lighting up smeared bodily fluids and fingerprints.

"These look to be recent. Any idea how many people were involved?" Long asked.

"We won't know for a while, but Braithwaite seems to have had a lot of company night before last. Apparently, he never got around to cleaning up."

On the closet shelf a wooden box with ornate scrollwork lay open, revealing a bag of cocaine and a crack pipe.

"Does it look like the perp took anything?" Long asked.

"Not that I can see. It's like Braithwaite came home and found him tossing the place," said White. "Whoever he was, we think he went out the back. The rear door was unlocked, and we found recent footprints in the yard. No signs of tire tracks. He must've parked down the street."

"And the neighbor didn't see anything."

"No ma'am."

"Wait a minute." Long returned to the living room. Beside the body lay an empty backpack. "Did either of you see a laptop anywhere?"

"No ma'am."

"What about his cell phone?" She patted Braithwaite's pockets with her gloved hand.

"Nope."

"I'll have to follow up with O'Meara, but I'll bet Braithwaite carried his computer home every night, which means our perp took it, along with his phone. The laptop probably belonged to Georgia Tech. Meanwhile, let's check the pawn shops around the city to see if they show up."

Long paced as she spoke. "So, Braithwaite arrived home unexpectedly. The intruder must have been searching for something else." She chewed her lower lip. "What would that have been?"

The three cops went back upstairs to the master bedroom. Long examined the closet again, kneeled, peered beneath the bed and pulled the cover back. As she stood, she glanced up and saw a mirror mounted into the tray ceiling. She raised her hand, quieting the investigators. "Do you gentlemen think you could take that down?" she asked. "Be careful. It'll be heavy."

Standing on four ladders, the techs located screws along the mirror's frame. With the help of Meacham and White, they lowered it onto the bed. Between two joists a cutout revealed a small video camera with a cable leading to an uplink.

In the hallway, they located an attic scuttle leading to a passageway barely large enough for an average sized man.

Long watched as the techs photographed the camera from above and below then carefully removed it for lab examination. "Braithwaite must have been uploading his home movies to the cloud."

A sick feeling came over her. A request for Braithwaite's internet backups might lead to FBI involvement, the last thing Long wanted.

"Do you think this is what got him killed?" asked Meacham.

"Maybe," she said. "Maybe not. I need to find out more about his research. You two get back to canvassing the neighbors, while I get a search warrant for Braithwaite's office."

"Uh, Sergeant," White grinned, "When you find those sex videos, you think me and David could, you know, watch them with you . . . maybe offer a little perspective?"

Long rolled her eyes. Turning back to the waterbed and the two-way mirror, she made a note to ask the medical examiner to check Braithwaite for signs of sexually transmitted disease.

As she left, her phone buzzed with a text from Brandon Markham, Long's former therapist and Grafton's father. *Beth, please call me.*

She closed the message and shoved the phone back into her pocket. She'd speak to him when she got home.

Last Gleaming

* * *

William knocked softly on Sean O'Meara's office door. O'Meara stopped in mid-sentence and apologized to the young man seated across from him.

"Hey, Uncle Sean. Sorry to interrupt you. It's only that . . . I had an appointment with Dr. Braithwaite, and he's not here. I tried his number, but it went to voicemail."

O'Meara rose from his desk, fumbling for words. "William . . . I'm afraid I have bad news. I went to Dr. Braithwaite's house earlier and found him on the floor in his living room. Someone murdered him."

William staggered and caught himself. "Oh my God! Why would anybody do that?"

"I don't know. It seems that he walked in on a burglar."

"That's horrible."

William stared about, unable to comprehend. "Who would want to kill a college professor? Who's going to take over his work?"

Sean indicated the younger man seated across from him. "William Wakefield meet Delbert Foster. Delbert was Dr. Braithwaite's graduate assistant. He'll be filling in until I can find a permanent replacement."

Remembering his manners, William shook hands with Foster, a tall skinny man with unruly brown hair, a receding chin and a prominent Adam's apple. Turning back to Sean, he said, "I . . . I know you guys are busy, and I hate barging in like this. It's only that I . . . I'd scheduled an interview with Dr. Braithwaite. Dr. Foster, is it okay if I get your number? I'd like to come back sometime when you're not busy and talk about your research."

"Sure," the man shrugged. "By the way, it's *Mr*. Foster. And you can call me Delbert. The best time to reach me is at night when I'm free to talk."

William felt foolish, trying to think of something else he could say to two men who had just lost a respected colleague. "Thanks. Okay if I call you this evening?"

"Sure."

Chapter Three

William Wakefield

Kennesaw State University
September 19, 2019

William strolled out of Sean's office and into the embrace of a sparkling late afternoon. He passed a cute coed peddling red tee shirts with white lettering that read, "See Bram run. Run, Bram, run."

He couldn't get the events of the past twenty-four hours out of his mind . . . making love to Misty, Dr. Braithwaite's murder and nearly coming to blows with his brother.

As he reached his Jeep, his phone rang. A female voice asked to speak to *Mr. William Wakefield.* Suspecting a sales call, he started to hang up.

She introduced herself as Atlanta Police Sergeant Elizabeth Long. "Mr. Wakefield, I'm investigating the murder of Garth Braithwaite, and I found a message you left on his answering machine about an appointment. How did you know Dr. Braithwaite?"

Nervously, he replied, "Sergeant, I'm a journalism student at Kennesaw State. My uncle, Sean O'Meara, was Dr. Braithwaite's research partner. I'd planned to interview him for my news writing class. I just now found out about his murder."

"I see."

"Uhm . . . if you don't mind, I was wondering if you could tell me how the search for the killer is coming."

He could almost hear the patronizing smile in her reply. "Nice try, young man, but I'm afraid I'm not at liberty to discuss an ongoing investigation."

As the call ended, William wondered why she had gone through Braithwaite's phone messages, if she thought his murder resulted from a botched burglary. He dialed his grandfather, Tom Williams, who had promised to pitch his story on Sean's research for the *Atlanta Journal-Constitution* Sunday edition.

"Hey," Tom answered.

"I suppose you heard about Dr. Braithwaite."

"Yeah. That's quite a shock. I tried reaching your Uncle Sean but had to leave a message."

"I just got a call from a Sergeant Long with the Atlanta police. She saw my phone message on Dr. Braithwaite's answering machine at Tech. I got the feeling she doesn't think this was a garden variety break-in. But she wouldn't answer any of my questions."

"She's not going to. I know Beth Long. She worked with Paxton Davis, an old friend of mine. She's a tough woman, all business."

William spotted a campus cop in the distance studying a parked car. "Do you have any other police contacts who might talk to me?"

"Maybe. I'll see."

William shook his head. "I just don't get it. How could something like this happen?"

"Braithwaite lived in West Midtown, son. Despite all the gentrification down there, there's still a lot of crime. I don't think this has anything to do with his work. He just . . . came home at an inopportune time."

"But it all feels so . . . random. Think of all the lives his research could have saved. And we're just brushing it off as some everyday occurrence?"

"You sound like you're getting angry, William."

He stopped for a moment. "I guess I am."

"*Good.* That'll make you a better reporter. Channel that anger. Just follow it wherever it takes you. Be ready for surprises."

"What do I do now with my article? I needed Dr. Braithwaite's perspective."

Tom paused. "What if you changed your scope? Let me call the paper and find out who caught the murder story. Maybe you can write a sidebar about Braithwaite's work, based on your interview with Sean."

"That would be great."

William paused. "Oh. When I was at Uncle Sean's office, I met Dr. Braithwaite's assistant, and he agreed to talk to me. His name's Delbert Foster. What kind of questions do you think I should ask him?" William retrieved a legal pad from his bookbag.

"Well, what do you know about him so far?"

"I know he was a graduate assistant. And he doesn't have a PhD."

"Hmm. See if you can find out how he landed the job as Braithwaite's assistant. *But don't lead with that.* You need to make him feel comfortable first. Start by asking about his background, where he came from, where he went to school. Get him talking. Then sound impressed and ask if his line of work usually requires a doctorate. Get his permission to use a recorder."

"And what if he doesn't take the bait?"

"Ask if he's *pursuing* a doctorate. Give him a chance to explain his situation. If he gives you an evasive response, then you'll know you're onto something, and you can follow up with Sean. Whatever you do, try not to spook him. If he sounds nervous, fall back on standard questions that appeal to his ego, like 'What inspired you to go into engineering?' Listen for what he says *and* for what he doesn't."

Despite their previous conversations about the art of interviewing, this seemed like a lot to take in. William felt completely out of his depth. "Okay. Thanks."

Tom continued. "The main thing I'd be curious to know is what Foster thought of Braithwaite. But don't come right out and ask him. I'm sure the cops have already questioned him about their relationship. He'll be reluctant to give a candid assessment of his murdered boss. The fact that you're Sean's nephew might work in your favor, given that Foster now reports directly to him, but it could work against you. Don't overplay it."

"Thanks, Pops."

William waited until after supper to dial Foster, expecting to get his voicemail. Instead, the man answered. William took a deep breath. He reintroduced himself and asked Foster if he'd reached him at a good time.

"It's as good as any. I'm just sitting here relaxing in front of the tube."

"Thanks. This shouldn't take more than thirty minutes."

"No worries."

Foster sounded so laid back William wondered if he'd smoked a joint. He pictured him sitting with his feet propped on his coffee table.

"Okay. Well, for starters, could you tell me a little about your background?"

"I got my B.S. and M.S. in electrical engineering at Auburn. I spent a couple of years with a firm in Atlanta, then applied for the PhD program at Tech."

"How's that coming?"

Foster paused. "I had to put it on hold for . . . uhm . . . financial reasons. Anyway, I'd taken a research methodology class from Dr. Braithwaite, and he offered me a job as his assistant."

"So, that's how you met him?"

"Yeah. He let me stay on after I put my degree on hold."

William scribbled furiously, adding a question mark next to this last comment. He didn't know much about university research policies, but it seemed unusual that Braithwaite would keep a graduate assistant who'd stopped taking classes. *Is he holding back something embarrassing. Could it relate to the murder?*

"So, when do you see yourself resuming your studies?"

"I . . . I'm not sure yet. Right now, I'm up to my eyebrows reviewing Dr. Braithwaite's notes and putting them in order."

"What was it like working with him?"

Foster's reply sounded like it came from a three-by-five card. "Garth was a highly respected member of the research community and an incalculable loss to Georgia Tech. His murder came as a blow to all of us. I'm sure your Uncle Sean is experiencing the worst of it."

William pivoted, hoping to catch him off guard. "Why did you choose bioengineering research? Don't private firms pay more?" He had no idea what they paid.

Foster's answer came quickly this time, as though he'd practiced it in front of a mirror. "I'd rather make a difference in the world than make a fortune."

William suppressed a snicker. He had yet to get a straight answer from the man. Figuring he had nothing to lose, he asked, "Why do you think someone would murder a research scientist?"

"According to the police, he came home in the middle of the day and surprised a burglar."

"I know that's what it looked like, but I'm wondering what this burglar might have been looking for."

"I . . . I have no idea."

"Okay. Well, that's about all I have. Is there anything you can think of that I should have asked?" Tom had taught him this standard closer. Sometimes it yielded surprises. This would *not* be one of those times.

"Nope. I believe that covers it."

"If I think of anything else, would you mind if I give you a call?"

"Anytime, my man."

Scanning his notes, William marked some of them for a follow up with Sean, particularly the PhD discussion.

Chapter Four

Harmon Wakefield

Rural Virginia/North Georgia
September 19, 2019

Harmon Wakefield slowed his mount to a walk, allowing his companions to catch up. At seventy-seven, he prided himself that he could still manage a horse, often riding at full gallop across the rolling fields of his 150-acre estate.

Gazing into the distance he descried a forested ridge and perhaps the beginnings of fall color . . . or maybe a trick of the late afternoon sun. Overhead a murder of crows dive bombed a red tail hawk.

From a nearby field came the sweet smell of new mown hay. He watched as a large tractor made its slow turn, and his thoughts drifted back to a time when he would have driven that tractor himself. The son of an Oklahoma oil rigger, Harmon enjoyed manual labor. It gave him the opportunity to stay in shape while contemplating the greater challenges of life. Business owner, former senator and political operative, his schedule still required a certain degree of stamina.

Abigail Martin, the more experienced rider of his guests, pulled alongside aboard a young stallion, her pale complexion flushed from the ride. "Harmon, you know I never grow tired of visiting this place, but something tells me this is *not* a social occasion."

Martin, a special assistant to the National Security Advisor, wore her steel grey hair pulled back in a bun. For today's visit, she had traded her signature straight-cut black dress and matching pumps for blue jeans, a Notre Dame sweatshirt and stylish boots. If she bore any resentment at having come all the way out here from D.C., she didn't show it. Harmon knew she had little time for a road trip when a simple phone call would suffice.

He leaned forward and caressed the mare's neck. His other visitor, an overweight man with thinning hair in his late fifties finally caught up. His pasty complexion spoke of days spent behind a desk, not on the back of a horse.

"You okay there, Scott?" Harmon asked, fearing he might have to explain to the board of Wycap Investors why their CEO died of a heart attack on the Wakefield plantation. "Abigail," he added, "as soon as Scott here catches his breath, I'm sure he can explain why I invited you here."

They waited patiently as Scott Weber regained his composure. "Ms. Martin, I'm sure you've heard of a defense startup called Night Flight Industries."

"Yes."

"A few months back, Wycap bought a majority of their shares."

"I remember that," she said. "That came as a considerable relief for the NSA. We feared they might never raise the capital to complete some very sensitive projects. We appreciate Wycap coming to their rescue."

"What you may not know, Ms. Martin, is that they've had some preliminary success with a radically new weapons platform."

Martin turned to Wakefield. "And this is what you brought me out here for? We couldn't have discussed this back at the White House with Pentagon representatives?"

"We could have," said Harmon. "We might even have invited some of the president's *trusted economic advisors* to join us . . . and by nightfall his buddy in the Kremlin would know all about it. Don't forget China's not our only enemy."

"Oh, come on. You don't think he's that dumb."

"As a matter of fact, I do. And Night Flight isn't ready to demonstrate this new system yet. We can't afford to tip our hand. We're awaiting tests on some key components. When we've ironed all that out, you'll have a skybox seat. But that's not our principal concern at the moment."

Wakefield watched the beleaguered hawk wing its way toward a distant stand of trees as more birds joined the attack. "What keeps me awake at night," he said, "are *two* things. As I'm sure you know, the Chinese and the Russians are hacking our computer systems with impunity, and their spies have infiltrated every research institution in the U.S. We could revoke their F-1 visas, but that takes time."

"You said you had two things," Martin reminded him.

"The component Night Flight needs is under development at MIT for a completely different application. Among the developers is an engineer we suspect of being on the payroll of the Chinese. By the time we get him out of there, it could be too late."

"And your solution is . . ."

"To stop the research by cutting off its funding and hire the rest of their team away to Night Flight. We're doing the same thing at other institutions."

"So? What do you need from me?"

"Tell her, Scott."

"Despite all our security measures, Wycap still faces the problem of hackers," Weber replied. "Another of our holdings has developed a secure network for healthcare providers, virtually impenetrable. We also think it'll help protect communications between defense contractors and the Pentagon. We're a long way and millions of dollars from completion. We can't ask our investors for more capital at this point without explaining why."

"And you want money from Uncle Sam," she replied.

"Uh . . . yes ma'am."

Martin stared silently at the corpulent investment banker then turned her gaze to Wakefield. "Seriously, Harmon. How long do you think it'll take some pimply teenager to break this new system? He'd need nothing more than Internet access, a case of energy drinks and patience, all in abundant supply for a kid living in his parents' basement."

"It's not the enterprising young nerd who concerns us, Abigail. Our biggest threat is a coordinated cyberattack from China, Russia, North Korea or Iran. Technologies such as these in their hands would have unimaginable consequences."

"And you think your new security system can prevent that?"

Harmon gave her a mischievous smile. "It doesn't have to keep them out indefinitely. Just long enough for Night Flight's team to bring their little project to fruition. By the time our enemies find out about it, they'll be so far behind they'll never catch up. It'll be Reagan's Strategic Defense Initiative all over again."

"The SDI never worked, Harmon."

"It didn't have to. The mere threat brought Gorbachev to the bargaining table."

"Harmon, the governments you just mentioned already have their spy teams covering every defense website in America around the clock."

"You're assuming this involves the Internet. It doesn't."

"And you want . . ."

"All we're asking, Abigail, is for your boss to loosen his purse strings and let a few coins fall into Scott's palm. It won't even be a rounding error in the NSA's budget. If the project fails, no one will ever know."

Martin nodded slowly. "I can't promise you anything, but I'll see what I can do."

As the party rode back to the farmhouse, the horses picked up the scent of the barn and quickened their pace. Harmon chuckled to himself. *They're like a CEO smelling a government subsidy.*

Martin brushed her hair back. "By the way, how are things coming with your new crop of congressional candidates?"

"I believe I've found some folks who will fit the bill quite nicely. There's a former Lockheed executive down in Georgia you might want to take a look at. His name's Bram Dennis. He's making a run for the Senate."

* * *

As Abigail and Scott departed, Evelyn Wakefield came out to wave them goodbye. Turning to her husband of fifty years, she said, "Harmon, I'm sure you made your points with your usual charm. You'll get the funding you need."

He gazed into her pale gray eyes and nuzzled her snow-white hair. Bending to kiss her, he thought, *Whatever else I may accomplish in this life, it will pale next to my marrying this incredible woman. She grows more beautiful every day.*

"Come on," she said. "Supper awaits us."

Retiring to the veranda, they seated themselves to bowls of vichyssoise. Their cook beamed with pride, as though she had just delivered twins. "Will there be anything else, senora?" she asked.

"Thank you, Paloma," Evelyn said. "We'll ring when we're ready for the coq au vin."

As he savored the cold soup, Harmon contemplated how far he'd come and the many small things he'd grown accustomed to, like elegant outdoor dining. Beyond the distant forest, the last fires of a brilliant sunset brightened an overhanging cloud.

Convinced that his daughter had married beneath her station, Evelyn's father, Henry Cabot, purchased the land in her name and hired an architect to design the brick mansion. Harmon recalled the old adage that the Lodges only speak to the Cabots, and the Cabots only speak to God. *I'm sure the old bastard bought this place thinking it would outlast our marriage.*

Evelyn interrupted his reverie. "Harmon, you're working yourself too hard. We have a son in the State Department, remember? Why can't you step back, relax, and let him take over your political machinations?"

"Darling, I'm as proud of Bill as you are, but he still has much to learn. For one thing, he needs to stop listening to all these globalists and disabuse himself of the notion that if we ply our enemies with enough theme parks and MacDonald's franchises, we can win them over to democracy and the free market. Guys like Xi and Putin never enjoyed the benefits of a prep school education or a Wharton MBA. They're nasty SOBs who play for keeps. They've been at war with us all along, and we keep electing presidents too dumb to see that."

"I know. I know. Harmon, I've heard you say that until I can recite it chapter and verse. Darling, I'm sure America will survive if you take just a few weeks off, The Sapsfords have invited us out to their place in Vail. Colorado's so beautiful this time of year."

"And it'll be just as beautiful in January."

She gave him a sharp look, "Don't you even think of getting up on skis again at your age."

"Okay. But let me wrap up some things first. After Christmas, we can take off and go wherever you want."

The mere mention of Christmas steered the conversation to their annual family gathering, one of the few occasions when their son and grandsons visited.

* * *

Harmon drifted off to sleep that night replaying his conversation with Abigail Martin and Scott Weber. Hours later, he awoke to the soft purr of the cell phone on his bedside table.

The digital clock read three a.m. He rose quietly, so as not to awaken Evelyn. As she snored softly, her back to him, he picked up the phone, grabbed his bathrobe and padded down the hall to his office.

"This better be damned important for you to call me at this hour."

"Sir, I don't know if you've heard the news. We have a problem in Atlanta."

By the time the conversation ended, Harmon gave up all thoughts of returning to bed. Instead, he started a pot of coffee, retreated to his sunroom, and awaited the dawn, wondering how this news would affect his plans.

* * *

A thousand miles away, Dean Scarborough sat at the wheel of a nondescript Buick he'd rented using a fake ID. Staring up at the bright green BP sign overlooking Joe Frank Harris Parkway, he wondered how he could have screwed up so badly. *I just needed to get my hands on some compromising information about Braithwaite.*

A careful planner under most circumstances, he wished he'd *never* contracted with Simon Wilhoite to hire a burglar. *What was I thinking? His man was supposed to get in, grab a few things and get out.*

As far as Scarborough knew, those items either remained in Braithwaite's residence . . . or lay on a shelf at an Atlanta police precinct awaiting examination. Now Wilhoite wouldn't even return his calls.

Scarborough had never met the thief and didn't know his name or where he lived. *The perfect cutout . . . And when the cops catch him, he'll give up Wilhoite, and Wilhoite will give me up.* How long before that happened, he couldn't begin to guess. But, given his complexion, he knew he'd never look good in an orange jumpsuit.

Soon the sun would peep over the ridge to his right. He had to move on before then, lest someone see him, someone who might recognize him later. *I could grow out my beard and let my hair get long. But then I'd definitely look like a fugitive.*

In a matter of weeks, perhaps months, he might return to Atlanta, but for now he would lie low in a remote cove on Carter Lake at a friend's cabin, the kind of friend who didn't ask questions. Scarborough closed his eyes and visualized a SWAT team descending on his Grant Park home.

He stepped out of his car, thinking a cup of coffee might help him think, then remembered that the twenty-four-hour gas station probably had a security camera and got back in. He dialed his client using a temporary phone he'd purchased at Walmart. The man answered after several rings. In clipped terms, Scarborough explained his situation.

"You did what!" the voice on the line exploded. "*What, in God's name, possessed you? I told you to get some leverage on the man, not kill him!*"

"I did that, sir. In the process, I discovered that Braithwaite had certain . . . sensitive information. I thought . . ."

"I don't pay you to think, you idiot! That's *my* job."

As he paused, Scarborough heard him cursing beneath his breath. "What you're going to do, right now, is disappear while I clean up your mess. And one more thing . . . *lose this number*. If I need you, I'll call *you*. Until then you don't know me. Are we clear?"

When the call ended, Scarborough stepped out and dropped the burner in front of his left front tire. He glanced about to make sure no one had seen him, then climbed back in. As he drove away, he felt a slight bump and imagined the sound the device had made as it ground it into the pavement. His other phone lay in a pouch under the seat. He'd removed its battery and stuffed it inside the rental papers in the glove compartment. For the time being, he would rely on other means of communication.

What he would do for a living, once he returned to Atlanta . . . *if* he ever returned, Scarborough would ponder as he tried to enjoy the serenity of the pristine lake. When he flunked out of Georgia Southern, he'd gone to work for his dad, as a private investigator, the only career he'd ever known. The old man died ten years ago. Now, with the loss of his biggest customer, a political fixer, Scarborough could hardly expect referrals.

The man said he would clean up the mess, which probably meant throwing Scarborough under the bus. Not waiting for that to happen, he would take matters into his own hands. Emergency cash, stashed in an old suitcase in the trunk, would cover his meager living expenses during his extended vacation. *The upside of not having a nine-to-five is that no one misses you when you don't show up at the office.*

* * *

Simon Wilhoite turned off his phone, not wanting to hear from Dean Scarborough *or* from Steven Saldano. He sat alone in his darkened den and replayed the final segment of the eleven o'clock news with the volume turned low to avoid waking his wife.

Atlanta police are still seeking help from anyone who might have information in the murder of Georgia Tech professor Garth Braithwaite.

Wilhoite shut off the television and stared at his reflection on the screen. Thick bags had formed beneath his eyes from lack of sleep. He rose and poured himself another scotch on the rocks, his liver-spotted hand shaking so badly he spilled it down his shirt.

Chapter Five

Misty Sax

Cherokee County, Georgia
September 23, 2019

    William Wakefield tossed his bookbag into the back seat of his Jeep and settled in behind the wheel. The day had been a total waste. Preoccupied with the Braithwaite murder, he'd sleepwalked through his classes, hearing nothing his professors said.
    As he reached for his keys, his phone rang.
    "Hey, Grandpa."
    In recent weeks, Harmon had taken to calling him at odd hours.
    "William, I understand you and Henry are coming up here to see us for Christmas."
    "Yes. I got a text from Dad. I haven't had a chance to discuss it with Mom."
    "I'm sure school is keeping you busy."
    "Yep, especially my journalism studies."
    "How's that coming?"
    "Pretty well. I've been interviewing Uncle Sean and his colleagues for an article I'm writing."
    "I heard the bad news about Sean's research partner . . . Garth Braithwaite."
    "Yeah. That's pretty messed up."
    "What do you know about it?"

Curious as to why Harmon would have such a keen interest in the matter, William became cautious. "All I know is what the police are saying, that Dr. Braithwaite came home and walked in on a burglar."

Their conversation drifted to other topics, with Harmon asking about Marie and Henry. When it ended, William dialed Misty and caught her studying for a test. He told her about Braithwaite's murder and his interview with Foster and asked if they could meet somewhere to talk.

"I was about to make supper for my grandma. She eats early . . . Why don't you come over?"

"No, I don't want to barge in . . ."

"*Come over, William.* We have plenty of food. Grandma wants to meet you."

"Okay. I'll be there in twenty minutes." He texted his mom to tell her he'd be late getting home.

When he arrived, he found Misty in the kitchen, stirring a pot of chicken chili. She invited him out onto the deck, where her grandmother sat sipping wine in a wicker recliner, surrounded by peonies and knock-out roses.

Esther appeared to have recently returned from the beauty parlor, with her flaming red hair and matching fingernails immaculate. She scrutinized William and pursed her lips. "So, Melissa tells me you want to be a writer."

It took him a second to realize she meant Misty. "Yes ma'am. My grandfather's an old newspaper man. He started out with a daily in Tampa back in the sixties when he came home from Vietnam. He almost got killed covering a string of murders in his hometown. Hearing his stories made me want to become a journalist."

"This grandfather of yours sounds like quite a man. Is he single?"

This brought a smile. "As a matter of fact, he is. He has a girlfriend, at the moment, but . . . you never know."

Changing the subject, he commented, "You have a beautiful place. How long have you been here?"

"I moved here with my husband Myron in 1968. This was all farmland back then. Myron worked for his uncle's garment factory in New York. The uncle relocated us to Atlanta . . . if you can imagine that. I told him I'd come here under one condition. He had to buy me a place where I could look out my back door and see *nothing but nature*. I was *so* tired of Brooklyn."

"Your flower beds are amazing, and that garden!"

"Oh, that's Melissa's. She always loved that spot. When she was little, she would say, 'Grandma, you could have a *whole farm* out here.' When she came to live with me back in May, you know what she did? She went out there and plowed it all up. She stayed up all night reading about vegetables and stuff. You should have seen the squash, the beans, the peas. She's planting collards and sweet potatoes now for the fall."

"I know you're glad she moved back here from Charleston . . . and so am I."

"Yeah." A sour expression passed over her face. She leaned toward William as though sharing a secret. "My son, he sells his company for *millions* of dollars . . . You know what he does? He moves his family to Charleston. Buys a big house and a yacht. Not one thought for his aging parents back here in Georgia. At least my granddaughter loves me."

She fixed him with a piercing gaze. "So, tell me, what kind of work do your parents do?"

"My dad works for the State Department, and my mom's a criminal defense attorney."

"Good. You should never be broke."

Esther's 1960s brick ranch backed up to a power line right of way, giving it a stunning view unobstructed by neighboring homes. A Titian sunset illumined the fading remnants of a summer garden, creating a perfect Renaissance landscape.

Misty arrived with two steaming bowls and placed them on a glass-topped table, then returned to the kitchen for her own serving and two more glasses of wine. As William studied her, any lingering doubt that he wanted to spend the rest of his life with her evaporated.

She took her seat beside him and said, "Grandma, I have something to tell you. I'm going to write your life story, and William's going to help me."

This produced a hearty laugh, "Who in the world wants to read my life story?"

"I do," said Misty, "and my children will if I ever have any. People need to know everything you went through, Grandma. We must never let them forget."

By the time Esther rose to turn in, the sun had set, and fireflies had begun their nightly ballet. Misty helped her back inside with the aid of a walker. When she returned, she and William snuggled on the chaise lounge and gazed at the stars.

"Wow. How could you ever think of leaving a place so beautiful?" he asked.

"Because I have so many things to do. Maybe someday I'll retire to a place like this."

"You know, I've wondered, if you're majoring in agronomy, why aren't you a vegetarian?"

"I eat meat. If you don't like it, that's fine. But I'm sick of people telling me I should abstain from it, as if it were some *moral imperative*. That's ridiculous. Every organism on this planet survives by eating something else. It's no more wrong for me to eat a chicken than to eat vegetables. It's the order of things."

Slowly, they drained their wineglasses as conversation drifted to a stop. Eventually, she rose and invited him back to her bedroom.

Later, as they lay between soft cotton sheets, catching their breath, William scanned the walls, filled with photos and drawings of plants and insects. "You have interesting taste in art."

"I took those pictures in our backyard. I had some photography and drawing courses in high school. When we moved to South Carolina, my mom sent me to an exclusive academy hoping I'd go to Wellesley or Sarah Lawrence." She chuckled. "You should have seen her when I told her I wanted to come back here and go to Kennesaw. I wish I had a photo of her face. I'd frame it and put it right there between the grasshopper and the praying mantis."

"You mentioned the other night you wanted to go to UGA and major in agronomy. When do you see that happening?"

Misty's mood changed, and her eyes glistened. "My grandma's health is failing. I don't know how long she has left, but when she's gone, I'm out of here."

William stifled an involuntary response, praying she hadn't noticed it. "Hopefully, that'll be way into the future."

He slid beneath the covers and caressed her body with his lips. "I kinda like having you here."

She paused as though composing her answer. "William, you're the sweetest guy I've ever known. You seem to genuinely care about other people. If I ever wanted to spend the rest of my life with someone, it would be you. But I just . . . have too much going on, right now, I'm not sure I'm ready to commit to a relationship."

Unable to think of a response that didn't sound like wheedling, he let it go.

"So," she asked. "What's the story with the murder of your uncle's research partner?"

"I don't know. The cops are saying he came home and surprised a burglar. It all seems so . . . cliché, especially when it happens to someone who's doing work that could save lives."

"I know you wanted to interview him for an article you're writing, but this seems to have taken on a greater significance for you."

William sat up, struggling to put his thoughts into words. "Maybe this *was* just a botched burglary. But I get the sense that there's something more to it. What did Braithwaite have in his home that a burglar would want?"

"William, shit happens. What if you spent all this time only to find out that all the killer wanted was Braithwaite's stereo. You can't spend the rest of your life living vicariously through other people."

"I'm a journalist. That's what I do."

"Then you'll have to accept that bad things sometimes happen to good people. Everything tends toward entropy. Things fall apart, mountains erode. *We all die eventually.*" She leaned close to him and ran her hand over his body. "Let's make the best of the time we have."

She climbed on top of him, and, for a while, took his mind off such weighty matters.

* * *

Simon Wilhoite slid in behind the wheel of his aging Cadillac. He'd had a stressful day and looked forward to crawling into bed with his overweight but compliant wife. The car sat in total darkness behind Wilhoite's pawn shop. He'd procrastinated on replacing the burned-out light above the back door.

As he turned the key, and the large engine came to life, he wondered again what had become of Steven Saldano. In his mind he replayed televised images of police and crime scene techs swarming in and out of Braithwaite's West Midtown bungalow like ants. *How did I ever get involved in this shit?*

Simon had ignored Dean Scarborough's text and phone messages and, when the man wouldn't take the hint, blocked his number. He had conveyed the instructions faithfully to Saldano. He never told him to kill Braithwaite. *Why did I hire that idiot?*

He pressed the radio button and tuned it to WSB. Atlanta Police were still seeking information that might lead to an arrest.

"Good," he said out loud, "Hopefully he's long gone by now with a new identity."

He flinched as a gun barrel pressed against his neck. "Not yet, Simon," came the low voice at his right ear. "You and I have a few things to discuss." Saldano's face appeared in the rear-view mirror. His ruddy complexion seemed to radiate in the sickly green light of the dashboard.

Startled, Wilhoite nearly pissed himself. *Why didn't I check the back seat before I got in?*

"Right now," said Saldano, "you're going to turn off the car and tell me who paid you to hire me for the Braithwaite job. I need his address and his phone number. And . . . Simon . . . don't even think of moving your hand toward that gun under your coat."

"His name's Dean Scarborough. He . . . he lives in Grant Park. That's all I know. I don't have his phone number. I swear."

"That's okay. I can find his address."

Saldano put a single .22 round into Wilhoite's ear. The flash momentarily illuminated the vehicle's interior, but its heavy doors, with their windows up, contained the sound.

As he shoved Wilhoite's lifeless body into the passenger seat and drove away, his headlights swept over two men standing in the shelter of a doorway across the street. *Ah shit!*

Pausing at a stop sign, he glanced back to see if they had noticed him. One of the men passed a small plastic bag to the other. *Just another street corner drug deal.*

He eased away, and the men parted ways as though nothing had happened.

Back at his motel room, Saldano brought up the app he had used to locate the home addresses he burglarized. He debated the wisdom of exposing himself to discovery, now that the only person who could tie him to Braithwaite lay dead in a darkened parking lot.

Counting the cash hidden in his battered suitcase lining, he realized he had nowhere near enough to set himself up with a new identity in another city. *This Braithwaite is going to pay me a lot more for the laptop and phone than he paid Simon.*

The following morning, he visited Scarborough's residence, posing as a delivery driver. He parked his nondescript rental van around the corner, stepped up onto the porch and checked the interior through a curtained window. Despite its clutter of antique furnishings, it had an abandoned feel.

Saldano considered breaking in and ransacking the place but decided to wait. He knew the man would return eventually. Instead, he left in search of a cheap apartment close at hand where he could lie low.

He returned several times over the next few weeks. Dressed as a homeless man, all but invisible to passersby, he wandered up and down the street each day, watching the house.

When a passing cop finally stopped him for questioning, Saldano again thought of giving up his quest. *But I need the fucking money.*

Chapter Six

Lisa Chu

Smyrna/Atlanta
September 24, 2019

Peeping from behind her locker door, Lisa Chu scrutinized the young man as he made his way through throngs of students changing classes. She studied the contours of his face, his impassive countenance, the compact movements of his body. Shorter than most ninth-grade boys, Henry Wakefield struck her as someone others might never notice.

They'd met in World History. Though he wouldn't raise his hand or speak up, his eyes never left the teacher. When called upon, his answers came out crisp, correct, and deferential. The two football players seated behind him would snicker and make rude comments. If he heard them, he gave no indication.

Their gaze met as she closed the locker, and he gave her a winsome smile.

"Hey," she said.

"Hey yourself." His pale blue eyes bore into hers.

"Are you ready for the quiz?" she asked.

He shrugged. "As ready as I'm going to be."

For the past two evenings they'd met at a corner table at Starbuck's. Lisa pretended she didn't understand her assignments to draw him out. He would amaze her with the clarity of his answers, the calm, modest confidence as he explained them.

Trailing down the hall behind him the two football players closed in like pack animals. The taller one, *Ryan something*, grinned at his companion and dropped his shoulder into the middle of Henry's back, knocking him into Lisa and causing her to drop her books.

"Getting a little sideways action there, Wakefield?" he asked.

Before Lisa could stop him, Henry pounced like a feral cat. In one move, he swept the boy's feet out from under him, slammed his face into the floor, rolled over and clutched him from behind in a choke hold.

The river of students parted like the Red Sea. Ryan's companion knelt beside Henry and pummeled his face, to no avail. "Let him go!" he screamed. Henry blinked but neither flinched nor let up.

A hall monitor, with the aid of another teacher, separated the young men as Ryan's eyes bulged, and his face grew purple. It took him several minutes to catch his breath. A football coach escorted Henry to the principal's office, while the hall monitor helped Ryan to the nursing station.

Lisa sat through her next class in stunned silence, hearing nothing the teacher said. When it finally ended, she texted Henry.

By the time he replied, two hours later, school had let out. *Hey. Sorry about all that. You okay?*

I'm fine. Can I call you?

Sure.

He answered with an exasperated sigh. "Hey."

"Hey. What happened to you?"

"I'm suspended for two days, and I've been kicked off the wrestling team. My mom's pissed. She's grounded me. She was going to take away my phone, but she needs a way to check up on me."

"I'm so sorry. Did they do anything to that *jerk*, Ryan? He's the one who started it."

"They probably sent him home with a lollipop," Henry said.

"I hate it that you're off the wrestling team. That's so unfair."

"I'm hoping they'll take me back . . . when I return to school."

"If you're grounded, how are we going to study?"

"My mom doesn't get home until six. You could come over here. It's a short walk."

"I'm not sure my parents would like that." She took a deep breath. "Let me see what I can do."

* * *

Seated in the KSU library struggling with chemistry formulas, William's thoughts strayed back to Misty. A text from his mom startled him. *Where are you? When are you coming home?*

What's up?

Her typed response came slowly. William drummed his fingers as he waited. *She texts as if she's drafting a motion to suppress evidence. I can almost hear her tapping frantically with one finger.*

I had to go pull your brother out of school, that's all. It seems he tried to kill one of his classmates. I'm back at my office. I want you to go home RIGHT NOW and check on him. Make sure he doesn't go anywhere.

William shook his head and typed, *Okay.*

* * *

As he entered the house, he heard a low murmur of conversation from Henry's bedroom, as though explaining something on the phone. Then a female voice responded. *This I have got to see,* he thought.

Pretending he didn't know his brother had company, William tapped lightly and opened the door.

"*Hey*," Henry shouted. He reached for a lamp as though to heave it at William.

"Whoa! Sorry. I didn't know you . . . um . . . had company."

A beautiful Asian girl sat on the bed beside Henry, an open textbook between them. She had her hand on his knee, yet they both remained fully clothed. *Clearly, this boy needs some coaching.*

Henry's face reddened. "How about knocking next time?"

William noticed Henry's black eye. *Nothing new*. He raised his eyebrows. "Are you going to introduce your friend?"

"Uh . . . yeah. This is Lisa. Lisa, this is my brother, William," Henry glowered. "I'm going to have to teach him a lesson about barging into my room."

"Hey, Lisa." William extended a hand. "Nice to meet you."

"Hi."

"We were just studying," Henry blurted.

"Uh . . . yeah. About that. Somehow, I don't think Mom's going to see it that way. If *she* comes home and finds you like this, you'll be grounded until after the next election."

Henry lowered his head and nodded.

"Hey, why don't I give Lisa a ride home? You stay here. When I get back, I can set you guys up on Zoom. You can meet online, and all Mom needs to know is that you're studying."

"I'm going with you," Henry said.

"Nope. You're grounded, and if Mom finds out you left here on my watch, we'll *both* be in deep shit."

"I think he's right, Henry." Lisa said. "I'll be in trouble myself if I don't get home soon."

William and Lisa climbed into the Jeep. As they made a left onto Atlanta Road, they passed Marie on her way home. Distracted by traffic, she didn't seem to notice them.

"So, Lisa. How did you and Henry meet?"

"We sit next to each other in World History."

"Okay. And you're helping him with his studies?"

"It's more like he's helping me."

"Cool." William paused, trying to think of what to ask next. "So, you're a freshman. Did you go to Campbell Middle?"

"No, my family moved here right before school started."

"Where are you from?"

"Hong Kong originally. We . . . ah . . . moved to Toronto a few years ago. My father taught there at the university."

"Hong Kong. Wow. How did you end up in Toronto?"

She paused, as though choosing her words carefully. "Ever since the Chinese government took over, the people of Hong Kong have lived under tighter and tighter restrictions. They tell us what we can do and what we cannot. My father wanted to do research that would improve our lives. The People's Liberation Army wanted him to help develop new spy equipment. He only pretended to go along. When the University of Toronto offered him a one-year fellowship, he took it. When we got there, he applied for asylum."

"Didn't the PLA see that coming?"

"Apparently not. They thought we would return. Besides, we left my grandmother there."

"What happened to your grandmother?"

Tears flowed down her cheeks. "We don't know," she said, in a voice so low William could barely hear her.

Anxious to change the subject, he asked, "So, what brought you guys to Atlanta?"

"My dad got a temporary visa to teach electronics at Georgia Tech."

"How do you like it here?"

She brightened. "The people I've met are very nice."

"Even my brother?"

"Especially your brother." She lowered her head and gave him a shy smile.

"I wonder if your dad knows my uncle. He's doing research at Tech." He stopped for a moment, thinking of Garth Braithwaite. "At least he was until somebody murdered his partner."

Lisa's eyes widened. "I heard about that. That was horrible. My dad told me he knew the guy."

"Yeah? Dr. Braithwaite and my uncle were developing a biochip that can diagnose and report viruses and malignancies. They wanted to find a way to restrict blood flow to tumors. Now my uncle's trying to find somebody to replace him."

A thought came to William. "What happens when your dad's visa expires?"

She shrugged. "I'm hoping we can stay here permanently. Toronto gets pretty cold in the winter."

"Maybe my uncle could talk to your dad about taking over Dr. Braithwaite's position."

* * *

Not wanting to return home amid a brouhaha between Marie and Henry, William texted Marie saying he was going over to his grandfather Tom's place.

Two years earlier, Tom had taken William on a cross-country trip. After dropping him off at LAX with a ticket to Atlanta, Tom continued his journey, writing stories and updating friends and family. He returned six months later with a new girlfriend, Brandy Spain.

To William, it seemed that she must have been beautiful once, but a lifetime of suntanning and smoking had taken its toll. Though ten years younger than Tom, she looked the same age.

"I had to get out of the house," he told her. "Henry got kicked out of school again for fighting, and I didn't want to be there when Mom got home."

"Can't say I blame you."

William followed her into the dining room where he found Tom.

"I have some news," Tom said. "David Meacham and Mark White are helping Beth Long with the Braithwaite murder. I don't know if you remember them, but they're the cops who investigated the break-in at my house in Midtown a couple of years ago. I was able to get Meacham's number."

"Do you think he'll talk to me?"

"I don't know, but we can try."

Tom pulled out his phone and dialed. He held his finger to his lips as it rang.

"Meacham," a voice answered.

"Officer Meacham, this is Tom Williams. I don't know if you remember me."

"Yeah. I remember." He sounded wary.

"I believe you spoke to my son-in-law yesterday following the Braithwaite murder."

"Your son-in-law?"

"Sean O'Meara."

"Dr. O'Meara is your son-in-law?"

"Yep. Small world, isn't it?"

"I'd say so."

"I was wondering what you might have found out about . . ."

"Say, aren't you a reporter?"

"I was."

"Then you know I can't talk to you about an ongoing investigation."

"Actually, this isn't for me. My grandson's writing for his school newspaper. He was wondering if you might have some time for an interview about your work."

A long pause followed. "I guess that's okay, as long as he doesn't expect me to talk about the Braithwaite case. When do you want to meet?"

"Let's ask him. He's right here."

Startled, William answered, "I could meet you on Monday. What would be a good place?"

"Monday's my day off. I live in Conyers."

"Are you available in the afternoon around four?" *My God. Conyers? It'll take me an hour to get there.*

Meacham agreed to meet him at a Pizza Hut off I-20.

When he hung up William asked, "What do you know about him?"

"Meacham? From what I've heard, he's been on the force more than twenty years. He's a good beat cop, decent investigator, but he'll be lucky to retire as a sergeant."

"You think he carries some resentment about that?"

"He might."

"What should I tell Mom about this interview?"

"You can text her from Conyers and tell her you'll be home late."

"Oh my God! She'll kill me."

"Yeah, but it'll take her mind off Henry for a while."

Chapter Seven

The Interview

Atlanta/Conyers, GA
September 25, 2019

    The medical examiner's report on Braithwaite yielded no surprises as to his cause of death. But, acting on Long's request that he examine the victim for STDs, he found a tiny, recent scar at the base of Braithwaite's penis. Otherwise, he would have missed the microchip inserted next to a small blood vessel. *Would that have anything to do with his research?* Long scanned the ME's notes again as she dialed.
    "O'Meara," the voice answered.
    "Dr. O'Meara, this is Sergeant Long. When we spoke the other day, you mentioned that your work with Dr. Braithwaite involved medical microchips."
    "Yes."
    "Can you think of any reason why Dr. Braithwaite would have a chip implanted next to his uhm . . ." She looked up the term. ". . . *internal pudendal artery*?"
    "I . . . I have no idea."
    "What medical conditions did you say you're studying?"
    "Under the terms of our grant, we're focusing on the detection and, ultimately, the destruction of certain types of tumors."
    "Was Dr. Braithwaite researching any other conditions you know of?"

"He . . . once mentioned a side project. It involved a means of *increasing* blood flow using a microchip. It sounded crazy to me, but he was the chip guy. My background's oncology."

"How did this topic come up?"

"At the time, we were discussing angiogenesis, the process by which tumors create their own blood supply."

"And?"

"And he said something about an idea he had to repair damaged or atrophied organs."

"Was he developing a microchip for that purpose?"

"I . . . I don't know. Like I said, it would have been a side project."

"Did he mention anything else about this idea?"

"No. That's all. He sort of . . . blurted it out, then went off on a different topic."

"Would he have used any of your research funds for such a project?"

O'Meara went silent, as though stunned by the question. "Sergeant, that would constitute fraud. It would void our grant and subject Garth, and probably me, to disciplinary and, perhaps, legal action."

"Do you know if Dr. Braithwaite might have developed such a chip before he died?"

"That seems unlikely."

"What would that involve?"

"First, he'd have to design a prototype."

"How would he go about doing that?"

"Once he completed his CAD drawings, I'm sure anyone with the right printing equipment could have done it. But I don't see how he could have reached the testing stage so quickly without a lot of help from a vascular specialist."

"If he *had* developed a prototype, how would he go about implanting it?"

"That would require surgery. Without FDA approval, I can't envision any competent doctor in the United States performing such a procedure."

Long considered this. "You say no competent *U.S.* physician would do it. Could he have developed the chip with a foreign specialist, possibly south of the border?"

"I suppose so. He took some time off a few months back."

Long scribbled a note to investigate any flights Braithwaite might have taken.

"Where would he have gotten funding for this, if it didn't come from your research grant?"

"Sergeant, if Garth was working on a permanent cure for erectile dysfunction, there is no end to possible funding sources. The market for such a product would be inestimable."

"Dr. O'Meara, I have another question I meant to ask you earlier. When we found Dr. Braithwaite, we didn't see a cell phone *or* a laptop. Is there any reason why he would have left them at his office?"

"I don't think so. The university bought that laptop for him. It was state of the art, and Garth took a lot of pride in it. He used it for evaluating complex CAD designs, and he did a lot of online gaming in his downtime."

"Thank you, Dr. O'Meara. I'll get back to you if I have further questions."

Long gazed down at her file and took a deep breath. She called her superior, Lieutenant Art Darnell, and reluctantly requested FBI assistance.

As she rung off, a text appeared. *Hey, do you suppose you could come over tonight and bring Grafton?*

Long hadn't spoken with her daughter's father, psychotherapist Brandon Markham, since the day of the Braithwaite murder. She thought about calling him to get his professional opinion, as a therapist, about what would motivate grown men like Braithwaite to seek sex from underage women. Suddenly she broke out laughing, recalling her own age difference from Markham.

As much as she enjoyed the older man's company, she couldn't picture him as a husband. From the beginning, they'd had a transactional relationship. He'd satisfied her needs, while his marriage precluded him from wanting anything more, or so she thought. Invariably, their most intimate conversations wound up with the two of them naked in bed.

Given her current stress level, Long could use the diversion, but that would necessitate dropping off Grafton at her mom's. Nancy would know immediately the purpose of the sleepover, and that would only lead to another argument. She smiled as she pictured Markham's trim body, hardened by a five-mile-a-day run followed by a rigorous workout.

Brandon, I'll have to make it another night, she replied.

She twirled the medical examiner's plastic vial between her fingers, unable to see the microscopic device inside. *How can something so small be so powerful that someone would pay so much for it?*

* * *

Tom and William's trip to Conyers took an hour and a half in traffic. Tom drove, while William made notes.

"Okay, what's the main thing you want Meacham to tell you?"

"I'd like to know how the police are coming with Dr. Braithwaite's murder."

"*Nope*. He made that a hard condition when he agreed to the interview. If you even mention Braithwaite, Meacham will probably get up and walk out. Just get him talking and don't interrupt him until he comes up for air. When he does, be ready with your next question. Now, tell me what you have."

"I'll start with some innocuous topics, like what made him decide to become a cop, the kind of training he went through . . ."

"Good. Remember what I taught you. Begin with things he'll *want* to talk about. Build trust by showing a genuine interest in *him* and his profession. Don't bring up any potentially sore subjects like his rank or any missed promotions. When he says something interesting, ask for specifics, but don't press him if he starts to clam up. Remember, you're not an investigative reporter . . . yet. He didn't have to agree to this interview. He's doing you a favor."

They arrived early and found the restaurant empty but for a couple of customers near the door. As they located a seat in a quiet corner, William tried to ignore the aroma of fresh-baked pepperoni pizza.

Through the front window they watched as a middle-aged man with a gray brush cut stepped out of a dark blue Ford Bronco. He wore a tan blazer, golf shirt and jeans.

"That's him," Tom said.

Despite his civilian attire, something in Meacham's bearing made him look like a cop, perhaps the way he walked with his hands out from his side.

"Right on time," said Tom.

As he stepped inside, Meacham stopped and removed his aviator sunglasses. He ambled over and extended a hand. "Mr. Williams."

"Good afternoon, Officer. It's been a long time."

He smiled. "Not long enough. This must be your grandson."

"Hi. I'm William Wakefield."

"Pleased to meet you. So, tell me what I can do for you . . . so long as it doesn't involve Braithwaite."

William pulled out his notebook and pen. "You don't mind if I take notes, do you? It helps me remember things more clearly."

"Sure. That's what reporters do." He grinned at Tom.

"So, if you don't mind, can you tell me you how became a cop?"

"I graduated from high school and joined the army. They sent me to Fort Gordon over in Augusta for MP training. When I got out, policing was all I knew, so I signed up for the Academy and eventually got a transfer to Homicide."

"What does your typical day look like?"

"Most of the time the job's pretty boring. I sit in a patrol car somewhere until we get a call. Then things can get . . . *unboring* ."

"What sort of calls do you get?"

"Even though my partner and I are with homicide, we take all kinds of complaints, noisy neighbors, domestic disturbances, sketchy-looking guys prowling around somebody's home. You never know where that'll lead. By the time we get there, the subject's usually gone or the caller's changed their story."

"So, what happens when you get called to a murder scene?" As he flipped a page, William made sure Meacham could see the notes he'd prepared for his interview with Braithwaite.

"We arrive, secure the scene and make sure we don't have a suspect hiding somewhere ready to jump us. If we see anybody who looks suspicious, Officer White takes him outside and questions him while I take pictures inside."

"What if there's no one there?"

"We call in the crime scene techs and put up yellow tape. Meanwhile, the lead investigator arrives and takes more pictures to make sure we get a complete visual record. When the techs arrive, they take *even more* photos, gather evidence, bag it and take it to the lab."

"What do you do next?"

"Usually, the lead investigator puts us out on the streets knocking on doors, finding out who might have seen what happened or knew the victim. Sometimes she'll call in more officers."

"You said 'she'. Your lead investigator's a woman?"

"Yes. Officer Mark White and I handle a lot of cases with Sergeant Elizabeth Long. Your grandaddy knows Sergeant Long."

As Meacham spoke, William thought he saw a flicker of disgust cross his face. *Does he resent working for a woman?* He bit his tongue to avoid mentioning that she had called him.

Examining his notes he asked, "So, when you have an *unknown* suspect, like with the Braithwaite case, what role do the crime scene investigators play in helping you make an arrest?"

Meacham responded with a smirk. "This isn't like television. The stuff the techs come up with hardly ever leads to an arrest unless we match DNA or a fingerprint with the national database. Finding a killer takes *police work*. The techs mainly help the prosecutor get an indictment and a conviction, *after* we've caught the bad guy."

William wrapped up with his standard question, "Can you think of anything I haven't asked?"

"You could ask me how I'm able to get up every day and put on my uniform knowing that most of the people I'm protecting don't really care for what I do."

"Okay."

Meacham leaned across the table. His eyes narrowed. "I do it because I want to make a difference. And even on my *worst* days . . . I still believe I do."

"I'm sure you do."

Meacham glanced at William's notes. "So, tell me what you thought of Dr. Braithwaite."

"Well, before I found out about his murder, I'd planned to interview him for a technology article I'm writing. I spoke with him earlier on Zoom but only briefly. He seemed like a smart man, able to explain his work in terms I didn't need a PhD to follow."

Meacham nodded. "And?"

"From what I could see of him, he seemed a bit vain, the way he dressed, his carefully combed hair, the earring, like he was preening for the camera."

Meacham raised his eyebrows. "Would you call him a lady's man?"

"I guess *he* thought he was."

William paused. "Officer, I don't know if you've spoken with Dr. Braithwaite's assistant, Delbert Foster, yet. I interviewed him the other day about his role in the microchip research. He mentioned that he'd dropped out of the PhD program, then he became evasive when I asked him how he was able to stay on as Dr. Braithwaite's grad assistant. It seemed strange at the time. It might not mean anything. I just thought you should know."

Meacham pursed his lips. "Might not . . . but I appreciate the information. You never know."

Meacham's phone rang. He gave the number a curious look then answered. The voice on the line came through clearly. William and Tom glanced at each other.

"Officer Meacham, this is Sean O'Meara. You asked me to call you if I remembered anything else."

Meacham glanced at Tom, then excused himself, rose from the table and moved out of earshot.

When he came back, Tom said, "Officer, thank you very much. We won't take up any more of your time. I need to get William back to Smyrna before my daughter rips my head off."

* * *

Walking out to the Jeep, William stopped long enough to text Marie, saying he would be late getting home.

As they pulled out of the parking lot, William asked, "Is it always that easy to get cops to talk to you?"

"I wish it were. I'm usually trying to get information about an open case. They won't talk to me unless they're asking all the questions or have a story they want to float on condition of anonymity. That's why it's important to build trust with them."

"Have you ever been coerced to give up a confidential source?"

"Nope."

"Would you?"

"Nope."

"Is it okay that I mentioned that part about Delbert Foster."

"Did you interview Foster off the record?"

"No."

"Are you hoping to get more information out of him later?"

"Probably not."

"Then it's okay. Who knows? It might help Meacham's investigation and make him look good. He might even remember that the next time you have questions for him."

"Meacham mentioned his partner, Mark White. I think you said you'd met him. What's he like?"

"Probably a good cop, though not very bright. Meacham seems to act as his mentor. White basically does what he's told."

Tom gazed out the window, then added, "I spoke to my contacts at the *AJC*. They liked the idea for your sidebar on Braithwaite's research, but they don't have room for it."

William let out a long sigh. "Thanks anyway." Why don't we call Uncle Sean and ask him about his conversation with Meacham?"

Tom pulled out his phone, called Sean and put it on speaker.

"Hey, Sean. William and I are on our way back from Conyers. You'll never guess who we were just chatting with."

"Who?" He sounded irritated that Tom had interrupted him.

"David Meacham. William was interviewing him at a Pizza Hut when you called."

Sean took a deep breath. "I wanted to tell him that I'd remembered something since . . . since the day of the murder. I didn't bring it up at the time. I was afraid it might damage Garth's reputation."

"Sean, the man's dead. What harm could it do him now."

"I don't want this getting into the news and embarrassing Garth's relatives back in California . . . but there were rumors about the reason he had to leave Cal Tech. Supposedly they caught him . . . uh . . . diddling a coed."

"Like that's something new," said Tom.

"We're talking about a fifteen-year-old exchange student with emotional issues."

"Ouch. Anything else?"

"Only that a couple of his grad students accused him of stealing their ideas and claiming them as his own."

Tom chuckled. "It sounds like Sergeant Long could wind up with *too many* suspects."

"*Oh*. I got the weirdest call from her earlier."

"Really?"

"The medical examiner found a microchip planted at the base of Garth's penis."

"What?"

William shook with laughter until Tom shushed him. "What's this all about?"

"All I know is that Garth had been developing a chip that increased blood flow."

"Yeah, I can see how that might have some financial and . . . uhm . . . *romantic* benefits."

"Yeah. Well, it certainly had nothing to do with *our* research."

"I understand, Sean. But if you do decide to wrap up that little project for him, please let me know. I'll volunteer as a test subject. I'm sure Brandy won't mind."

William could hold back no more. "Pops, please! I don't want to hear it."

Then a thought came to him. "Uncle Sean, when I interviewed Delbert Foster, he mentioned that he dropped out of the doctoral program at Tech, but that Dr. Braithwaite kept him on as an assistant anyway. Is that typical in such cases?"

"I don't know. But it does sound kind of strange when Garth had so many other grad assistants he could use."

"Do you think Delbert might have had something on Dr. Braithwaite . . . perhaps the proverbial naked pictures?"

"William, I wouldn't know anything about that. Guys, I have to go. I have work to do."

As they pulled into Tom's driveway, William asked, "How would I go about seeing Dr. Braithwaite's home?"

"Why?"

"I'm getting a very different picture of him from what we just learned. Perhaps seeing where he lived and died might help. Do you think you could find out his address?"

"Okay. But if your mom asks, you don't remember where you got it."

* * *

FBI Special Agent Mike Prillaman shut off his recording and silently thanked himself for getting a wiretap on Sean O'Meara's cell phone. Unsure what to make of everything he'd heard, he jotted the names *Tom* and *William* below those of Garth Braithwaite, Sergeant Long and David Meacham. *Why would Braithwaite be researching a cure for erectile disfunction, and what might that have to do with his murder?*

Chapter Eight

The Feds

Atlanta
September 26, 2019

Beth Long set down her order, two "naked dogs," fried rings and an orange soda. Since coming back from maternity leave, she'd eaten at Atlanta's Varsity Drive-in at least twice a week, a habit that made controlling her weight more difficult.

As she settled into a hard plastic chair, her phone rang in her pocketbook. "Long," she answered.

"Sergeant, this is Debra Galway."

Long took a second to recognize the name. She'd left countless apologetic messages for Braithwaite's sister, to no avail.

"Ms. Galway, I appreciate your calling me back. I won't take much of your time. I'm just trying to get some background on your brother."

Galway took a deep breath. "I don't know what I can say that'll help. Garth and I hadn't spoken in . . . several months."

Long caught a hesitancy in her voice, as if she were choosing her words carefully.

"What can you tell me about Garth's tenure at Cal Tech?"

"We didn't talk a lot about that. It was all way over my head."

"What was he like outside of work?"

She paused and asked, "What can I say? He was so full of life, a photographer, a runner, an avid skier. He joined my husband and me at Tahoe last Christmas."

Something in her responses sounded disingenuous, as though she'd rehearsed them.

"Do you know if he was seeing anyone?"

"He mentioned various girlfriends in the past, but never brought any of them over to meet us."

Long decided to do a little fishing "I understand Garth named you his executrix."

"Of course. I'm his only heir." This time, she seemed more comfortable, handling the softball question with ease.

Time to shake her up. "Ms. Galway, why did Cal Tech fire Garth?"

"I don't know anything about that."

Clearly she did. *What's she hiding?*

"Ms. Galway, If I were to contact one of Garth's former colleagues, what do you think they might say?"

"I'm telling you I don't know why they fired him. It all seemed so sudden."

"Thank you anyway. I'm sure you're going through a very rough time. I want you to know that my team and I will not rest until we bring your brother's killer to justice."

"I appreciate that."

"If I think of anything else, would you mind if I called you?"

"No."

With that, the woman hung up, leaving Long convinced that she'd lied about his abrupt departure from his former employment.

As she stared out at the parking lot, Long's phone rang again *M. Prillaman-FBI* flashed on the screen.

"Hello."

"Sergeant, this is Special Agent Mike Prillaman with the FBI."

Long had met the man on several occasions, but for some reason he still felt the need to introduce himself every time.

"Yes, Agent Prillaman."

"We got word back from Microsoft on Professor Braithwaite's One Drive account."

Long drummed her fingers. *Finally. What took these guys so long?* "Tell me you have good news."

"I'm afraid not. When our agents opened it, they discovered someone had wiped the files."

"*Shit.* Don't they have a backup?" Long knew nothing of such things.

"No ma'am. One Drive *is* a backup." His tone sounded patronizing. "By the way, when you spoke with Dr. O'Meara, did he say anything about scientists in other countries doing competing research?"

"No."

"Did he indicate that he or Dr. Braithwaite had travelled abroad in the past year?"

These sounded to Long like strange questions, given what little she had on the murders. *What does this guy know that I don't?* "No. I don't suppose you've had any luck tracing Dr. Braithwaite's phone or computer?"

"No ma'am. According to a gentleman we spoke with at Georgia Tech, Dr. Braithwaite had a school-issued laptop with a tracking app, but it won't light up until someone logs in. As for the phone, we believe whoever has it removed the battery."

"Figures." Long took a deep breath. She made a note to call the university's IT department to find out more about the app. "So," she asked, "where do we go from here, Agent Prillaman?"

"We're interviewing Braithwaite's former colleagues at Cal Tech to see if they know anyone who might have had a motive to kill him. We've also spoken with his only known family member, a sister in Bakersfield, Debra Galway. She wasn't much help."

Long wasn't about to let him know she'd spoken to Galway. "What about the rumors of orgies at his place? Don't you think it's a bit suspicious that Braithwaite's home movies disappeared right after his murder?"

"You don't know that Braithwaite ever *had* any sex videos."

"We found a hidden camera with a network uplink."

"Sergeant . . . *we never found anything on his One Drive.*"

Of course not, you idiot. Someone removed them. "And you don't find it strange that someone would wipe his drive right after his murder?"

"Perhaps."

"Who would have had access to his account?"

Prillaman paused, as though ruminating. "I suppose someone who had his One Drive ID and password."

"Yeah. I guess so. Did anyone *you* interviewed mention Braithwaite's . . . proclivities?"

Prillaman sighed. "No, Sergeant. No one we spoke to mentioned anything like that. We'll keep searching. If we find anything, I'll let you know."

"Thank you, Agent Prillaman."

He'd already hung up.

Long's suspicions turned to Debra Galway. *As Braithwaite's executrix, would she have access to his cloud accounts? Why would she erase his files? What might he have stored there besides sex videos?*

Long stared at her meal, no longer hungry. She didn't trust the FBI *or* Prillaman. This investigation needed real police work, but the moment she brought in the FBI, everything became mired in bureaucracy and hidden agendas. Lieutenant Darnell told her she could continue her investigation, *provided she coordinated with the feds.*

Staring out the window and across the Downtown Connector, she contemplated the Georgia Tech dorms backlit by the late afternoon sun. *Why would the feds be so quick to jump on a routine homicide?*

Long missed her old boss. Lieutenant Paxton Davis, now retired, spent his days at his lake house in North Florida. He'd been more a mentor than a supervisor. *Maybe I'll give him a call.*

Then another thought came to her. Braithwaite's murder might be a federal matter, but no one said anything about his possible involvement in child trafficking. Long looked up an old friend of her dad's now with the Special Victims unit. Sergeant Sid Cosgrove, when they last spoke, patrolled the West Midtown neighborhood, including the seedier areas of Howell Mill Road and Northside Drive.

He answered on the third ring. "Beth Long! I heard you were back from maternity. How old is that little girl of yours now?" She heard him pause to recall the name. "Grafton."

"Grafton's fine, Sid. She's three years old and I'm the one going crazy, chasing her around the house every night, keeping her out of trouble, then worrying about her all day."

"Yeah. As I recall *you* were quite the little hellion at that age. What can I do for you?"

"What do you know about a child trafficking operation in West Midtown? Delivers teenage girls to select locations in a white limo."

"You're working that Braithwaite murder."

"I was . . . before the feds swooped in."

"Does that mean you'll be turning over what you have to them?"

"Nope."

"Good girl. But I'm afraid I can't help you much on the trafficking thing. I've heard some vague rumors about this white limo operation, but so far that's all we have. Supposedly, they cater to a very select clientele. We don't know where they are or how their customers contact them. They might as well be ghosts. The damned NSA should be so secure. If we find anything, I'll get back to you."

"Thanks, Sid," said Long. *He'll get back to me sooner than Prillaman will.*

She took a deep breath and gazed at her meal. Though it had gone cold, it would have to tide her over until supper. She ate as much as she could stomach and contemplated her next move. As she dropped the remains into a trash can and stacked her tray, another idea came to her. She pulled up a number on her cell.

Long knew Amy Springer from their student days at Georgia State. A medical social worker, Springer became an advocate for Atlanta's sex workers while interning in the emergency room at Grady Memorial Hospital.

"Amy, this is Beth Long."

"Wow, Beth! It's been a long time. What can I do for you?"

"I was wondering if I might get your professional advice on a case I'm pursuing."

"Okay . . ."

Long filled her in, and Springer promised to get back to her.

As Long reached her car, she stopped and dialed David Meacham. "Hey, just checking in. Did you and Mark get anything else from Braithwaite's neighbors?"

"Yeah. One of them claimed he saw Bram Dennis sneaking out of Braithwaite's place early one morning, a few days before the break-in."

"Bram Dennis the state senator?"

"Yeah. You never know what shit you'll get when you start knocking on doors."

"Yeah. Did you find out anything else."

"Oh. It seems that Braithwaite's *research assistant* is not a professor or even a doctoral student."

"So?"

"That kind of raises the question as to why Braithwaite would hire him. I mean, why wouldn't Braithwaite get one of the other professors or one of his students to help him? Sounds fishy to me."

Long pondered this for a moment. "Okay. Maybe I should pay Mr. Foster another visit."

"What if we could check his bank accounts?"

"I'll have to leave that to the FBI."

* * *

Tired of waiting for Dean Scarborough to return to his Grant Park home, Steven Saldano fell back on his professional skills. A quick survey of Scarborough's back yard found it so shielded from view that he could get in and out unseen.

The security system logo had grown old and faded, indicating to Saldano that Scarborough had probably stopped making payments. He shrugged it off and picked the lock. Once inside, he sprinted to the foyer, where a small mountain of mail had accumulated beneath the slot in the front door. He scooped the envelopes into a contractor-size trash bag, never stopping to scan them. Though he wore surgical gloves, he touched nothing else.

As he exited, Saldano stopped long enough to snap pictures of photos lining the mantel. One of them *had* to be Scarborough.

Back at his tiny rental unit, he sifted through his haul. The bills included several with unpaid balances stretching back over the past three months. The one account Scarborough had kept up to date was his cell phone service. Saldano took a deep breath as he texted.

You don't know me, Dean, but you need to call me right away. Simon Wilhoite hired me to retrieve some sensitive items for you. You won't be hearing from him. You're dealing with me now. If the police find me, we're both going down together.

* * *

Ensconced in the solitude of his friend's lake cabin, Scarborough decided to reach out again to his client.

"I thought I told you to lose this number," the man shouted.

Scarborough interrupted him. "The burglar has my name and my phone number. He knows where I live, and he's demanding that I pay him for stuff he stole."

"Listen . . ."

"No. You listen. If the police catch this guy, he's gonna give me up. *And you need to know that I'm not going down alone.*"

The man paused. Scarborough could almost hear him gathering his thoughts. "How did he get your number. Tell me you weren't dumb enough to give it to Wilhoite."

Scarborough searched his memory. "No. I didn't."

"This guy's a burglar. He might have broken into your home and found it somewhere."

"He could have."

"Do you have security cameras?"

"Yes."

"And the service never notified you?"

"I've had so many false alarms, I asked them not to, but I left the cameras running in case of a real break-in. I could call them."

"Bad idea. Give me their number. I have an investigator, an ex-cop. I'll have him contact them."

Chapter Nine

Subterfuge

Atlanta / Rural Virginia
September 26, 2019

Sean O'Meara slowed to a jog, caught his breath and cooled down. Running five miles a day had produced few results, especially around his waistline. Age had gained on him.

His phone buzzed in the pocket of his running shorts. He opened the text to find a video of his wife and daughters. "Hey, Daddy!" squealed eleven-year-old Mary Frances. They sang a loud rendition of *Happy Birthday to You*, accompanied by dancing emojis.

"We love you, Dad," said Lauren, now eighteen and a freshman at Emory.

"Come home soon," his wife Kathleen added. "We have a big surprise for you."

As he shoved the phone back into his pocket, it vibrated again with a voice mail he'd missed earlier.

"Hello, Sean. This is Harmon Wakefield. I know we haven't seen each other in a long time, but I have something I'd like to run by you."

Sean barely knew the man. They'd met once, at Marie and Bill's wedding twenty years ago. *How did he get my number, and what would he want to talk to me about?*

He started to dial but thought the better of it. *Should I ask Marie what her ex-father-in-law might want? Better yet.* He pulled up a list of recent calls and hit the call-back button.

"Uncle Sean!"

"Hey, William. Do you know why your grandfather would call me?"

"Pops?"

"Your other grandfather."

"No. I could reach out and see what he says."

"I'd appreciate that."

"By the way, happy birthday."

"Thanks, William."

"You guys have any plans for tonight?"

"Yeah. They're taking me to Canoe for dinner. I'm not supposed to know that, but I noticed the reservation on Kathy's phone."

"Are you still available for an interview tomorrow?"

Sean held the phone away as he sighed. He appreciated William's interest in his work and wanted to encourage his journalistic aspirations. And he *had* promised him.

"Sure. Why don't we meet at the OK Cafe off I-75 at West Paces? My treat. We could get there a little early and avoid the rush."

"Sounds great."

"By the way," William asked. "How did things go with Dr. Chu?"

"Oh. Thanks for putting me in touch with him. We spoke yesterday. He seemed interested, and we scheduled a formal interview for this afternoon."

* * *

As he dialed Harmon, William wondered what a retired Virginia senator would want with a biotech researcher in Atlanta whom he hardly knew. *Is this why he wanted to know about Dr. Braithwaite?*

"William," Harmon answered.

"Hey, Grandpa. What you been up to?"

"Nothing much, chatting with some old friends. How about you?"

"I've been pretty busy with school, and um . . . I met this girl."

"Great. Tell me about her."

"Well, her name's Misty. She's beautiful . . . and very smart. I met her in my math class. She plans to transfer to Georgia and study agronomy. Right now, she's living in Cherokee County with her grandmother, Esther."

"Agronomy?"

"Yeah. She wants to get her master's and go into research."

"Wow. I'm impressed. I'd like to meet this girl."

"Maybe I could bring her up there sometime on a road trip."

"Absolutely. Now, tell me again what *you're* studying."

"Journalism. I'm interviewing science and engineering professors for my blog site. I'm also writing for a campus magazine."

"If you want to learn engineering, why aren't you at Georgia Tech?"

"No way! I'm barely passing freshman math. I think I'll stick to writing about the work other people are doing . . . you know . . . like Uncle Sean."

"Do you know if the police have a suspect yet in the Braithwaite murder?"

"Not that I know of."

"This must have put Sean in an awful bind."

"I'm sure."

"I was thinking about your Uncle Sean the other day. I know someone who'd like to speak with him. Owns a company that develops biomedical devices."

"What's their name?"

"MedChip Labs."

"Cool. That might interest him. What kind of devices?"

"Ones that identify new viruses."

"Wow."

William grasped for something else to say. "Oh. I almost forgot. Henry has a new girlfriend. Her name's Lisa Chu. And her dad's an engineering professor at Georgia Tech. I gave Uncle Sean his name, and he's interviewing him to replace Doctor Braithwaite."

"Really?" Harmon paused, and William heard a voice in the background.

"Hold on," said Harmon. "Your grandmother wants to speak to you."

"Sure." Footsteps echoed on the kitchen tile. Evelyn cleared her throat as she picked up the phone.

"Hey, Grandma."

"Hey, William. Your dad tells me you and Henry are coming up here on Christmas Eve."

"Uh, actually, I think we're flying up the next day. Mom wants us to go to mass with her and Pops, his girlfriend and the O'Mearas."

"Good enough. Your grandfather and I are looking forward to having you. You boys can go horseback riding. Do some skeet shooting."

"That'll be great. We'd love that."

They chatted for a while as he caught her up on latest news. As she hung up, William still found Harmon's call to Sean puzzling. He Googled MedChip Labs and spent the next hour perusing their filings and press releases.

* * *

Harmon Wakefield sipped Pappy van Winkle on ice and studied the image of Bram Dennis frozen on his laptop. The man exuded the self-confidence a televangelist as he tucked an errant blonde curl behind one ear.

The camera, it seemed, loved the Georgia legislator. He represented a district northwest of Atlanta, one of the most conservative in the state. Its voters loved him as well and had re-elected him twice by large margins.

Peering from a corner of the screen, political operative Homer Starke laid out his case like a used car salesman. With his thick glasses and gaping mouth, he reminded Harmon of Mr. Magoo.

"I'm telling you, Harmon, this guy's the real deal. Before running for office, he spent fifteen years in management at Lockheed-Martin. He's a deacon in his church. He's tough on crime, and he scores one hundred percent with groups like the Family Research Council. He's an upstanding citizen all the way around. He'll make us a great U.S. senator."

Harmon only cared about the Lockheed experience, the rest being nothing more than a sop for ignorant voters. He needed support for his work on the China front and didn't trust the incumbent, a stock exchange executive appointed to fill an unexpired term.

"And you're sure, Homer, that this man has not even a whiff of scandal, no meth addiction, no dead hookers."

"I'm telling you the pope should be so clean."

Just out of view of the camera, sat Harmon's wife, Evelyn. She'd been his closest political adviser since his first run for Congress. He glanced at her for her appraisal of what they'd heard.

She gave him a skeptical look.

"Okay," said Harmon. "I'll give it some thought. In the meantime, I think I'll check out Senator Dennis myself." The buzz of his cell provided a perfect excuse to cut the meeting short. "Homer, I've got another call coming in. I'll get back with you."

"Sure. I just . . ."

Harmon closed the Zoom connection, reached for his phone, glanced at the ID and accepted the call.

"Hey, Sean."

"Hey, Harmon. I got your message. What can I do for you?" He sounded wary.

"William's been telling me about your work down there in Atlanta. Sounds impressive. He also mentioned the sudden death of your partner. I was sorry to hear about that."

"Yes."

"I was wondering if you've had any luck finding a replacement."

"I think so, a Dr. Gordon Chu."

"I see. That was quick."

"I guess it was. William gave me his name. It seems Gordon's daughter is a classmate of Henry's."

"Tell me about Chu."

"He was born in Hong Kong and emigrated to Toronto with his family a couple of years ago. He's been teaching at Georgia Tech on a temporary visa. He likes the area and wants to join our project. He has excellent credentials."

"Well . . . I *had* called to tell you about a private sector opportunity I thought might interest you. You'd be doing the same kind of work but making a lot more money."

Sean took his time answering. "I appreciate your thinking of me, Harmon, but my work here at Tech is very important to me, and to Kathleen. When I'm done with this project, I'll probably go back to teaching oncology at Emory."

"Well, if that should change, please let me know."

"I will . . . and uh . . . thanks again."

"My pleasure."

Harmon's next call went to Abigail Martin at the NSA. He got her voicemail, hung up and dialed his son office at the State Department.

When Bill answered, Harmon said, without preamble, "I need everything you can find out about a Dr. Gordon Chu, engineering professor at Georgia Tech."

"Okay. Can you tell me anything else?"

"I don't know if you heard, but somebody murdered Sean O'Meara's research partner, Garth Braithwaite, two weeks ago. Police still have no suspect. Sean's hiring this Dr. Chu to replace him. They're working on a medical microchip, and we desperately need to keep it away from the Chinese."

"Are you saying Dr. Chu is a PLA agent?"

"I don't know, but we can't take that risk. We have good reason to believe that the Chinese are developing bioweapons at their facility in Wuhan."

Bill sighed into the phone. "What makes you think Sean's research has anything to do with virology? Last I heard, he was searching for a cure for cancer."

"The technology he's developing could have all manner of medical uses. *We need it for defense purposes.*"

"Dad, don't you have *other* defense projects? I thought Abigail was getting NSA funding for you."

"First of all, I haven't heard back from her in a while. And now we have intelligence that the Chinese are experimenting with new virus strains in Wuhan. The last thing we need is for them to get their hands on *anything* that would protect them from a pestilence *they've* unleashed on the world."

"Yeah. I've seen that *intelligence.* So far, it amounts to nothing more than rumors of a flu-like disease. The last thing the president wants to do is spook people."

"I'm not talking about spooking *anybody*, son. We need to get ahead of this, and it's going to take *time*. I need to know that Sean O'Meara isn't providing crucial research to a PLA asset."

"Look, I can't spend my time chasing down phantom commies for you. The cold war is over. Doesn't Mom have work for you to do around the house?"

"*You think the cold war is over? Whose propaganda are you listening to?*"

"*Dad*, we have no reason to believe that China's research in Wuhan has anything but medical purposes."

"Everything China does, medical or not, has *military* purposes. To think otherwise is delusional."

Bill started to say something, then sighed. "Let me see what I can do."

He called back, an hour later, to say that Chu, as far as anyone could tell, had no connections with China's Ministry of State Security or the People's Liberation Army.

"I don't care, son. I want his visa revoked . . . yesterday."

Harmon disconnected without another word and made more calls. Within an hour he'd located one of the many private donors for O'Meara's research grant.

As their cook brought them supper in the arboretum, Harmon asked Evelyn, "So, what were your impressions of Bram Dennis?"

"He sounds too good to be true. How many of these born-again, family-values conservatives have turned out to be philanderers, or worse? You don't want to throw your support behind somebody like that Senate candidate from Alabama, the one who raped all those young women . . . And I wouldn't trust Homer Starke any further than I could throw him."

She paused, as though delicately framing her next comment. Quietly, without inflection, she said, "Harmon, what really troubles me is that you would blithely assume that this Gordon Chu is a PLA agent. For all you know, he's exactly what he says he is. Nor did you consider Henry's feelings in any of this. From what William says, Henry seems to care very much about Chu's daughter, Lisa. *And what right do you have to interfere with Sean O'Meara's research, just so you can pressure him into coming to work for one of your companies.*"

Harmon made no reply.

Chapter Ten

The Memoir

Cherokee County
September 27, 2019

Esther Sax clutched her sweater against the autumn chill and pulled her blanket higher. The late afternoon sun reflected in her face, softening the lines about her eyes. Sitting on her patio, she watched as Misty pulled weeds from her fall garden. She reached for her oxygen mask and took a long pull.

William raised his Fuji for a candid shot, then turned to capture Misty's intent expression as she used a trowel to dig out a stinging nettle.

"Look at her," Esther said. "All her life she's been like that. Whatever she wanted she pursued as if nothing else mattered. Can you believe she wants to go work on a kibbutz?"

"She told me that." *What would it take to change her mind?*

Laying his camera on the patio table, William slid his notebook from his backpack. "Mrs. Sax, Misty has told me so much about you. I'd like to find out more if you don't mind."

She gave him a dismissive wave. "Why should I mind? And by the way . . . if you're going to sleep with my only grandchild, the least you can do is call me 'Esther.'"

Hearing this, Misty stared at her, wide-eyed. "Grandma!"

"I'm not deaf, you know, I hear you two in the middle of the night. You're not as quiet as you think."

William took a moment to recover, sliding Misty a guilty look. "Uh . . . Esther, then," he said. "You don't mind if I take notes, do you? It helps me remember details later."

"Enough already! I don't mind."

"I understand you were born in Poland. I was wondering if you could share some of your earliest memories."

Her gaze shifted to a time and place far away. "Huh! Earliest memories. The few I recall, were of that damned camp." She shook her head.

"Auschwitz?"

"Yeah. Auschwitz."

Her left arm still bore the tattoo, a stark reminder that this woman, someone's daughter, someone's wife, someone's mother, Misty's grandmother, had once been treated as nothing but a number.

William paused, wondering what to ask next. "We can take this slowly if you like."

She pursed her lips and shrugged. "How much time do you think I have? If I don't talk about it now, when will I?" She paused and took another drag on the oxygen. "All I remember from that time are fragments, like torn photographs. I remember a woman. I think she was my mother . . . my first mother."

"Your first mother?"

"I must have been about three when the Germans arrested my parents. Somehow, we became separated after we got to the camp. I don't even know my real name. An older woman . . . Rebekah . . .hid me under some loose floorboards and named me Esther. She let me out at night to relieve myself. She cleaned me, shared her food with me. My God, what they would have done to her if they caught her! She was my second mother . . . She told me once that my name meant *star* in Hebrew, that Esther was a brave queen who saved our people."

Her expression remained impassive. What she saw through her welling tears William couldn't imagine. "You know, it took me a long time to remember how to cry."

She wiped her eyes and continued. "I had no papers. I didn't even know my real birthdate, so I took Rebekah's, July 6. In the days before the Russians came, the Germans finally killed Rebekah. Why they didn't find me I'll never know.

"After the war, some people rescued me and took me to the West. I have no idea who they were. From there they shipped me to New York with some other children. I was eight years old. A couple in New York, Hannah and Joe Abramowitz, adopted me. When I got there, the first thing I did was run and hide under the bed until they convinced me I could come out. Hannah was my third mother. She and Joe were the kindest people I ever knew. They taught me English and eventually sent me off to school."

"How did you meet your husband, Myron?"

Esther smiled for the first time, as though she'd found an old picture at the bottom of a drawer. "Myron Sax . . . I was in college when I took a job as bookkeeper for a garment manufacturer. That's where we met. Myron was a salesman . . . *such a salesman*. I tell you the man wouldn't leave me alone. He spent so much time in my office, it's a wonder he sold anything.

"We married in 1960. When Myron took a job here in Atlanta, I told him I would move south with him under one condition. I was sick of the city. I wanted to live in the country, with trees and open sky. So, he brought me here. You should have seen this place. There was not another house in sight. That road out there was nothing but dirt. So much for New York."

"That's quite a story. What would you say it taught about humanity?"

She considered for a moment. "Human beings can be brave, like Rebekah. They can be compassionate, like Joe and Hannah. They can be smart and funny, like my Myron. But put them together in a mob, give them a charismatic leader who promises them a better life, and they turn into animals." She sighed, "Maybe they're afraid. Maybe they need something that makes them superior, or their lives become meaningless. What can I say?"

"Do you ever worry that all that could happen again?"

Esther smirked. "What do you think all that stuff in Charlottesville was about?"

William froze for a moment, suddenly recalling the Unite the Right marchers, their antisemitic rants, and the murder of a peaceful demonstrator. Returning to his notes, he asked, "What was it that kept you going through all that?"

"First it was Rebekah, then Joe and Hannah, then Myron and our son Jeff." She watched her granddaughter working with such quiet intensity. "Now it's Melissa."

Without knowing why, William asked, "Esther, do you believe in God?"

"No. Joe and Hannah took me to temple, and I would hear the rabbi speak, but he could never explain to me how this God of his could choose a people and then abandon them."

"Do you believe in life after death?"

She lifted an arthritic finger and crooked it in Misty's direction. "You see that young lady over there? She's my life after death."

William could think of nothing else to ask.

Misty, brushing dirt from her hands, knelt beside her grandmother. "Grandma, I think this is enough for one day. Let me help you back inside."

In stunned silence, William settled onto a chaise lounge and awaited Misty's return. She came back with a blanket and squeezed in beside him.

"How much of that did you know?" he asked.

She shrugged. "Some."

"I hope I didn't upset her."

Misty bit her lower lip as a tear formed in the corner of her eye. She clasped his hand, "She needed to get it out . . . Thank you for doing this."

"Sure. Tomorrow morning I'll write it up and we can talk about it."

"I can't tell you how much this means to me."

"That part about her not believing in God, did you know that?"

"I'm not surprised."

"So, how do you feel about that?"

"You mean, do I believe in God?"

"Yes."

"I don't know. My dad's not very religious. My mom raised me Jewish. I think it was all a status thing for her. I had my Bat Mitzvah, all that. But lately . . . I don't know . . . How about you?"

"Same thing, I guess. My mom took Henry and me to church most Sundays, sent us to Catholic school, and all. It was just . . . what we did. We never really talked about it. I'm pretty sure Henry doesn't believe anymore." William snickered. "If he does, he's pretty pissed at God. In fact, Henry's generally pissed at everybody."

He pulled her close and nuzzled her hair.

"William, I'm all sweaty and dirty. I need a shower."

"You smell great. Just sit here with me for a while."

She let out a sigh. "Okay."

"So, tell me more about your parents. You said your dad sold his company for enough money to retire with a beach house and a yacht. What kind of business was it?"

"Oy. There you go again, *Mr. Reporter*. My dad and a friend designed a tracking device for vehicles. He came up with the idea while delivering pizzas at UGA. Landscaping and delivery companies used it to route their trucks and make sure they only went where their dispatchers sent them. Parents used it to keep tabs on their kids. Can you believe my mom had him put one in my car?"

"You must be very proud of your dad."

Misty took a moment to compose her answer. "Sure. Why not? He built a fortune. He even made the *Inc. 500.* Yeah, I was proud. At some level, I guess my mom's proud of him too. She sure is proud of all that money."

"You mentioned that your parents split up for a while."

"Yeah. They called it a *trial separation*. Not that it made much difference. I mean, he stayed gone all the time anyway. We only saw him late at night and early morning."

"You sound angry."

"Wouldn't you be?" she asked.

William gazed out at the last remnants of the sunset. "I guess so. Our situation was pretty much the same. I'm sure that at some level I resented my dad. He travelled so much that sometimes we wouldn't see him for weeks. Over time I thought about him less and less. I came to the realization that I was building my own life, and that it didn't depend on him."

Misty scrutinized him. "I guess we have that in common."

"What brought your parents back together?"

She smirked. "I suppose *I* did. I made my mom's life pure hell. I screamed at her when I didn't get what I wanted. She grounded me more times than I could remember. Finally, one night I snuck out. I met an older boy at the end of the street. He wanted to take me up to the lake with him. I convinced him to go to the mall instead."

She averted her gaze. "He tried to make me suck his dick right there in the parking lot," she said with a triumphant smile. "I nearly bit it off. He screamed like a little girl and let go of me. I had the door halfway open when he backhanded me across the face. I yelled for help and ran inside."

"Did he come after you?"

"No. The chickenshit drove off and left me there. I had to call my dad to come get me. He took me home. And then my parents called the police."

"What was that like for you?"

"I wanted to crawl inside a hole and die."

"What did the police do to the guy?"

"Nothing. He had to go to court. The judge let him off with a warning. He went back to school and bragged to his friends that he'd fucked me in his parents' car."

"So, he got away with it?"

"Nope. A few weeks later he showed up on crutches with his arm in a sling. Someone had jumped him where he worked, broke his kneecap, his collar bone and his nose."

"Oh shit! That's some serious payback."

"Yeah. They never caught the person who did it. But I knew it was my dad. We never talked about it. I just knew."

"Wow. Your dad sounds like a hell of a man."

"Yeah."

"So, your parents got back together."

She chuckled. "*Oh yeah*. Would you believe I came home from school one day and found them fucking?"

"Oh my God. Poor baby. I can't even imagine. Not that I'd want to."

"Yeah. I'm afraid I'll carry that visual for the rest of my life."

One by one, stars appeared, until they filled the firmament.

"Tell me," he asked. "When you were little, what did you want to be when you grew up . . . And don't tell me you wanted to be an agronomist."

She gave him a rueful smile. "I wanted to be an actress or a fashion model, like all the other little girls."

He brushed back a strand of hair from her brow. "Why?"

"I suppose I wanted people to think I was beautiful."

He pulled her to him and kissed her. "You *are* beautiful, Misty, more beautiful than you know."

"I appreciate your saying that. I just never thought of myself that way." Tears gathered in her eyes. "The only person I ever remember telling me that was my grandma."

He wrapped his arms around her and held her tight for a long while.

* * *

As William reached the turnoff to his neighborhood, an idea came to him. Continuing down Atlanta Road, he made his way to West Midtown. With the help of Waze and the address Tom had given him, he located Westparc Village and the home of the late Garth Braithwaite. Unable to gain entry, he stood at the gate and snapped several pictures.

The row of two-story bungalows sat on the smallest lots William had ever seen. *Braithwaite's must be the third on the left.* There, in the middle of a narrow strip of grass, stood a *For Sale* sign.

An idea came to him. He located a matching sign near the gate and scanned the QR code, hoping to get a text from the realtor by morning.

For good measure, he texted Misty. *Hey, give me a call sometime tomorrow.* He added, *I need your help with something,* then changed it to, *I have a small adventure in mind.*

Chapter Eleven

The Witness

Atlanta
September 30, 2019

Despairing of a breakthrough in the Braithwaite case, Beth Long immersed herself in another investigation, the murder of pawn shop owner Simon Wilhoite. She had no witnesses, scant forensics and no apparent motive. While examining pawn records, security footage and crime scene photos she received a call from Amy Springer.

"You wanted to know about child trafficking in the West Midtown area?" she asked.

"Yes."

"I think I have something for you."

"Shoot."

"At about three this morning, a motorist saw a young woman lying on the side of Collier Road near Northside Drive and called 911. It appears someone beat her up and dumped her there. The victim had no ID but gave her name as Mandy Carter."

"And?"

"She claims she's eighteen but looks more like thirteen."

"Okay. What about her condition?"

"The ER doctors tell me she has a fractured cheekbone. All I got from her were monosyllabic answers through clinched teeth."

"Is she still at Grady?"

"Yes. They treated her injuries and admitted her for observation. They think she ingested drugs of some sort."

"Okay. As soon as possible, I need to question her. What did she tell you about her assailant?"

"All I got was that he's a white male named Dan in his mid-fifties."

"Did you find out where Mandy lives?"

"No."

"Did she tell you how or where she met this Dan?"

"I asked, but she refused to answer."

"Have you called Child Protective Services?"

"What can they do with her? As far as we know she's eighteen."

"Thanks, Amy. Have the police questioned her?"

"A Sid Cosgrove came by. He couldn't get anything out of her either."

"Is he still there?"

"Yes."

"Can you get him for me?"

When Cosgrove came on, Long said, "Sid, I'm on my way there. Can you wait around?"

"Sure."

* * *

Springer met her at the emergency room entrance. Long hadn't seen her old friend in years. She'd put on weight and dressed like an aging sorority girl.

Nothing she had said could have prepared Long for the sight of Mandy Carter. Her short, red hair appeared dyed, and one whole side of her pale, freckled face, what little Long could see around the gauze and ice pack, had swollen twice its normal size and resembled an overripe eggplant. The other side appeared untouched.

Long could not imagine how a girl so young could have endured so much. *What horrors must she experience on a daily basis?* Overcome with anger, she pictured her daughter, Grafton. *This 'Dan' better pray I'm not the one who finds him.*

"How do you deal with this?" she asked Springer.

She shook her head. "I've seen worse."

Numbed by painkillers Mandy slid in and out of consciousness. Interviewing her would have to wait.

Long found Sid in the cafeteria drinking coffee with a couple of uniform cops. With his casual clothes, long hair and drooping moustache he looked out of place.

"So," she asked, "what do you think?"

"Given the circumstances, we believe Ms. Carter's in the sex trade, but we can't prove it."

"Did you run her through Missing Persons?"

"Of course. We came up empty."

"What kind of family would just let her disappear and not report it?"

"You got me."

Long pondered for a moment. "I could get the number of the caller from the 911 operator and have David and Mark question them to see what else they may have noticed on Collier Road, but it's a long shot. You think Mandy might be part of the white limo operation?"

"Who knows? I see this shit all the time. We shut it down one place. It pops up somewhere else."

"So, there's nothing you can do?"

He pursed his lips. "I could flash some pictures of her and ask around some of the clubs and street corners," he said, "see if anyone recognizes her."

"You think they'd tell you?"

"They might. Child trafficking, underage drinking, that's the kind of trouble they don't need. There's a bigger problem, though. If she's part of this white limo operation, she probably doesn't frequent those places anyway. She'd be too conspicuous."

"I need you to do whatever you can. Now that the FBI is involved, Lieutenant Darnell wants me to share with them everything I have on Braithwaite."

"I heard about that. What do you suppose would bring the Feebs in on a local murder?"

"Prillaman claims it's related to Braithwaite's research. Part of his funding came from federal grants."

"So, what do you plan to do?"

"That's where you come in. I'm thinking if *you* could take over this white limo investigation, we could say it has no relevance to Braithwaite's murder. And we wouldn't have to share anything you discover with *Special Agent Prillaman*."

Sid smiled. "You know, your daddy would be mighty proud of you."

She felt a blush creeping into her cheeks. "Thanks."

Then another thought came to her. "From what I could see of Mandy's face, the good side at least, she's beautiful, childlike. Whoever her pimp is, he'll come looking for her . . ."

"I'm way ahead of you. I have a couple of undercover cops hanging out down the hall. If he shows up, we'll grab him."

* * *

As Long left to pick up Grafton from her mom's house, she got a call from Mike Prillaman.

"Hello, Sergeant. I thought I'd check to see if you'd found out anything more about the Braithwaite murder."

She considered stonewalling him, but Darnell *had* ordered her to collaborate. She decided to throw him a bone instead.

"The only thing I have of interest is the fact that Braithwaite's assistant, Delbert Foster, was *not* a professor or even a doctoral student. In fact, he dropped out of Tech, but Braithwaite kept him on anyway. That seems unusual. It makes me wonder what he might have had on Braithwaite. Given his engineering experience, why wouldn't Foster get a better-paying job in industry?"

"Thanks, Sergeant. I'll look into that."

Long struggled to hide her sarcasm. "Sure. And let me know what you find out." Whatever his motivations, Prillaman cared nothing for Mandy Carter or *any* of Braithwaite's other victims.

Amy Springer had proved a big help, but Long needed an expert opinion on the mind of a pedophile. She texted Brandon Markham. *If you're not busy tomorrow night, I can drop Grafton off with my mom.*

Long dreaded explaining to her mother why she needed to keep Grafton for the night, especially when it involved Grafton's father, whom Nancy regarded as pond scum.

* * *

Posing as Mr. and Mrs. Williams, William and Misty toured the home of the recently departed Garth Braithwaite. The listing agent had met them at the gate. In keeping with their ruse, they'd dressed as they would for a job interview.

The realtor, a perky blonde barely older than either of them, prattled on with such inane comments as, "This is the kitchen," as if they didn't know.

William snapped pictures of each room, using the excuse that he and his bride would peruse them later. He made a point of capturing a closeup of the carpet, where Sean had found Braithwaite. Someone had either replaced it or gotten out the blood stains.

Warming to her role, Misty asked, "So, tell us how this place came on the market."

The agent paused, as though bringing up the precise message her broker had crafted. "The previous owner was a single college professor who passed away. We're marketing it for his estate."

"Oh my God. He didn't die here did he?"

The agent manufactured a reassuring smile. "Oh no. I believe he died at the hospital."

When they reached the master bedroom, William snapped several pictures of the mirror attached to the ceiling.

The agent blushed. "The estate wanted to sell the home as is, I believe we could get them to remove that."

William flashed Misty a wolfish grin. "Oh no. I believe we'll keep it."

"So, how long have two been married?"

"Just last week."

"And are you already starting a family?"

Misty feigned outrage. "Do you think we got married because I was pregnant? What kind of slut do take me for?"

Mortified, the agent apologized repeatedly. When they reached the front door, she recovered long enough to ask, "So, what do you think?"

"We'll talk it over and get back to you," said William. "Right, darling?"

"You'll want to move quickly," said the agent. "We're anticipating a bidding war."

As the Jeep pulled out of the neighborhood, William and Misty convulsed in laughter.

"Seriously," she asked, "what do you plan to do with what you've learned on this little foray?"

"This confirms that Braithwaite was into some kinky shit."

"And you plan to publish that?"

"Not until I learn more, like what his research had to do with his murder. I might need your help again."

* * *

Miles away, at a small park in Atlanta's Morningside neighborhood, Delbert Foster sat on a bench reading a book in the waning afternoon sun. The sweat stains forming beneath his armpits had little to do with the weather. If anyone had noticed him, they'd see that he hadn't turned a page in the fifteen minutes he'd been there.

An elderly Asian woman strolled up with a small dog. Short and heavyset, she sat on the opposite end of the bench and caught her breath. She never so much as glanced in Foster's direction. Leaning over, she caressed her pet and said in a low voice, "Continue reading. Do *not* look at me."

He flinched but did as instructed.

"I received your message." She scanned the crowded park, stroked the dog and gave Delbert a smile that never made its way to her eyes. To nearby joggers and sunbathers, she would have seemed unremarkable, someone acknowledging a stranger with a casual greeting. "What do you know about this replacement O'Meara is interviewing?"

"He's Chinese," Foster muttered under his breath. "Name's Gordon Chu. Came here from Toronto. That's all I know."

"Okay. You need to work quickly then before he takes over and replaces you. Give me everything you can get your hands on. You will upload weekly reports to the One Drive account we provided, encrypted of course. Understood?"

"Uh huh."

"I trust you will find your reward satisfactory."

"Thank you."

The lady set her dog on the sidewalk, stood and strolled away. When she had crossed the street and rounded a corner, Foster closed his book and departed in the opposite direction.

* * *

Mei Ling Hsu replayed her conversation with Foster as she filled a tea canister with black leaves. She dipped it into a steaming ceramic pot and let it steep, a ritual she'd followed every day since she and her son came to the U.S. in 1999.

The son, a Chinese embassy official, died of pancreatic cancer, but Mei Ling stayed on, thanks to his foresight in helping her obtain U.S. citizenship. When the brew reached the proper color for her taste, she added a shot of bourbon, an American custom she'd acquired.

At seventy-nine, she no longer got out much. Her knees ached as she settled into her battered armchair and gazed out her picture window onto Virginia Avenue. The place reeked of dust, mold and Sichuan spices. It reminded Mei Ling of her childhood home.

A burner in a drawer beside her buzzed with an incoming text. As she reached for it, her white terrier, Bobo, climbed into her lap, curled up and closed his eyes.

She read the cryptic message from her PLA contact at the consulate in San Francisco and typed her reply. Within the hour it would arrive in Beijing amid the latest diplomatic communiques.

* * *

Long made the mistake of telling Grafton she would spend tomorrow night with her grandmother. It took her three readings of *Good Night Moon* to get the three year old to sleep. Her phone rang as she prepared for bed . . . Sid Cosgrove.

"We think we've found Mandy Carter's pimp," he said.

"You caught him?"

"Not exactly. He showed up at the hospital around six. We had a plain clothes officer in scrubs at each end of the hall. They moved in and nabbed him before he could escape. We took him downtown for questioning, but we had nothing we could use to hold him. He kept saying he was just a friend who heard about Mandy's *accident* and wanted to come see her."

"You say you grabbed him in the hall. Did Mandy hear you?"

"I don't think so. She seemed unconscious at the time."

"So, what's next?"

"The good news is we have his name and where he lives. The bad news is he knows we're watching. He'll sit tight for a while, hoping we'll lose interest."

"Who is he?"

"A limo driver named Franco Balboa. No priors. Has an apartment on Piedmont at Sydney Marcus and parks his cars over on Northside Drive. And, get this, he owns *three* white limos. We have his picture and the license plates. We're asking around to see if anybody recognizes him, but I'm not optimistic."

"Can you send me his photo and a couple of shots of his cars. And pull his vehicle registrations. I want to know if they're all in his name and what liens, if any, they're carrying."

"What about Mandy?"

"The hospital told me they could hold her for another day or so, but then they'll have to cut her loose. We're trying to locate her family, but she won't cooperate. Keeps claiming she's an adult. I'm afraid we're going to lose her."

Exasperated, Long could think of nothing else to ask. "If only we could get our hands on Braithwaite's videos and see if they include this Balboa character."

"Yeah." said Cosgrove. "So, how are you coming with the Simon Wilhoite murder?"

"No joy there either. He left his store after dark, and someone ambushed him in his car. He'd parked it behind the building in an area not covered by the security camera. Meacham and White are trying to track down some of Wilhoite's recent pawns."

Long opened her laptop and studied a recent photo of the man, apparently in his eighties, judging from his sparse, white hair and gaunt, spotted face.

"Anything taken from the store?"

"Not that we could tell."

"Doesn't sound like a robbery," Sid said.

"Nope."

Chapter Twelve

Mandy and Franco

Smyrna/Virginia
October 1, 2019

Availing herself of an Indian summer day, Beth Long went for an early-morning run before reporting for duty. As she approached her first mile, her phone shuddered in her armband. She slowed down, caught her breath and took the call.

"Hey, Sid. What's up?"

"Our girl Mandy is in the wind."

"Oh shit!"

"It gets worse. As soon as I found out . . ."

The phone buzzed again. "Sid, I hate to interrupt you. I've got David Meacham calling."

"Take it. I'll hold."

"Beth . . ." Meacham sounded out of breath. "You need to come over to Madeira Limousines on Northside Drive. There's been a shooting. The address is . . ."

"I know where it is. I have Sid on the other line."

"Call me back then."

"Sid, there's been a shooting at the limo service on Northside . . ."

"I'm on my way there now."

* * *

Madeira Limousines turned out to be little more than a parking lot behind a shopping center near I-75. Surrounded by razor wire with a padlocked gate, it contained the three white stretch limos and a tiny building. The gate stood open, and between two cars lay a body.

Meacham donned his gloves, knelt beside the short, swarthy corpse and scanned it without touching anything. Long, Cosgrove and Mark White stood a few feet away. Long guessed Franco's height at about five-two and his age somewhere south of thirty.

"What do you see, David?" Long asked.

"One in the chest and another in the forehead, low caliber from the size of the holes. No exit wounds. Judging from the powder burns, the shooter must have been up close. Looks like a professional hit, somebody Franco knew. We'll know more when the techs get here."

"Check his pockets."

"Here's his wallet. No sign of his keys."

"Somebody took his everyday car."

"And they're probably over at his place now ransacking it."

"David, call for backup. Sid and I are on our way there."

Long and Cosgrove arrived to find Balboa's Cadillac out front and his apartment door ajar. A set of keys lay on the living room floor, amid piles of papers. Clothing littered the carpet in both bedrooms. Prescription drugs and toiletries filled the bathroom sink beneath a recently broken mirror.

"You think whoever trashed this place got pissed when they didn't find what they were looking for?" she asked.

"Yeah. Otherwise, they'd have left sooner. Let's get some pictures, call in the techs and have them dust for prints."

A thorough examination turned up some smudged latents, but Balboa's intruder had left no trace. As Long slid a drawer back into place, she noticed it seemed a bit short for the depth of the chest. Removing the back panel, she found a compartment less than an inch thick, with manilla envelopes taped to the inside. They contained dozens of polaroids of young women performing various sex acts. In none of them were the johns clearly identifiable.

Sid shook his head. "I guess old Franco liked to advertise his product."

"Or he may have had a more disgusting purpose in mind," Long said.

"Either way, this is probably what our killer wanted . . . I can't believe this shit."

"I'd sure like to know who the men are in these pictures."

"Yeah. Well, good luck with that."

"We need to find out who these young women are, as well," she said. "Every one of them is in danger."

Sid set the photos down. "I'm certainly not putting *these* out on the street. What good can come of it? The best we can do is put out an APB on Mandy as a material witness in Balboa's murder."

"That'll put a target on her."

"It's already there."

Long paced the room, dangerously close to a breakdown. "Sid, if we can find even *one* of these girls, maybe they can tell us where Mandy went." She stopped in mid-stride. "I have a better idea. I'll take them to Amy, see if she recognizes any of them. She may have worked with one of them in the past. And meanwhile, I'll have David and Mark continue checking with Braithwaite's neighbors. *They have to have seen something they're not remembering.*"

Fighting back her gorge, she put the photos back in their envelopes. "Sid, we're going to find Mandy Carter right away. And we're going to find her alive, *whatever it takes.*"

"Do you think Darnell will make us bring in Prillaman?"

"Not unless we tie Balboa's murder to Braithwaite."

"And if we do?"

"Then at least we'll have a clearer idea as to who hired the burglar and why."

"What do we do next?" he asked.

Long thought for a moment. "I'm meeting with an old friend tonight. Let me see if he has any suggestions."

* * *

Mike Prillaman sat at his desk, picking at a take-out salad. Try as he may, he could not decide what to make of Beth Long's communique regarding Delbert Foster. *Is the woman trying to send me on a wild goose chase while she works the Braithwaite murder on her own?*

An exhaustive background search on Delbert Foster turned up nothing more than an apparent appetite for gambling. The absence of any obvious qualification for his research assistantship troubled Prillaman, but he had no way of gauging its significance without speaking to someone at Georgia Tech.

Scanning his notes from previous conversations with Long, he dialed Sean O'Meara's personal line.

When the man came on, he sounded distressed.

"Dr. O'Meara, this is Special Agent Mike Prillaman. I hate to bother you, but I was wondering if you might have a moment to discuss Delbert Foster."

"No," he shouted. "I don't." He paused as though composing himself. "You'll . . . You'll have to call back later." With that he hung up.

Prillaman swiveled his chair and gazed out at a perfect autumn sunset. *What the hell was that all about? If Beth Long is tampering with federal witnesses, I will have her ass.*

As he considered whether to call Art Darnell, his phone rang, an unidentified number with a 202 area code.

"Prillaman."

"Agent Prillaman, this is Abigail Martin with the NSA. Can you call me back on a secure line?"

* * *

Shadows crept across the well-manicured lawns and winding streets of Westparc Village. A young couple parked their Jeep at an abandoned shop across from the entrance, pulled out two bicycles and tailgated a homeowner through the gate.

As they meandered past the brick-and-stucco McMansions, they saw residents returning from work, pulling into their garages and retreating to the sanctuary of their comfortable abodes. A lone jogger stopped and caught her breath. As she reached for her key, William parked his bike and said, "Hi. My wife and I are thinking of putting a contract on the Braithwaite place and wanted to check out the neighborhood. How long have you been here?"

She eyed him suspiciously then smiled at Misty. "I've only been here a couple of months."

"I understand Dr. Braithwaite got shot in his own living room."

"Yeah. I heard about that from a neighbor."

"Did you know him?"

"No. Like most people around here, I don't socialize much."

"Has there been a lot of crime here?"

"Not that I know of."

"How do you suppose a burglar could get in here in the middle of the day?"

"I have no idea . . . Look, I've gotta go."

"Thanks."

At the end of the cul-de-sac, William and Misty stopped and spoke to an elderly man raking mulch around a newly planted shrub.

Misty stopped at the end of his driveway as William circled back to her. "That's going to be gorgeous."

"Yeah . . . Thanks. The idiot landscapers put a red maple here, too close to the foundation. It died in a matter of months."

"How long have you lived here?" William asked.

"About a year. This was the first house in the neighborhood. I moved here from Connecticut to be near my daughter."

"We're looking at the place down the street, Dr. Braithwaite's. Did you know him?"

"No, and I didn't want to." When neither William nor Misty replied, he added, "You should have seen all the fancy cars coming and going. They parked all along the street and would stay here all night. The neighborhood association wouldn't do a damned thing about it."

"What do you suppose was going on there?"

"No good. There was this long, white limousine that would pull up and drop off a bunch of party girls. From what I could see, none of them could have been more than sixteen."

William glanced at Misty. "Tell me about Braithwaite's other guests."

"Men. They looked to be middle-age, well-off from what I could see. There was this one guy who showed up maybe twice. Looked just like that politician. I forget his name . . ."

Misty interrupted him. "Bram Dennis, perhaps?"

"Yep. I told the cops that. I don't think they believed me."

As they loaded their bikes onto the back of the Jeep, William tried to reach Sean. His call rolled to voicemail. "Maybe I should call David Meacham, see what he might have found out."

"Maybe you should focus on your studies and let the police do their jobs."

"You sound like my mom."

"That's because she's right. Look, if you want to keep on sleuthing around murder scenes, that's your business, but I'm done. This was fun, but you're on your own from here."

* * *

Kathleen Williams O'Meara, known to her family as *Kathy,* pulled into the garage of her Druid Hills home, drained from a long day at Emory Midtown Hospital. Another young patient had lost her battle with leukemia. Twenty years into her career as a pediatric oncologist, Kathy still had trouble coping. On her way home she pulled into a gas station and cried until she had no more tears. Numb, she couldn't even recall the rest of her drive.

Now, more than ever, she needed the listening skills of her calm, compassionate husband. What greeted her as she walked into her kitchen startled her. Not once in their married years had she heard Sean curse or raise his voice.

"Sean, what is it?"

"I just got a call from Gordon Chu. Homeland Security revoked his visa. They're sending him back to Canada."

"Why?"

"He wouldn't say, but something tells me Harmon Wakefield's behind this. That bastard!"

Stunned, Kathy stammered, "Harmon? Sean, what are you talking about?"

He sat at the kitchen table and placed his head in his hands. "A few days ago, Harmon called me, out of the blue, and left a message. I couldn't imagine what he wanted, so I made the mistake of calling him back. He said he'd heard about Garth's murder. He seemed to think this might put a halt to my research. He offered me a high-paying private sector job. I declined, of course, but I made the mistake of mentioning Gordon."

"What did Harmon say?"

"He said to call him back if anything changed."

"And you believe he somehow got Gordon's visa revoked?"

"What do you think? He probably called his toad of son, and Bill pulled some strings. That's all it would have taken."

"What are you going to do?"

"I guess I'll have to find somebody else?"

"What about this Delbert Foster?"

"He doesn't have the experience that Garth and Gordon had and he . . . seems to lack commitment. I guess he'll have to do until I can find someone better. I hope my research funding holds out. If we get any further behind . . ."

Kathy wrapped him in her arms and laid her head on his shoulder. "Honey, I know how much this means to you. Believe me, it means every bit as much to me."

* * *

Damp with sweat, Brandon Markham struggled to catch his breath. Raising up on one elbow, he ran his fingers through Beth Long's thick brown locks.

"You have such beautiful hair. Why won't you wear it down?"

"Are you asking me as my former therapist or as an occasional lover?"

"Both."

"I put it up when I'm in uniform to keep it out of the way."

"It seems to me that it's *become* part of your uniform, your coat of armor."

"Alright. *That's enough*. I came over to talk about Braithwaite, remember. What motivated him?"

"I can hardly psychoanalyze a dead man."

"If you could, what would you ask him?"

Markham took a long breath as he contemplated his answer. "It would take several sessions. I'd begin by exploring his childhood. I would probably need to bring in a repressed memory specialist. I might order a brain scan."

"And what would that tell you?"

"Probably nothing."

"So, you don't know. Why didn't you just say so?" She closed her eyes, struggling to concentrate. "What motivates people like Braithwaite and his buddies?"

"Could be the thrill of getting away with something. More likely, its having power over someone."

"But what about the fear of getting caught."

"They're scared as hell of getting caught. We've all heard stories about what happens to child molesters in prison. But that doesn't stop them."

She sat up and pushed away the sheets, ignoring Brandon's appreciative assessment of her body. "The real question is, how do you stop these people?"

"You don't."

"That's not the answer I came here for, Brandon."

"There *is* no way to stop them. There's no *cure*."

"And you expect me to settle for that?"

"Look, you're already doing what little you can. You chase down these vermin, arrest them, and hope some bleeding-heart judge doesn't put them back on the street. But as long as there are pedophiles, we'll always have child trafficking.

"You're dealing with violent sociopaths, no different from serial killers, most of them *very* intelligent, with a high rate of recidivism. They know they'll get caught eventually, but they can't stop. It's a compulsion."

"Who are these creeps?"

"Many of them are powerful, successful people, like clergy and politicians. They hide behind a mask of respectability, knowing their flock will continue to believe them, no matter what. Those are the folks you need to go after. Find them, expose them and make them pay."

"How do I do that?"

"Ask your friend, Amy Springer. She works with the victims. It'll take time. You'll have to build trust with them."

He kissed her softly on the lips. "Beth, my concern is for *you*. We both know what's driving this obsession of yours."

Heat rose to her face. "I told you that in confidence, Brandon. Our professional relationship ended the first time you fucked me."

"But we were making so much progress."

"Yeah. From transference to codependency."

Chapter Thirteen

Deportation

Smyrna/Virginia
October 4, 2019

Henry Wakefield paced the sidewalk outside Starbucks like a lion in a cage. Lisa should have been here an hour ago. She'd never been late for their afternoon study sessions. Each time he dialed her number his call went straight to voicemail. As he tried again, his phone rang. He fumbled it and caught it in midair.

"Hey. What happened?"

Her voice came though so softly he could barely hear it. "Henry."

"What happened?"

She sobbed. "We're moving back to Toronto."

"What?"

"My mom texted me to come straight home from school. When I got here, I found them sitting at the dining room table looking as if someone had died."

The air rushed from Henry's lungs. "You're moving back to Canada? Why?"

"Someone came to see my dad today on campus. They told him his visa had been revoked."

"How can they do that?"

"I don't know," she moaned. "I had a big fight with my mom. She won't let me go anywhere."

As they spoke, Henry failed to notice the sun sliding westward or shadows growing longer. His phone buzzed with an incoming call, his mom. He ignored it.

"I have to go," Lisa said. "I have to help my mom with supper."

"Will I see you tomorrow at school?" he asked.

"No, Henry. We'll be packing. My dad's calling a mover. This . . . This is goodbye, Henry."

The line went dead.

"Motherfucker!" he screamed, ignoring stares from passersby.

Henry set out, oblivious to his destination. When his phone rang again, he answered without checking the caller ID.

"Henry, where in the hell are you?" his mother yelled.

He hung up without answering and found himself at the entrance to a cul-de-sac. At the end of the street stood the home of Tom Williams and his girlfriend Brandy.

Brandy answered his knock. "Hi, Henry," she said affectionately. Are you here to see your grandpa?"

She seemed nice enough, Henry thought. His grandfather certainly saw something in her. But to him she just looked old, thin and wrinkled. Her tattooed arms looked like rawhide, and her breath smelled of alcohol.

"Yes ma'am."

"Let me go get him."

"Hey, Pops," Henry said when Tom came to the door.

"Henry, where have you been? Your mom called. She's worried about you."

"It's a long story."

"I'm listening."

Last Gleaming

* * *

Tom called Marie and told her he'd bring Henry home. When they arrived, Henry went straight to his room without a word.

Tom kissed his daughter on the forehead.

Tears welled in her blood-shot eyes. Tendrils of mascara lined her cheeks.

"Dad, I don't know what to do with him. I thought giving him some space might help. If anything, he's become even *more* sullen. I spoke with Bill last week about Henry moving back in with him, but with all his travel he's never there."

"Look, Henry's had a rough day."

She stared at him, incredulous. "*Henry's* had a rough day?"

Tom filled her in on what little he'd gleaned from their conversation.

Marie shook her head. "No. No. This is just his latest outburst. He's getting worse and worse." She collapsed into a chair and put her head in her hands. "Maybe what he needs is a more structured environment."

Tom gave her a quizzical look. "You thinking about sending him off to a military school?"

"Well, maybe that's what he needs.'

The garage door opened. Returning from school, William walked in and dropped his bookbag onto the couch.

"Hey, Pops. What's up?"

"Henry came to see me earlier, and I brought him home."

Turning to Marie, he asked, "Mom, what's the matter?"

She shook her head. "I don't want to talk about it."

Tom changed the subject, "I wonder what could have caused Dr. Chu to lose his visa so abruptly."

"What?" William shouted.

When Tom had explained, William went to Henry's door and knocked.

"Go away," he cried.

"It's me."

A long silence followed.

"Is it okay if I come in?"

Another long silence. William tenuously opened the door.

"Man, I am so sorry. What the fuck happened?"

Henry rubbed his bloodshot eyes. "I don't know. She called and said her family had to move back to Canada."

"That sucks. Can you call her back?"

"No. She had to pack. They're leaving tomorrow."

"Well, her parents will probably turn in early tonight. Text her and see if she can talk."

"What good will that do? I'll never see her again."

William shrugged. "Maybe you can Facetime her later in the week. Maybe, when this all gets worked out, they can return."

Henry stared at William as if he'd lost his mind. "They're moving, dude. She's *gone*."

"Have you thought about calling Dad?"

Stunned, Henry slowly nodded.

* * *

Worried that his casual mention of Gordon Chu to Harmon may have set in motion Chu's precipitous departure, William changed into a tee shirt and track suit. He needed time to think. On his way out the door, he yelled to Marie that he was going for a run.

"Don't be long. Your grandad and Brandy have invited us over for supper."

Prowling the twilit streets, William replayed in his mind his earlier conversation with Harmon. *How do I get him to admit it without coming right out and asking?* He pulled out his phone and dialed.

"Hey, William."

"Hey, Grandpa."

"How is everybody?"

"I'm doing fine. Henry's not in a very good place."

Harmon's tone grew cautious. "What happened?"

"His girlfriend's dad lost his visa. They're moving back to Toronto."

"That's too bad."

William stopped and stared at his phone. *'Too bad' can mean a lot of things. Does he feel bad for Henry, or has he already rationalized that the loss of a girlfriend is a small price to pay in his geopolitical games?* "What do you suppose could have caused that? It seems so . . . sudden."

"Yeah. Well, that happens sometimes. Perhaps Homeland Security discovered something about Dr. Chu that caused them some . . . concern."

"Dr. Chu was *not* a PLA agent, Grandpa. Lisa told me they left Hong Kong to get away from those guys."

"And I'm sure that's what her dad told *her*."

William bit his tongue. "I suppose you're right. I just thought you might want to know. Anyway, I've gotta go."

In a matter of minutes, William had found all the answer he needed. Pondering what he should do with that information, he texted Marie. *I'm walking over to see Pops. I'll see you and Henry when you get there.*

He arrived to find Tom in the kitchen cooking vegetarian spaghetti while Brandy set the table.

"Would you like a glass of wine?" Brandy asked. "I have Pinot Gris and Chianti."

William politely declined. "Before Mom and Henry get here, I'd like your advice on something."

"Ask away," said Tom as he stirred Marinara into a pan of sauteed onions and peppers.

"I'm afraid I screwed up by mentioning Dr. Chu to Grandpa Harmon. I just spoke to him, and I got the impression that either he or Dad pull some strings to get Dr. Chu's visa revoked. What can I do?"

As Tom contemplated this, Brandy set down a plate, came over and hugged William. "First of all, it's not your fault. You don't even know that that's what happened. Why don't you talk to your Dad and see what he says?"

"Assuming I could even get him on the phone, I'm not sure he would give me an honest answer."

"At least, give him a chance," she said. "And, until you know for sure, I wouldn't say a thing to Henry. That'll only upset him more."

"She's right," said Tom. "And, by the way, when are you bringing this young lady over to meet us . . . Misty?"

"Soon."

After careful consideration, William told Tom and Brandy about his visits to the Westparc neighborhood with Misty. "All I got from this was a glimpse into Braithwaite's private life. I had no idea he was a pedo. You think this had anything to do with his uh . . . side project."

Tom came and sat beside him. "Let's not jump to conclusions. Let the police investigation play out."

"You think they'll talk to me if I tell them what I found out?"

"Son, whatever *you* know, the police already know. They're way ahead of you. Drop this for now. Focus on your studies. If you get bored, go to the courthouse in Marietta and sit through some trials. Take notes. Interview the cops. When the trial ends, maybe you can get the DA and the defense attorney to talk to you. Talk to your mom about everything you hear. It'll get her mind off her problems with Henry and perhaps help her better understand your interest in journalism."

"I'll ask her what trials she has coming up."

"Good . . . And you might want to think about a double major, one that would allow you to pursue your writing career while making a decent living. Perhaps PR."

* * *

Harmon brushed his sorrel mare and dried her with a large towel. He could have handed her off to one of his grooms, but he preferred to do this himself.

His phone rang again, and he answered, irritated at the interruption.

"Hey, Harmon. I wanted to follow up with you and see if we can count on your support for Bram Dennis."

Homer Starke's voice grated in his ear. Something bothered him about Dennis, but he couldn't put his finger on it. He needed all the votes he could get in the Senate. "Homer, I can get you a half mil in soft money."

"You won't regret it, Harmon."

"I'd better not."

As he hung up, a text appeared from Abigail Martin. *I believe I may have something for you, Harmon. Consider it a Christmas present.*

* * *

Shadows lengthened as traffic inched along Cherokee Street bringing office workers home to Atlanta's Grant Park neighborhood.

Streetlights winked on one by one. Unnoticed among the cars, a lone bicyclist pedaled northward toward the adjacent Cabbage Town neighborhood.

Steven Saldano had spent another fruitless day surveilling the home of Dean Scarborough. Burglaries and petty thefts had helped him pay his meager rent and stock his pantry but would never fund his move to the West Coast or the return of the lifestyle he'd once enjoyed.

Sitting on a sagging couch in his cramped living room, he pulled out one of his burners and texted Scarborough. *Time to light a fire under this bastard.*

* * *

Eighty miles away, Scarborough set down his book and rose to toss another log on the fire. Despite the cool weather and peaceful surroundings, he hadn't slept since his text from the burglar. He put the battery back in his cell phone and reread it.

You don't know me, but you need to call me right away. Simon Wilhoite hired me to retrieve some sensitive items for you. You won't be hearing from him. You're dealing with me now. If the police find me, we're both going down together.

According to news reports, police still had no suspects. *If only I had some idea who Simon hired, I could pass that on to Homer.*

Scarborough thought back to the time he first met Homer Starke, recalling his disappointment after hearing so much from his dad about the man. At first sight, he reminded Scarborough of a homunculus. Yet, in the eighteen years since then, Homer had risen from a Hart County commissioner to political king maker at the state level.

For reasons he never explained, Homer hired Scarborough to find out as much as he could about a Georgia Tech researcher rumored to have hosted wild parties involving wealthy business owners and under-age females. Scarborough's research included frequenting bars along Northside Drive and picking up prostitutes, the younger the better.

When one of them offered him information in exchange for a bump of coke, Scarborough happily obliged. Getting Wilhoite to hire a burglar to search for damaging photos or videos had seemed like a stroke of genius . . . at the time.

Scarborough punched in Homer's number. When another message from the burglar appeared, he read it and began to hyperventilate.

Maybe you didn't understand me, Dean. I'm not going away without my money. You owe me, asshole. Clock's ticking. Call me back, or I will find you.

Scarborough considered deleting it, then recalled that the sender still had no idea as to his location.

The call to Homer rolled to voicemail. When Scarborough's frantic appeal went unheeded, he again removed the battery and decided to try later. *When I asked Homer for help, he said he'd look into it. What's keeping him?*

As Scarborough contemplated this, a text arrived from Kevin Murphy, owner of the cottage where he'd hidden out for nearly a month. *Hey man. I wanted to give you a heads up. I'll need the place for New Year's Eve. I'm bringing my new girlfriend up there for some alone time.*

* * *

Working late at his office, Delbert Foster pulled out his phone and opened his cryptocurrency app. His day had gotten off to a profitable start. *The old bat's as good as her word.* Mei Ling had transferred another $25,000 into his account. Using a burner, he texted her his appreciation.

Braithwaite's murder had come as a shock. Whether it related to the biochip project or to his late-night escapades, Delbert had no idea, but he now slept with a gun on his nightstand and peered over his shoulder wherever he went. The Atlanta police seemed to have no inkling as to the killer's identity or his motive.

Delbert had discovered Braithwaite's home movies when the man accidentally forwarded him the wrong link. While that knowledge *had* provided him the means to ensure his job security, it might also cost him his life.

Reaching into his desk drawer, he shook out a couple of Tums and chewed them as he paced his tiny workspace. Foster's more immediate concern, what to do when Braithwaite's successor discovered how little he'd contributed to the research, abated with the sudden deportation of Gordon Chu. Delbert remained confident in his ability to bullshit Sean O'Meara, a doctor with no understanding of electronics.

For now, he would continue downloading and studying Braithwaite's designs, working late nights in his modest apartment with his deadbolt locked and a chain on the door. As he reached for his phone to make the call that would brighten his bookie's day, Sean O'Meara appeared in the doorway.

"I need you to come to my office. Gordon's agreed to get on a call with us before he departs for Toronto. We're going over his notes to see what we can salvage."

"Sure . . . Uhm, I don't mind."

Foster arrived in Sean's office to find Chu staring out from a large monitor Sean used for conference calls. It seemed to Foster that the man had aged in their brief time together, though it might have been the exaggeration of the pores and lines in his face from sitting close to the camera.

As O'Meara and Chu launched into a dry, lengthy discourse on the use of biochips to counteract angiogenesis, another text popped up from Mei Ling. Foster nonchalantly reached into his pocket and shut it off, praying she didn't try to call him.

Chapter Fourteen

Home for the Holidays

Rural Virginia/Atlanta
December 25, 2019

Bill Wakefield's State Department limo picked up William and Henry at Dulles and dropped them at the circular drive in front of Harmon and Evelyn's country home. William stretched and yawned.

Henry stared across moonlit fields blanketed in snow. On his face, William glimpsed something resembling a smile. It had been so long he'd forgotten what it looked like.

Five hours earlier, they'd kissed their mom goodbye at Hartsfield-Jackson. Their grandparents wanted them here yesterday, but at Marie's insistence, they stayed in Smyrna to attend Christmas Eve mass.

The front door flew open, and there stood Bill, Harmon and Evelyn, framed in a scene worthy of a Hallmark card. To William it seemed none of them had aged since the last time he'd seen them, more than two years ago.

A thick aroma of baked ham, cranberries and sweet potato casserole flowed out to greet them. "Merry Christmas, boys," Harmon yelled, "get in here before the food gets cold."

Later, as their cook, Paloma, cleared the dishes, William and Henry decamped to the den, where Harmon kept an X-box and a large-screen TV for their visits. As they lost themselves in a game of Fortnight, a heated discussion arose in the adjoining parlor, Bill and Harmon arguing over foreign policy.

"But if they don't know what we're doing, they'll simply assume the worst, and hit us first," said Bill.

"And if we let them in on our latest weapon systems, they'll steal them and use them against us. When will you boys learn that Xi and Putin are *not* our friends? They aren't even honorable adversaries. You keep thinking that if we send them enough Hollywood movies, we can turn them into Americans."

"Dad, this is not *Charlie Wilson's War.* The NSA is not going to fund your global vendettas. Abigail was just putting you off."

"Son, we're already at war. Your buddies at the State Department are just too dumb to see it. The Russians are hacking our hospitals, and the Chinese are developing biological weapons."

Bill let out an audible sigh. "We've been over this. There's no proof that Putin's behind the hackers. All we need is tighter cybersecurity. And Xi is not about to unleash some disease that will wipe out his own people. The best way to avoid a war is through cooperation."

"And while you're *cooperating* with them, they're stealing our technology so they can use it on us."

William's interest in the video game faded. He and Henry wandered into the next room, bringing the conversation to a halt.

"Henry," Harmon said, "your dad tells me you're a straight A student and that you want to go the Naval Academy when you graduate."

"Yes sir."

William stared at his brother, dumbstruck. *When did he decide that?*

"Well," said Harmon, "when the time comes you won't have to worry about recommendations."

Bill beamed at his younger son. "Henry, do you mind if we tell everybody your other news?"

Henry took a moment to reply. "Sure . . . I mean, I guess it's okay."

"Well, go ahead."

"I've been accepted into Wellington Academy for the spring semester. I'm not returning to Georgia."

As they congratulated him on getting into Bill's old prep school, no one seemed to notice William sinking into the nearest chair. *Why am I always the last to know?*

He stood and excused himself. Halfway down the hall he ducked into a half bath, locked the door and pulled out his phone.

"It's about time," Marie said. "You were going to call me when you got there, remember?"

"Did you know Henry wasn't coming home?"

"Yes, William. Your dad and I spoke last night. I was too upset to talk about it this morning when I took you two to the airport."

She paused. "This has been a long time coming. Henry's been angry at me ever since I left your dad. I don't know what he expects me to do. I'm not moving back to D.C., and he can't stay at your dad's condo while he's out of town for God knows how long. I guess he figures by being at Wellington he'll at least be close to Harmon and Evelyn."

Her voice trembled. "Henry doesn't like me very much right now, William, and, to tell the truth, I don't like him much either. Maybe Wellington will straighten him out."

"Are you there by yourself?"

"Yeah. Your grandfather and Brandy went up to Asheville this morning and won't be back until tomorrow."

"Really?"

"Yeah. No shit! I never thought I'd see the day when my dad had a better sex life than I do . . . What am I talking about? I don't have a sex life."

Anxious to change the subject, William said, "Hey. Why don't I change out my ticket? I can be home tomorrow night."

"No. Your grandparents have been looking forward to this for months. You can't duck out on them like that."

"They'll be fine. Let me discuss it with Dad."

Before he could hang up, Marie tumbled to his plan. "You just want to come home so you can see that girl . . . Misty."

"Well . . . Why don't I bring her by and introduce her to you?"

"Yeah. Why don't you? I've been asking you for months. I'm starting to think she doesn't exist."

With that, William said goodbye and dialed Misty. As he said goodbye, someone knocked on the bathroom door. He opened it to find Henry.

"You planning to spend the night in there?" he asked.

"Sorry. I wanted someplace private to make a couple of calls."

"How's Misty?"

"She's fine. Her parents are in town for the holidays to see her and her grandmother."

"Cool . . . You called Mom?"

"Yeah."

"How was she?"

"Lonely."

Henry nodded.

"Why didn't you tell me about all these plans, about you coming up here to go to school?"

"Well, it all happened so fast." Henry glanced back at the parlor, where Bill and Harmon had gone back to arguing politics.

"What makes you think military school will be any different from Campbell? Hell, it seems to me it'll be a lot worse."

Henry shook his head. "At Campbell, I'm an outsider. Most of those guys have known each other since elementary school. At Wellington, at least, I won't be the only new kid."

"Yeah. Well, you won't have me there to get you out of trouble."

"Maybe that'll be a good thing."

"Let's hope."

For the first time in as long as William could remember, his brother hugged him. He feared he'd crack a rib.

When they returned to the parlor everyone stared as though they'd been gone for hours.

"What were you guys doing back there?" Bill asked. "You came here to see your grandparents."

William wrestled with guilt, wanting nothing more right now than to be on a plane flying home to Misty. He went to the closet to retrieve his ski jacket, gloves and cap.

Treading quietly onto the patio, he found himself in another world. The full moon and stars reflected on a thick blanket of snow as far as he could see. Beside the shed stood a fir he and Henry had planted as boys, now more than twenty feet tall. Harmon had decorated it with enough lights to dim the grid.

Brushing off a chair, William sat and pulled up his knees for warmth. He took a deep breath and let it out, watching the fog dissipate as it drifted toward the roof line. Behind him the sliding glass door opened.

"Son, what are you doing out here?" Bill asked.

"I needed some fresh air."

"Your whole family's wondering where you are."

William felt a warmth rising to his face. "It's not exactly our *whole* family, now is it, Dad?" He studied his father's profile, silhouetted against a wreathed window, and waited for his response.

"William, I know I haven't been there for you and Henry over the years."

"Haven't been there? My childhood memories of you are from interviews on C-SPAN. Do you even remember our birthdates? Every year on your wedding anniversary, Henry and I watched Mom, sitting alone, quietly drinking herself into a stupor. How the hell will either of us make a decent husband or father? The closest thing to a role model we have is Pops."

Bill started to say something, then stopped. "Son, the work I do is more important than you'll ever know."

"Yeah? Well, you weren't too busy to revoke Gordon Chu's visa. Did you think I wouldn't figure that out? Did Grandpa Harmon put you up to it? Lisa was the first girlfriend Henry ever had. Did you ever stop to think about that?"

Bill said nothing as he wiped a tear from his cheek.

This only made William angrier. "Why did you ever get married? You weren't a father. *You were a sperm donor*. I'm changing out my ticket and flying home tomorrow."

He stormed back into the house, ignoring his grandparents' startled looks, and retreated to his bedroom. He doused the light and buried his face in his pillow.

Minutes later, there came a light rap at the door. Reluctantly he opened it. Evelyn stood there, decked out in her ski attire, hand raised to knock again if needed.

"Are you up for another moonlight stroll?"

William pulled her to him in a tight embrace. "I am so sorry, Grandma. I love you very much."

"Then get out here. We're going for a walk."

"I need to apologize to Dad first."

"He's already left. You can call him tomorrow before you leave. Put on your hiking boots. You'll need the traction."

Evelyn led William along a path recently shoveled and salted to a wooden bench Harmon built years earlier. "Let's sit here for a moment."

Gazing up at the stars, her face glowed angelic in the moonlight. Her neatly coiffed hair seemed to reflect the wintry scene. "William, I don't know what you said to your father, but it upset him very much."

"Grandma, I am so sorry." In the heat of the moment, he'd said so much more than he intended.

"Don't apologize to me. Save it for him."

William wiped tears on his sleeve. "It's just that . . ."

"You don't need to explain. I raised my son to believe in himself, that he had a mission in life only he could discover. Ten generations ago, your ancestor, John Cabot, came to America. He made his fortune dealing in *slaves* and *opium*. He founded one of the richest families in Boston. Everything you see here came from that. I taught your father that we can't change our past, or where our money came from." She leaned toward William, looking him in the eye. "It's what we *do* with our blessings that matters.

"When I met your grandfather, his name was William Harmon. I'd recently read an old novel I had by Oliver Goldsmith . . ."

William laughed. "*The Vicar of Wakefield?*"

"It sounded much more . . . elegant. I married that man, because I saw in him something my father did not, someone driven by ambition and a desire to serve others . . . In time, and with a lot of work, he became a good husband. I'm afraid your father did not.

"You can't do anything about that either. You can't change your parents or who they are. You must love them and forgive them . . . not for their sake, but for yours. Only then can you move past your childhood and become a man and someday, perhaps, a good husband and father."

William thought of Misty and wondered what it would take for him to make a good partner for her. He couldn't even picture them having children.

He and Evelyn returned to the house without another word. As he drifted off to sleep, he heard Henry climb into the other bed.

"Next time I see you," he said. "I'm going to kick your ass into the middle of next week."

"You're on," William mumbled.

* * *

Delbert Foster's Christmas proved even more miserable than William's. Cold and alone, he wandered the park where he'd met the Chinese woman, hoping to see her walking her little dog. *This is so stupid. I should be out celebrating with my friends. Why hasn't she returned my calls? What happened to her? She must live somewhere nearby.* He scanned the darkened streets thinking he might spot her.

Countless scenarios played out in his mind. In the one that replayed again and again, the FBI had arrested her. *How long will it take them to discover her connections . . . including me? I am so screwed.* He pictured them, as he'd seen on so many TV shows, barging into his office in blue windbreakers and yelling at him to step away from his laptop.

He had to do something. Without the old woman's payments, his gambling debts had mounted. *If I don't pay them soon, the FBI will be the least of my worries.*

That morning, in desperation, he had located the number for the Chinese visa office in Atlanta. The CIA, no doubt, tapped their embassies and consulates. He wondered if the same applied to their travel bureaus.

Scanning the park for anyone who might notice, he dialed. The operator who answered sounded sleepy. He gave her his name and explained the nature of his research at Georgia Tech. "I'd like to speak to someone about travelling to your country, preferably a scientist doing work similar to mine." He gave her the number for his latest burner. He prayed she could read between the lines.

Hours later, as he prepared a meager repast, the phone lit up. The caller inquired, in flawless American English, "Mr. Foster??"

"Yes."

"I believe we have a mutual acquaintance."

"Yes."

"Unfortunately, we haven't been able to reach her of late."

"Oh."

"In her absence, we are prepared to deal with you on a more *direct* basis."

When the call ended, Delbert let out a deep breath. He went to his kitchen for a bottle of tequila and a joint. *Hopefully, I can placate my creditors until I get my next payment.*

As if on cue, his phone rang.

Chapter Fifteen

The Return

Smyrna/ Cherokee County
December 26, 2019

Harmon drove William to Dulles without a word about the scene he'd made the night before. As he waited to board, William tried to reach his dad. When the call went to voicemail, he left a message apologizing. He told him he loved him and asked him to call back when he got a chance.

Five minutes later, Bill returned his call. "Hey. Sorry I couldn't pick up. I was online with our embassy in Beijing. I told them I needed to step out."

"I didn't mean to interrupt your meeting."

"No, no, no. Calling you back was more important."

William cracked a smile. "More important than world peace?"

"At the moment, yes."

"Dad, I want you to know I'm sorry about the things I said last night."

"Don't be. They . . . needed saying."

"You've done so much for Henry and me over the years."

"William, I've been generous with *things*. That comes easy for me. I need to be more generous with myself. Maybe I can fly you and your girlfriend . . ."

"Misty."

"Misty. Maybe you two could come up here for the weekend and stay with me in Georgetown. We could tour the Smithsonian."

"That would be great. I'll ask her. While you're at it, maybe you could do something for Lisa Chu."

Bill took a long time replying. "That's a bit more complicated," he sighed. "Let me see."

The gate agent announced boarding for the flight to Atlanta. "Look, I've gotta go," William said. "I love you."

"I love you too."

As he placed his travel bag in the overhead, it occurred to William that Bill, for all his many shortcomings, always knew what to say in any situation, an important asset for an aspiring politician. *Maybe he'll say the right thing for the Chus."*

The plane landed at Hartsfield-Jackson at eleven p.m. Marie met him at the top of the escalator. William felt like shit for making her come out at that hour.

Exhausted, he texted Misty in the car to let her know he'd returned. He arrived home, undressed and fell asleep before she replied.

* * *

He awoke hours later to a persistent ringing. He pried open his eyes to find his bedroom lit only by his phone. The caller ID read *Misty*.

"Hey," he managed through parched lips. He stood, opened the blinds and gazed out on a cold, gray morning.

"Well, at least you're alive," she said.

"If you say so."

"You came home early."

"Yeah. My mom was here by herself. She's having a rough time. Henry isn't coming home."

"What?"

"Dad got him into a military prep school in Virginia."

"I can see how that might upset her."

"You haven't met Henry. Trust me. She'll get over it. Besides, it's the best thing for both of them."

"You told your mom you were coming home just so you could console her?"

"Yep."

"And she bought that bullshit?"

"Nah."

"Good for her. Tell me about your trip."

"Later, when we're by ourselves. Say, is it okay if I come over there now?"

"I'm tied up with my family at the moment, but I can come by your place this afternoon. That'll give *you* a chance to spend some time with your mom and give *me* a chance to meet her."

"Okay. What about your grandma? I thought your parents were going back today."

"No, they're staying over for New Year's."

"Maybe I can meet them."

"Maybe . . . if you play your cards right."

When she hung up, William threw on some old clothes and sauntered into the kitchen in search of breakfast. He found Marie emptying the dishwasher. As he reached to hug her, he caught a whiff of stale cigarette smoke.

"Mom, you *said* you were going to quit."

"*Don't even start.* Your aunt came over yesterday, and I got an earful from her."

Fine wrinkles showed about her mouth and eyes, like a fracture on a windshield. Her teeth and fingernails had a yellowish cast. She seemed to have aged before his eyes.

He shook his head and retreated to the shower.

***

Following lunch at the Battery, William and Marie shopped the after-Christmas sales at Towne Centre Mall, which improved her mood considerably. As they returned home carrying bags of clothes, Misty texted him saying she'd be there in twenty minutes.

Bundled against the cold, William swept leaves from the deck and wiped down three patio chairs. He closed his eyes and luxuriated in the scent of wood smoke riding on the crisp, dry air.

When Misty arrived, he introduced her to Marie, and Misty filled them in on her parents' visit. Marie went to the kitchen and returned with three wine glasses and a bottle of Chardonnay, ignoring the fact that Misty and William were underage.

"My grandma keeps asking about you," Misty said. "And I showed my dad your write-up from her interview. He liked it very much."

"Really? That was back in September."

"Yeah. I should have gotten it to him sooner." She examined her clasped hands for a moment. "You know, it's the first time I've seen him cry since my grandfather died?"

Marie sipped her wine and studied her prospective daughter-in-law. "William tells me you're an agronomy major."

As Misty described her career goals, the two women became engrossed in a lively conversation, totally ignoring William, until his phone interrupted them.

William's cousin, Lauren O'Meara wanted to know if he and Misty could meet her and her new boyfriend at Café 290 in Sandy Springs. Misty called her parents to get their okay, and William told Lauren he'd see her at seven.

On the way over, he explained to Misty that Lauren, daughter of his Uncle Sean and Aunt Kathleen, was studying secondary education at

Emory. "She's one of the brightest people I know, and perhaps the most competitive."

They arrived to find the venue bumping to the sounds of Joe Gransden and His Big Band. At a back table William spotted her seated beside a tall, dark-complected man with a full beard, whom she introduced as Hari Vogel.

"What an interesting name," Misty shouted above the crowd noise.

"My dad's Jewish and my mom's Hindu. They met at NYU."

"Where did you grow up?"

"In Scarsdale. My parents teach at Iona University."

"Oh, I know Scarsdale." Misty wrinkled her nose. "My mom wanted me to go to Sarah Lawrence."

"That's right down the road from our house."

"If you don't mind my asking, what religion are you?"

He shrugged. "I believe in a higher being. I'm just not sure which one. I'll get back to you on that."

Lauren took his hand and gazed at him as if he were one of her pupils. "Yeah. I'm still working on catholicizing him."

"Great," said Hari. "That way, I can feel guilty before thousands of gods."

"How did you meet?" Misty asked.

"Hari's my statistics professor," she said. "He's pursuing a PhD in economics."

William watched the way Hari looked at his cousin. *Sounds to me like that's not all he's pursuing.* "What are your plans when you graduate?" he asked.

"I'd like to work for one of the major think tanks in Washington."

"And perhaps become a member of the President's Council of Economic Advisors," Lauren added. "If he behaves himself, maybe I'll move up there with him."

Misty turned to William. "Hey, maybe your dad can make some introductions."

"Yeah. I'll mention that next time I see him."

Hari, twenty-one, ordered a Jack and Ginger. The club management, not as broad-minded as Marie, carded him. William, Lauren and Misty ordered Diet Cokes.

"So," William asked Lauren, "how's Delbert Foster working out?"

"Great, as far as I know. Dad's still trying to find another researcher to replace Dr. Chu. Right now, he's making do with Delbert."

William's thoughts returned to the questions that had gnawed on him for months. "Have you heard anything more about the Braithwaite investigation?"

Lauren shook her head.

As the drinks arrived, Misty's phone rang. Unable to hear her caller over the band, she excused herself and stepped outside. She returned in minutes, ashen, her eyes filled with tears.

"It's my grandma," she choked. "She fell, and my dad thinks she broke her hip."

William jumped to his feet. "Where are they taking her?"

"North Fulton." Misty insisted she could drive there from William's house, but he refused. They arrived at the hospital to find a middle-aged couple waiting in the emergency room.

Misty ran to her father, a thickly built man of medium height with graying black hair. Her mother, slender and attractive, embraced her. Feeling like an intruder, William had begun backing toward the door, when Misty stopped him.

"William, I want you to meet my parents, Jeff and Barbara Sax."

Jeff explained that Esther had gone back to her bedroom when they heard her fall and scream. William shook his head, not knowing what to say, whether to stay or go.

At length, an ER physician came out and told the family that Esther had suffered a hip fracture. "It's too soon for a prognosis. We've given her a sedative, and she's resting peacefully."

As Misty gave the doctor a detailed explanation of Esther's medical conditions, Barbara thanked William for bringing her straight there. He explained that Misty had left her car at his mom's house, and Jeff said he'd bring her by to get it in the morning.

* * *

William rose at seven the next day, having tossed all night. Misty and her dad arrived at eight. She told him they needed a few minutes. Jeff thanked William again and drove away.

"William," she said, "I can't tell you how much I appreciate your being there for me last night. But . . . I need to spend the next few days with my family."

Devastated, William could only nod and tell her he hoped Esther got well soon, which sounded lame as he said it. He asked her to give him a call later and watched her as she backed out of the driveway.

* * *

Homer Starke dialed the number for Dean Scarborough's latest burner. It took five rings before he answered, his voice thick with sleep.

"Hey, Homer. Any news."

"My investigator finally got ahold of your security footage from the break-in back in September."

"What did you find?"

"We make your burglar out to be about five-six, athletic build, tanned face and black hair. He wore a ball cap and dark glasses, but we were able to map the bone structure of his face. A search of all the available databases turned up empty. It appears the man's never been arrested. For good measure, I had my man check out the number on your texts. It belonged to a burner sold at a convenience store on Memorial Drive in Atlanta."

"So, what do I do now? I need to be out of here tomorrow. I borrowed this place from a buddy of mine, and now he wants it back."

Starke let out a deep breath. "Try to stall him if you can. But you'll probably have to meet with this burglar to get Braithwaite's laptop and phone. And for that you'll need to be in Atlanta."

Homer paused, hating what he would say next with every ounce of his being. "Find out how much the bastard wants. I'll wire it to your account. But don't pay him until you check back with me."

Chapter Sixteen

New Year's Eve

Roswell, Georgia/Atlanta
December 31, 2019

Esther opened her eyes to find three blurred images floating above her bed. *Where am I?*

As the faces came into focus, she recognized Misty, Jeff, and her daughter-in-law, Barbara. When she opened her parched mouth to speak, she found it blocked by an oxygen mask. It gave out a loud hiss.

Jeff leaned so close she could make out the hairs in his nose. His voice trembled. "Don't try to speak, Mom. It's okay. You're going to be fine. We're here. We're not going anywhere." His smile seemed forced. "We're going to celebrate the new year with you."

Again, Esther tried to speak. She felt the caress of a hand on hers. From the doorway came Misty's voice. "Excuse me, nurse. My grandma's awake."

Another face floated into Esther's field of vision, this time a woman in pale blue scrubs. "Hello, Mrs. Sax. I'm your nurse, Sally. Let me get you something."

A hand removed the mask and fed Esther a few bits of crushed ice.

"Take it slowly, now," the nurse said.

The ice tasted like ambrosia. Esther caught her breath. "Where am I?" she croaked.

"You're in the hospital, Mom," Barbara said.

Esther closed her eyes. *Now I'm "Mom." Before I was always "Esther."*

"Mom, you took a spill, that's all," added Jeff.

"When was that?"

"Saturday. You've been here three days. Don't try to move. They put a pin in your hip."

Esther winced. It seemed so long ago. "Where's Myron?"

"Dad passed away two years ago. Don't you remember?"

"Oh . . . Yeah."

"Mr. Sax," the nurse said, "Your mom needs to rest now."

Jeff nodded. "We're going to step outside, Mom, and let Sally take care of you." Tears filled his eyes.

Misty leaned over to kiss her grandmother on the forehead.

"Where's your nice young man?" Esther asked.

Misty bit her lip. "I'm sure William's out celebrating the new year, Grandma."

"So, you think you could bring him to visit me?"

"I'll see."

* * *

Outside the door, Misty buried her face in her dad's chest. He wrapped her in his arms and stroked her hair. For Misty it brought back a flood of memories, him picking her up and taking her inside when she fell off her bicycle, comforting her when she had nightmares, kneecapping a date who had slapped her and left her at a shopping mall in the middle of the night.

"How long will you guys be able to stay?" she asked.

"I'll be here at least until your grandma comes home. Your mom needs to go back tomorrow. She has some things to take care of in Charleston."

The nurse came out of the room. "Mr. Sax, your mom's gone back to sleep. She's likely to be out for a while. Why don't you folks go home? Get some rest. I'll call you tomorrow morning and let you know how she's doing."

"Well, Melissa," said Barbara, when the nurse had left, "this young man of yours seems to have made quite an impression on your grandma."

Trailing her family down the hall, Misty retrieved her phone from her pocket. Her most recent text from William had been at six p.m. She hadn't answered any of them. She wondered if perhaps he'd gone out with friends. She wanted so badly to call him now but had no idea what to say.

As they made their way through the lobby, she passed a small television mounted on a wall. A man and a woman, bundled against the cold, shouted into microphones. They wore gaudy eyeglass frames that flashed *"2020."* In the background, beneath a brightly flashing ball, people stood shoulder to shoulder, partying in the streets of Times Square. A digital clock in the corner of the screen read *11:59:27.* Barbara and Jeff stopped to watch.

In the far corner a tall, slender figure sat hunched over, asleep, on a vinyl couch. Tousled brown hair spilled over a heavy woolen coat. Though she couldn't make out his face, Misty recognized him in a flash. Blinded by tears, she brushed past her parents.

"William," she screamed, ignoring the disapproving stare of a desk attendant.

Bleary eyed, he looked up.

She knelt to kiss him. "How long have you been here?"

"I don't know," he mumbled.

"Why aren't you out celebrating?"

"I needed to be here."

Shouts from the television drifted down the corridor. "Four . . . three . . . two . . . one."

"Happy New Year, baby," said Misty, kissing him again and again. "I love you so much."

From behind her came Barbara's voice. "Welcome to 2020, William. It should be an interesting year."

* * *

Dean Scarborough sat alone in his Grant Park home oblivious to the New Years' festivities, the smiling hosts in their heavy coats and scarves, the revelers, many in garish costumes. In a news break earlier, Bram Dennis had announced his candidacy for the U.S. Senate, smiling into the camera, perfect teeth reflecting the afternoon sunshine, blonde hair swept back and graying at the temples.

Scarborough could hardly care. Police still had no suspects in the murders of Garth Braithwaite or Simon Wilhoite.

For months, Scarborough's only concern had been to save himself from arrest as an accomplice. Now he had to face a blackmailer whose identity he still hadn't discovered. His agony at wondering when the man would phone him again had given way to a fatalistic determination to get it all over with.

The man had promised to call at midnight and arrange a spot where they could meet, and Scarborough had the go-ahead from Starke. He caressed the bag of money beside him. *What if he doesn't bring Braithwaite's laptop and burner? What if it's all a trap to lure me into a secluded spot, kill me and take the money?*

A small pistol, a .22 revolver his father gave him years ago, hung heavy in his pocket. Scarborough had taken it into the woods at the lake and fired it into an empty plastic paint bucket to see how it felt. It sounded like a firecracker. Astounded that it still worked, he wondered if he could kill a man with it.

A sudden knock made his heart leap. Slowly, he recovered and glanced at the satchel. He left it where it sat and crept softly across the carpet.

Standing to one side of the door, he called out, "Yeah. Who is it?" His voice, echoing in the empty hall, mocked his attempt at bravado.

"Open up," said the voice. "I brought what you wanted."

Scarborough pulled the gun from his pocket and held it at his side. Slowly he reached for the knob.

Chapter Seventeen

The Suspect

Atlanta / Hartwell, GA
January 1, 2020

Beth Long pushed her daughter's stroller along a sidewalk, as a frigid blast stung her face. Grafton, wrapped in sweat clothes, mittens and her favorite knit cap, babbled a running commentary on everything she saw, seemingly immune to the cold. She stared up at Beth with her apple-red cheeks and crooked a finger at something in the distance.

The thought of having the whole day to spend with her daughter gave Beth a warm smile. Rising early, when most of Atlanta lay sleeping off New Year's Eve, she'd bundled Grafton and all her paraphernalia into her aging Toyota van and fled downtown for the suburb of Kennesaw.

Beth could almost forget that, two and a half months on, she still had no idea who killed Garth Braithwaite or why, no leads in the Franco Balboa murder and no clue as to where Mandy Carter had gone, or if she were still alive.

Amy Springer had reviewed the photos found at Balboa's place but couldn't identify any of them. Beth tried to drive those thoughts from her mind, if only for the time being. She could make more calls tomorrow.

At the end of the cul-de-sac stood Grafton's father, Brandon Markham. As the three strolled along the sidewalk, Long already regretted allowing him a visit.

"Dada," the three-year-old squealed, as she squirmed out of her restraints.

Long stopped and strapped her back in to keep her from climbing out and running to him.

When he asked if he could hold her she relented.

"Brandon, you can't just expect to show up every few weeks and take up with Grafton where you left off. Being a daddy is a full-time job."

He gave an exasperated sigh. "It's just that I'm busy, and I have so few opportunities to see her. She's my daughter too."

"No. She's *my* daughter. *You're* just the baby daddy."

She stopped. "I'm sorry, Brandon. But we've talked about this. Besides, you already have two daughters, or have you forgotten?"

Seeing his wounded look, she apologized again. "Look, when I said I was pregnant, you asked me what I wanted you to do. I told you *nothing*, and I meant it. I'm okay with you coming by to see Grafton, but I'm raising her myself."

"It's only that . . . I want us to be a family."

"Brandon, you *had* a family. How did that work out for you? *You're* the one who chose to tell your wife about us."

"I couldn't go on living a lie."

"You mean the lie you told when you took your oath as a psychotherapist, or the one you lived for more than a year before you found out I was pregnant."

"Exactly," he sighed. "You don't have to live with me if you don't want. You could move somewhere nearby, and we could get together more often. I could take you guys places. I could come to Grafton's dance recitals, that sort of thing. I could even help with your living expenses. You won't have to work. You can stay at home and spend more time with our daughter."

"What if I don't want to move to Buckhead?"

He scanned the 1960s, working class homes, some with aluminum siding, some with vinyl, a few still bearing their original asbestos shingles. "I guess I could move out here."

"You wouldn't do that in a million years. Besides, my mom's head would explode. She doesn't want to see your face."

"I understand, but will you just think about it?"

"Fine. *I'll think about it.*"

"Good. Anything new in the Braithwaite case?"

"Not really. We had a potential lead, a young woman we believe was in the sex trade, but now she's disappeared. We have an APB out on her as a material witness to the murder of her pimp."

"Tell me about her."

They walked on for a while, returning to where they'd started. "Okay," said Long. "I'll call you sometime next week."

He replied with a bittersweet shrug.

Back at the house, Beth found her mother preparing for her annual New Year's Day celebration. She wiped sweat from her face with a calico apron. In a few hours, her home would buzz with a cacophony of chattering guests.

Mixed fragrances of collard greens, black-eyed peas, ham hocks and corn bread clung to Beth's Georgia State sweatshirt like an old blanket from the closet of her childhood. Having friends and family over for food and football had been a tradition dating back as far as she could remember.

Her dad would invite other off-duty cops. They'd drink and watch bowl games while their wives sipped wine and gossiped in the kitchen. When Beth, who could barely heat up a frozen dinner, offered to help, Nancy assured her she had matters in hand.

As Beth went off duty last night, she'd heard units responding to a shootout in Grant Park. A homeowner answered a knock to find a gunman on his porch. He took a round to the chest before pulling his own gun and killing the unidentified assailant. He now lay in ICU at Grady. Relieved not to have caught this case, Beth pushed the memory from her mind.

* * *

David Meacham and Mark White hadn't been so lucky. The Grant Park homeowner, Dean Scarborough, though expected to survive, underwent emergency surgery and hadn't awakened.

The two officers spent New Year's morning scouring area neighborhoods, with dozens of other cops, showing photos copied from the fake driver's license found on the dead man's body.

A beat cop working the Grant Park area identified the John Doe as a vagrant he'd seen outside Scarborough's home weeks earlier. At the time of the shooting, however, the dead man wore a black pullover, gray slacks and a reefer jacket, hardly the standard attire of a homeless man. Meacham wondered if the cop had been mistaken.

As the search broadened northward into Cabbage Town, Meacham knocked on the door of an elderly Black man who said he recognized the deceased as his next-door neighbor, though he'd never spoken to him and didn't know his name.

By early afternoon, police had located the owner of the house, a doctor living in Druid Hills. He identified the man on the fake driver's license as his tenant, who had called himself Heyward Brown.

The landlord gave Meacham and Chief Investigator Tim Ellis permission to search the house. Inside, they found a laptop and a burner, apparently Braithwaite's. They also found, lying under the corner of a rug, a driver's license bearing the name *Steven Saldano*.

A search of the phone revealed a list of numbers, which Ellis copied before bagging it with the laptop and sending them downtown for further analysis.

"Anything else, Tim?" Meacham asked.

Ellis smiled. "Nope. Go home and watch some football."

* * *

The last of Nancy's guests departed, and Beth set to work cleaning the kitchen, while Nancy and Grafton watched a children's TV program. As Beth settled into her dad's old recliner her phone rang . . . Meacham.

"David, this better be good."

"Guess who we just heard from?"

"Look, I'm in no mood for . . ."

"Braithwaite's laptop."

Long came up out of her chair. "What?"

"You remember that IT kid over at Georgia Tech, Ryan, Brian, whatever?"

"Yeah. The one who gave me the laptop's MAC address."

"Not only did he have the address, but Braithwaite apparently downloaded a tracking app and set it up to notify both him *and* the kid. The kid was at home playing video games when his phone lit up. He still had my number and called me."

"Where's the laptop?"

"Downtown in Property."

"What!"

"Tim Ellis and I were out knocking on doors around Grant Park searching for anyone who might recognize the home invader who got shot this morning. Tim decided we should broaden our search. We located the place the perp had rented in Cabbage Town and found the laptop there. I opened it out of curiosity. That must have set off the alert. The kid wanted to wipe the computer. I told him not to do it until we had a chance to see what's on it."

Long permitted herself a fist pump. "And you said the perp's name was . . .?

"Steven Saldano. We verified his real driver's license with the DMV. His permanent residence turned out to be a luxury apartment uptown. I haven't spoken to the leasing company yet."

"What's the Grant Park homeowner's name?"

"Dean Scarborough. He's still in ICU."

"Is he awake?"

"Nope. Ellis told Mark and me to go home while he *finished up*. He's probably downtown right now holding a press conference and taking all the credit for nabbing Saldano. Meanwhile, I'm still hanging out at Grady keeping an eye on Scarborough."

"You say you found Braithwaite's phone. Did you find one belonging to Saldano?"

"Nope. If he had any burners of his own, he ditched them before going to Scarborough's place."

"Okay. *Good job, David*. See what else you can find out."

Already moving, Long grabbed her woolen cap, overcoat and gloves before Meacham disconnected. "Mom, do you think you could watch Grafton for me? I need to run out for a bit." She closed the front door behind her before Nancy could reply.

Enroute to Grady she dialed APD Headquarters and had them put her through to Tim Ellis.

"Tim, this is Beth Long. Where are you?"

"I'm sitting on my couch watching the Sugar Bowl, Beth, with a bunch of my friends."

In the background she heard a man shouting, apparently at the football game, and someone else laughing. "Hey," she said. "I'm sorry to bother you. I wanted to find out what you have on the Scarborough investigation."

"Scarborough shot an intruder in his own doorway. The perp turned out to be Steven Saldano. He had a .9 mm Glock belonging to Garth Braithwaite, your murder victim up in West Midtown. It was a righteous kill, as far as I'm concerned. I hope Scarborough survives so I can pin a medal on him."

"I understand your team found a satchel full of cash sitting on his sofa."

"So? Maybe he was planning a little post-holiday shopping."

"Seriously?"

"Beth, I don't care if he planned to spend it all on hookers and blow, he had a right to defend his castle."

"This was no home invasion, Tim. I believe Scarborough and Saldano knew each other. Saldano had something. He promised to swap it with Scarborough for the cash."

"Didn't the feds take over that case?"

"Fuck the feds."

It took Ellis a second to respond. Long could hear the grin in his voice. "You know, Beth . . . I like your attitude . . . as long as you aren't asking me to leave this bunch sitting here in my living room watching bowl games. Last time I did that they cleaned out my refrigerator *and* my liquor cabinet."

Someone jeered at him in the background.

"No, no," she said. "You go back to watching your game. I just wanted to let you know I'm on my way to Grady. I'm meeting David Meacham and Mark White there. When your boy, Scarborough, wakes up, we'll have a few questions for him."

"Okay. Just go easy on him. As far as I'm concerned, he's an upstanding citizen."

"I also need that list of numbers from Braithwaite's phone."

Ellis went quiet for a moment. "Sure. Braithwaite's your case. I don't see how his burner has anything to do with Scarborough."

"I intend to find that out."

* * *

Long parked outside the emergency room. Meacham met her at the door.

"Is he awake yet?" she asked.

"Nope, but he was starting to come around."

Long's trip proved a waste of time. Scarborough, though disheveled and foggy from anesthesia, managed to stick to his story. He'd never met Steven Saldano and had no idea why the man would show up at his door on New Year's Eve with a gun.

"And you never met Garth Braithwaite."

"Nope."

"Mr. Scarborough, we will prove that Steven Saldano killed Braithwaite. He stole Braithwaite's laptop and phone. You intended to use that money on your sofa to pay off Saldano, but he double-crossed you and you shot him. We're going to open that laptop and see what's on it that you wanted so badly. When we trace that information back to you, I will *personally* arrest you as an accomplice to Braithwaite's murder. Is that clear?"

She gave him a moment to let it all sink in. "Now, Mr. Scarborough, you need to think before you lie to me again."

His lips slowly parted. "No," he croaked. "I never met Saldano or Braithwaite."

Outside in the parking lot, Meacham asked, "So, do you believe him?"

"Not yet. I need to see what's on that laptop, and I need you and Mark to get to work identifying the numbers listed on Braithwaite's burner. What have you found on Saldano?"

"No priors. No known occupation. He had an unexpired lease on a fifteenth-floor luxury apartment in Buckhead and a Porsche sitting in his reserved parking spot. I'd say the man was very good at whatever he did. That dump he rented in Cabbage Town was simply a crash pad while he cased Scarborough's place."

"Let's take a ride up to Buckhead and see how the other half lives."

"Don't you need to call that FBI agent and let him know we've found Braithwaite's killer?"

Long chewed her lower lip as she pondered. "You're right."

She reached Mike Prillaman's voicemail and left an intentionally vague message about uncovering a lead.

"Good," she said. "That buys us some time."

"You might want to call Lieutenant Darnell too, just to cover yourself."

"That'll wait. Let's roll."

* * *

Homer Starke replayed his recording of the evening news and shook his head. Every Atlanta TV station led with the story of Dean Scarborough killing Steven Saldano on his doorstep. Homer now had the name of Braithwaite's killer.

He stood and poured himself another bourbon on the rocks. He threw the empty handle into a garbage can and gazed through his

French doors at the waning moonlight rippling on the waters of Lake Hartwell.

The reporter on the scene mentioned a large sum of cash found in Scarborough's living room and speculated that Saldano intended to rob him. Police, they said, had no idea how Saldano knew about the money and no evidence he and Scarborough knew each other.

"That fucking idiot!" Homer shouted. His words echoed through the empty five-bedroom home. "Maybe this'll buy us some time." He downed his drink, returned to the bar and opened another bottle.

He had tried to reach Scarborough earlier, with no success. From what the reporters said, he would probably remain at Grady for a few more days. *The only people talking to him right now are the police. How long before they trace this all back to me? How do I get to Scarborough before he spills his guts?*

Homer picked up his phone and dialed another number.

Chapter Eighteen

The Break

Atlanta/Virginia
January 2, 2020

The next morning, Prillaman returned Long's call.

"Mike, I believe we have Garth Braithwaite's laptop and phone." She did her best to keep from sounding smug.

"What! Where did you find them?"

"In a cheap rental down in Cabbage Town occupied by the late Steven Saldano."

"Who's Saldano?"

"We think Saldano was Braithwaite's killer. We don't know for sure. He had no priors, and his fingerprints don't show up on any of the databases."

"How did he die?"

"A Grant Park homeowner shot him in what he claimed was a home invasion."

"Any connection between this homeowner and Braithwaite?"

"None that we know of. Saldano's last known residence was a posh uptown apartment. We searched it."

"And?"

"No phone, no computer, nothing of interest, with the exception of an empty safe."

"Any idea what he was looking for at Braithwaite's?"

"Once I see his laptop, perhaps I'll know."

"Where is it, and where is Braithwaite's phone? I'll come by and pick them up *now*."

"They're in Property. You can have the phone. We're done with it. But I'm afraid I can't release the laptop to you until we copy off some files we need in an unrelated matter."

"What unrelated matter?"

"One that has nothing to do with Braithwaite's murder."

"If those files are on Braithwaite's computer, then *I* need them, and I need them *now*."

"And you shall have them as soon as I download my copies." Long grinned maliciously as she pictured his mounting anger.

"I can get a federal warrant, Sergeant."

"Knock yourself out, Mike. And in less time than it'll take you to get that warrant, you can come down here and we'll look at the laptop together. We'll need you to bring Braithwaite's password, the one your team used to hack into his One Drive account. I'm betting it'll open his laptop."

* * *

Prillaman met Long at police headquarters on Peachtree Street, along with Sid Cosgrove and a computer technician. Prillaman stood a good inch shorter than Long, which went a long way toward explaining his insecurities.

The technician disabled the laptop's Wi-Fi to prevent it from synching to the cloud and logged in using the same password as the now empty One Drive account. Using Explorer, he found hundreds of cached backup files. Before Prillaman could object, he copied them onto an external device.

"I'll take that," said Prillaman.

"Nope," said Cosgrove. "You're investigating Braithwaite's *murder*. I'm investigating him for child trafficking. You get the laptop and the cell phone only."

As Prillaman strode out, visibly irate, Long shared with her colleagues a triumphant smile.

She and Cosgrove spent the next two hours skimming through Braithwaite's personal videos, ignoring his CAD files, spreadsheets and Word documents.

Returning to Grady, they met Mark White and David Meacham.

"David, did you have any luck with the contacts on Braithwaite's cell?" Long asked.

"Nope. We're pretty sure they're all burners."

"Figures. How many pedophiles are going to give out their home numbers?"

"How did it go with the laptop?"

Cosgrove described the videos of Braithwaite's parties with as few graphic details as he could manage.

"Do you think you'll be able to identify any of the men?" Meacham asked.

"Not yet. Let's see what the lab can do."

White snickered. "Why don't you let me and David take a look at them?"

Ignoring him, Meacham asked, "Do you think Scarborough may have been one of them?"

"There's nothing to indicate he was."

"So how do you want to play this?"

"David, what do you do when you're holding a shit hand in poker?"

"Well, sometimes I bluff."

"And that's exactly what *we're* going to do."

When they arrived at Scarborough's room, they found him alone, finishing off a bowl of runny oatmeal. From what Long Could tell, he hadn't combed his thick shock of light brown hair and had developed a five o'clock shadow.

"Mr. Scarborough, do you remember me?" Long asked. "We met yesterday. You were still a bit woozy from your surgery."

He gave her a vague stare but said nothing.

"Mr. Scarborough, we've gone over Garth Braithwaite's laptop." She paused to study his reaction. "And we found some interesting home videos."

"He probably saved them for a little late-night viewing," White added, winking at Meacham.

Scarborough's eyes shifted from one cop to the next. "I don't know . . ."

"We also broke into Dr. Braithwaite's phone," said Long. "Do you have any idea why it would have contained your number?" *It's a shot in the dark, but the best I can do.*

Scarborough appeared genuinely bemused.

"Don't answer that question," said a voice behind them.

The officers turned to find a small, thin man decked out in a chalk-striped three-piece suit. He wore his shoulder-length brown hair swept back. A gold ring gleamed in each ear, and a bouquet of heavy cologne filled the small room.

"Who are you?" Long asked.

"I've been retained to represent Mr. Scarborough." He proffered a gold-embossed business card that read, "Marcelle Lacroix, Esq."

"Mr. Lacroix," Long asked, "Mr. Scarborough here just came out of sedation. *Who hired you to represent him?*"

"That is not your concern, Sergeant. Mr. Scarborough is recovering from serious injuries and is in no condition for interrogation. I'm sure that, as soon as he is, he'll be more than happy to cooperate with your investigation . . . in my presence."

A glow of relief spread over Scarborough's face.

***

The four cops rendezvoused in the parking lot beside Meacham's Bronco.

"So," he asked, "where do we go from here?"

Long stared into the distance, her face a mask of disgust. "We go nowhere, David." She ran her hand through her hair. "We're at a dead end. The Braithwaite murder is an FBI matter. As far as the APD is concerned, Steven Saldano acted alone. You can rest assured that if the feds find out differently, they won't be sharing that information with us. We have nothing on Dean Scarborough, and Tim Ellis has already ruled the Saldano shooting a justifiable homicide. So, let's see . . ."

She turned to Cosgrove. "How about you, Sid? What do you have so far on the white limo child trafficking case?"

"Something between 'Jack' and 'Squat.' I'll let you know if that changes."

"Well, I guess that about sums it up, David," said Long. "Braithwaite's murder is officially solved, and the trafficking, if it surfaces again, will be Sid's case. If it's okay with you, I have other pressing matters."

"But," pleaded Meacham. "What about Braithwaite's neighbor claiming he saw that Senate candidate, Bram Dennis, leaving Braithwaite's house following one of his late-night orgies?"

Long stared at him, exasperated. "And what am I supposed to do with that revelation, David? Run to the press? Unless Sid wishes to pursue it, we're done here."

Meacham's face reddened. "Sergeant, this is bullshit, and you know it! Do you really think Scarborough had all that money sitting there on his couch so he could buy Girl Scout cookies? Saldano stole Braithwaite's laptop and tried to use it to blackmail the men who were doing those little girls. We can tie both Scarborough *and* Dennis to Braithwaite's little sex ring."

"David, you need to calm down. We have nothing on either of those men, and, unless you want to tangle with Marcelle Lacroix, we need to drop this matter . . . for now at least."

* * *

Still fuming over their conversation, Meacham sat in his car for a half hour assessing his options. Braithwaite's murder had *not* been just another thwarted burglary. The sex videos from his bedroom proved that. There were others involved, Bram Dennis among them, and probably Dean Scarborough. *How could the APD punt a case like this to the feds? They don't give a shit about those little girls, forced to have sex with a bunch of sick old men. If Long won't do anything about this I will.*

He pulled out his phone and looked up the reporter whose grandson had interviewed him. It rolled to voicemail.

"Mr. Williams, this is Officer David Meacham. When you have a chance, please get in touch with me. I have some information that might interest you."

As he hung up, a call came in about a suspected corpse in Virginia Highlands.

***

As he walked his English bulldog, Otto, past the tiny, nondescript brick ranch, Ed Lanier couldn't help glancing in its direction. He despised the woman who lived there, though he knew her only as the *Wicked Bitch of the East*.

As far as Ed knew, she lived alone. From his home, two doors down, he'd never seen anyone coming or going from her gloomy abode. Her daily forays included strolls to the park and to the nearest market, always accompanied by her yappy little mutt.

Whenever the animal came near Otto, it would try to attack the bigger dog. On the one occasion when Otto snapped back, the woman screamed at Ed, threatening to call Animal Control.

Mercifully, Ed hadn't seen her in weeks. He quickened his pace, hoping to avoid an encounter. As he passed her place, however, a sickening odor rocked him. Otto seemed to notice it too. Ed stopped, unsure what to do. Instinctively, he knew what had happened. As a Vietnam vet, he recognized the smell of death.

He backtracked, hoping to get upwind, pulled out his phone and dialed 911.

***

Meacham arrived to find White waiting beside his car. An unmistakable stench greeted them as they donned disposable masks. Meacham, not wanting to puke in front of his partner, took the precaution of putting a daub of Vicks beneath each nostril.

When no one answered their knock, White took a five-pound sledge to the front door, which gave easily. They cleared the rooms, breathing through their mouths as much as possible. The sole occupant, an elderly

Asian woman, lay face up on her bedroom floor in an advanced state of decomposition. The desiccated body of a small dog lay beside her. Bite marks on the woman indicated she'd died first, and the dog had gnawed on her in his efforts to avoid starvation.

With no clear cause of death, White called in crime scene techs while Meacham stepped outside to catch his breath and survey the street. Ed Lanier met him there and gave his statement.

The woman's non-driver ID listed her as Mei Ling Hsu. Neighbors reported seeing her come and go but knew nothing about her. The only indications of family Meacham and White could find included a picture of a young man, presumably her son, and an old letter referring to her as "Mom."

A search of missing persons reports produced nothing. The only other items of interest in the residence were several burner phones, which White sealed in evidence bags and took with him.

He arrived at the property room to find a smiling Mike Prillaman. "Thank you, Officer. I'll take those."

* * *

Harmon stoked his fireplace, savoring the blend of maple and hickory. He leaned over to kiss Evelyn, who sat knitting at the end of the couch. They shared a small reading lamp, the only illumination in the parlor other than that emanating from the hearth.

As he returned to his recliner and settled in with a biography of Bill Donovan, his cell phone rang. Annoyed that he hadn't shut it off, he checked the display, and his scowl melted.

"Abigail Martin, as I live and breathe."

"Hey, Harmon. I haven't forgotten about our little pony ride a few months back. I'm still working with our budgeting team on your request."

"I appreciate that."

"I've also been working on something else that touches on that topic."

"Pray tell."

"I got word about an hour ago of a major arrest going down in Atlanta tomorrow morning. Back in September, one of our moles at China's San Francisco consulate intercepted transmissions between a known PLA operative and a research scientist at Georgia Tech. Obviously, this conversation cannot go beyond us."

"I understand completely. This research scientist have a name?"

"Delbert Foster, former assistant to Garth Braithwaite, the research engineer murdered in Atlanta a few months back."

"Any connection between Foster and the Braithwaite murder?"

"None that we know of."

"Any indication that Foster had *fellow travelers* at Georgia Tech?"

"The FBI doesn't think so. We're working with an agent down there named Mike Prillaman. He's been following Foster for several weeks now. An audit of Foster's bank accounts came back this morning, showing tens of thousands in transfers from an account tied to China's Ministry of State Security. Apparently, Foster worked with a Chinese American named Mei Ling Hsu. The feds *were* planning to pick her up at the same time as Foster."

"Holy shit," Harmon exclaimed, catching a disapproving look from his wife.

"We received word about an hour ago that Atlanta police found Mei dead in her home, apparently from natural causes. They believe she'd been there a while. They pulled a bunch of burners from the bottom of her closet. Prillaman has them now. One of them had a number in its call history that matched Foster's. Agents will arrest him first thing in the morning and hold him as a flight risk. I just thought I'd let you know."

"Abigail, you have no idea how much I appreciate that. Next time I'm in Washington, let me take you to lunch."

"Make it dinner."

As he hung up, Harmon began calling various contacts in biomedical research. He finally had what it took to pull Sean O'Meara's funding and redirect it to MedChip.

Chapter Nineteen

Connecting the Dots

Atlanta/Marietta
January 2, 2020

Despite what she'd told her colleagues, Long had no intention of backing off the Braithwaite case. She would pursue it, even if she had to do it off the books.

As she pulled onto Peachtree Street heading south, her cell phone rang. The display read, "L. Gwynn." She'd stored the Narcotics officer's number two years earlier when he helped her solve a multiple homicide in Midtown.

"Lyman! It's been a long time."

"That it has, Sergeant. That it has."

"To what do I owe the pleasure?"

"Are you still working that pawn shop shooting?"

It took her a second to register. "Simon Wilhoite?"

"That's the one."

"As a matter of fact, I'm heading back to the office now to pick up my case files. I thought I'd go over them at home tonight after I put my daughter to bed."

"Well, I have something that might help. We made a drug bust over in that area a couple of days ago. Now the perp's trying to trade a little information for a suspended sentence. I got the go-ahead from the DA's office."

"And this information . . ."

"He says he and another man witnessed the Wilhoite shooting. It looked like a contract hit. Dude shot him from the back seat of his own car."

"Did your informant see the shooter's face?"

"Yes ma'am. Identified him as that guy got killed over there in Grant Park night before last, Steven Saldano."

* * *

Long pulled Wilhoite's ledgers, one by one, from the evidence boxes. Starting with the date of his murder, September 19, she worked backwards, searching for names she might recognize.

Fifteen minutes in she found it, a redemption dated September 5 for $25,000. She couldn't make out Wilhoite's scrawled description of the item, but the payor's name, in clear block print, read "D. Scarborough."

She had him. Security footage would show Scarborough handing Wilhoite a large sum of cash. This, alone, wouldn't prove a connection to Saldano, but Long could feel it, the knowledge that she had the perp. It glowed inside her like the buildup to an orgasm.

Unsure of her next move, she called her mentor and former boss, Lieutenant Paxton Davis. She stepped into a stairwell to avoid eavesdroppers.

Paxton spoke with a calm demeanor far different from his pre-retirement days. In the background Long heard a light splash and the cries of birds. Apparently she'd caught him fishing for his supper. She explained what she had on Scarborough.

He gave this some thought and said, "Scarborough's $25,000 payment don't make him an accomplice to the murders of Wilhoite or Braithwaite. Hell, you'll have a tough time nailing him on the burglary.

He could just say he bought a bunch of stuff someone had pawned to Wilhoite."

He thought about it some more. "But Scarborough doesn't know what you have or don't have. If you threaten him with conspiracy and murder charges, maybe he'll roll over on the burglary and tell you who hired him. It's a long shot."

Long stopped to process this. "Yeah. Scarborough didn't pay all that money just so he could pick up a used laptop and a phone. *Somebody had a special reason to want them*. I'm convinced he's a cutout."

She laid out, in graphic details, what she'd found on Braithwaite's laptop and told him about Mandy Carter and Franco Balboa. "Franco is dead, and Mandy has disappeared. If we're going to bring down this child trafficking ring and put its customers away, we need Scarborough to come clean on who hired him. He doesn't even have to admit to setting up the break-in."

"Who's his lawyer?"

"A Marcelle LaCroix."

"Oh Lord. Good luck with that."

"You know him?"

"I know Marcelle. He don't come cheap. Nowadays he only represents top shelf crooks. *Somebody* hired him, somebody with power and *lots* of money, somebody Scarborough wouldn't even think of diming out."

"What do we do?"

"You'll have to find out who's paying LaCroix. And that won't be easy. He doesn't have to tell you a thing . . . And *find Mandy Carter* before Franco Balboa's killer does."

Changing the subject, he asked, "So, how are things going with *Lieutenant* Art Darnell?"

"As well as you might expect. I give him a wide berth, just like you told me. But I'm not sure how long I can continue to work this white limo investigation with Sid. I'm supposed to be turning over everything I find on Braithwaite to the FBI. It's like Darnell doesn't want anything to do with it, and I have no idea why."

"Just don't let him know what you're doing. And if he asks, this is Sid's case. He has a problem, he can take it up with Sid's boss."

Long concluded the call and pulled Marcelle LaCroix's card from her wallet. When he answered, she laid out, in stark detail, her discovery among the Wilhoite files, embellishing it with vague references to evidence that Scarborough had contracted with Wilhoite on behalf of an unknown figure.

LaCroix tried to call her bluff, but Long heard the uncertainty in his voice.

"Counselor, in a moment Sid and I are going to walk into his boss' office. He's been after Sid for months to wrap up this case. I'm sure he'll find these latest developments quite interesting, interesting enough to get a warrant for Scarborough's phone and email records. The only thing that might prevent that would be for you and Mr. Scarborough to offer at least a *partial* confession in exchange for a *possible* reduction of charges."

As the lawyer began blustering, she hung up, hoping he might take her not-so-subtle hint.

An hour later, LaCroix called back. "Sergeant Long, you can stop harassing my client now. He and I just met with the district attorney."

Scarborough had confessed to approaching Simon Wilhoite, a known fence, about acquiring stolen jewelry and electronics. He claimed they never discussed a burglary and that he'd never met Steven Saldano before the man tried to break into his home. Nor had he heard of Garth Braithwaite until he saw the news account of his murder. He stopped short of implicating anyone for hiring him and said that he planned to sell the stolen goods to unsuspecting buyers.

Long couldn't help wondering how close she had come to nailing Scarborough as an accomplice to the break-in. Now, by copping a plea, he would get a one-year sentence, at most. She wanted to scream. Instead, she would reach out to Sid Cosgrove to see if he'd heard any more on Mandy Carter.

As she started to dial him, her phone vibrated with a text from her boss, Art Darnell. One of the youngest lieutenants on the force, Darnell had risen through the ranks as a protégé of Deputy Chief Austin Murray, who maintained a constant lookout for sycophants in his own image.

Paxton and Murray had been bitter enemies, leading to an open feud that predated Long's promotion to sergeant. When Darnell took over as her boss, Long did everything in her power to stay off his shit list and off Murray's radar without compromising her integrity or her commitment to the job.

As she walked in, Darnell greeted her with a smile, much as a snake might a chipmunk.

"Good morning, Sergeant. Please come in and shut the door."

With an old-school flattop and white wall haircut, he dressed and carried himself as though prepared for a press briefing. "I received a call late yesterday afternoon from the FBI. It seems you have not complied with my instructions to keep Special Agent Prillaman abreast of your work on the Braithwaite murder and cooperate fully with him on *his* case."

As she opened her mouth to reply, he raised a hand and continued. "I also understand you insisted on copying files from Braithwaite's laptop and pulling call information from his phone before turning the equipment over to Mr. Prillaman."

"That information was germane to a child trafficking investigation unrelated to Dr. Braithwaite's murder."

Darnell leaned across his desk and fixed her with a stare. "Sergeant am I to understand that you are now requesting a transfer to Special Victims. If so, I'll see what I can do."

"That's not what I meant. I merely . . ."

"Never mind, Sergeant. As it turns out, your willful disregard for my orders has had no deleterious effect on Agent Prillaman's investigation." Darnell paused, savoring the moment before delivering his final blow. "Early this morning, *Sergeant*, the FBI, *with no help from you*, arrested Dr. Braithwaite's assistant, a Communist Chinese agent named Delbert Foster. They believe he may have hired Braithwaite's killer but will pursue that matter at their own pace."

He leaned back in his chair and studied her dispassionately. "You might also want to know that Foster had been blackmailing Braithwaite. Something to do with his misuse of research funding to pay for some experimental cosmetic surgery down in Mexico. That, *Sergeant*, is *real* police work."

Long felt her breath catch and fought the urge to gape in astonishment. The news that Prillaman had arrested Braithwaite's assistant as a spy only infuriated her more. Now, the smug bastard would never return the laptop and phone. Nor could anyone interview Foster until his trial concluded.

The participants in Braithwaite's debauchery could continue to molest young women, confident that they'd never see the inside of a courtroom. *It's as if somebody's pulling strings to protect these creeps, someone who has nothing to do with Chinese espionage.*

Darnell continued, "Naturally, the FBI would like you to turn over any information you have that connects the Braithwaite case to this . . ." He checked his notes. "Dean Scarborough. I trust you will have them to him by noon."

Before Long could recover, he added with an ugly smile, "By the way, in recognition of your *many contributions* to this case, I have one final task for you."

Chapter Twenty

The Announcement

Atlanta/Marietta
January 3, 2020

William and Misty arrived at the hospital to find her grandmother awake, sitting up in bed, and talking to Misty's dad. Esther picked at something that might once have passed for meatloaf. Clearly, the hospital staff wanted her out of there as soon as possible.

Seated in a vinyl upholstered recliner, Jeff flashed them a quick smile and returned to his point. "Mom, the doctor says we can take you home tomorrow. I've already hired someone to care for you around the clock."

Esther pursed her lips. "And why, pray tell, do I need a caretaker, when I have Melissa?"

"Mom, Misty has her classes, remember? Besides, you need a trained nurse, at least until you can get back on your feet."

"So, now you can afford to spend some of your fortune on your mother. I'm touched."

Misty intervened. "I'll be there to take care of you at night, Grandma. And William can help."

"I'd love to," William said.

Esther closed her eyes. "Thank God! I can't wait to get out of this place."

"You'll recover faster at home, Mom," Jeff added.

"I'll come over tomorrow and help Misty get the place ready for you," William said.

Before Jeff could demur, Misty jumped in. "We'd appreciate that very much."

As he left, William passed a television in the lobby. A newsbreak announced the closing of the Garth Braithwaite and Simon Wilhoite murder investigations. The banner at the bottom identified the spokesperson as Atlanta Police Sergeant Beth Long.

William studied the face of the woman he had spoken with briefly on the phone. With her brown hair pulled back in a bun and her crisp Class A uniform, she spoke slowly and deliberately. William's immediate impression of her was that of a classic beauty trying desperately to look professional.

"The Atlanta Police Department has now concluded that Dr. Braithwaite came home unexpectedly and surprised a burglar named Steven Saldano. We have recovered Dr. Braithwaite's laptop and other personal belongings following the unrelated shooting of Saldano at a home in Grant Park on New Year's Eve.

"Witnesses have also identified Mr. Saldano as the killer of pawn shop owner, Simon Wilhoite. *It appears that Saldano acted alone in both instances, and the two murders have no bearing on each other.*"

To William this seemed like a tidy ending to a very complicated investigation, *too tidy*. Long's expression seemed odd to him. Every muscle on her face confirmed that she didn't believe a word she said. She looked like a hostage reading a prepared statement at gunpoint.

She paused, and her face hardened into a look of grim determination, as if she were fighting back tears. "We are still seeking information in the murder of limousine operator Franco Balboa. If you know anything about this matter, please contact the Atlanta Police Department and ask for Sergeant Elizabeth Long. *I will do everything in my power to protect you.*"

Remembering his brief call from Long the day after Braithwaite's murder, William pulled out his phone and found her number. He started to dial it but decided to add her to his contact list. He'd ask Tom how best to approach her.

The news broadcast cut to an image of FBI agents, in their iconic blue windbreakers, removing boxes from a residence. "This morning," the announcer intoned, "the FBI also took into custody Garth Braithwaite's research assistant, Delbert Foster. They have not yet made a statement."

As the agents marched him away in handcuffs, Foster appeared thin and haggard, as though he'd quit eating and immersed himself in drugs. To William, his evasiveness during the interview now made sense. He again wondered how Foster managed to land a research position without a doctoral degree or enrollment in a graduate program. *Did he have something on Braithwaite, something he used to blackmail him? Something that someone else would kill to keep from coming out?*

William thought of calling Sean but opted for Tom instead.

"Hey. I just heard about Delbert. What do you know?"

"It's total bullshit, Pops. The APD pressured Sergeant Long into closing the case. This reeks of politics."

"Could be. If so, there's nothing else she can do."

"How do you think Foster's arrest will affect Uncle Sean's project?"

"It sure doesn't look good. With all the issues he's had, I can't imagine he'll continue to get funding."

"Grandpa Harmon tells me our universities are *full* of Chinese and Iranian spies."

"He may be right. When it comes to that sort of thing, he has better sources than I do. By the way, I just spoke to David Meacham. He agrees that the APD announcement is a coverup. He gave me a wild story about Braithwaite having orgies at all hours of the night with a bunch of underage women and making home movies. He thinks someone hired Saldano to retrieve those videos."

"Why would a burglar go to all that trouble to steal Braithwaite's DIY porn?" William asked.

"Maybe he planned to use it for blackmail . . . or perhaps one of Braithwaite's guests wanted to get rid of the evidence. Statutory rape is pretty serious business."

"Uhm . . . Misty and I rode our bikes around Braithwaite's neighborhood a few months ago. We met an old man who told us he saw men coming in and out of Braithwaite's house. He said one of them looked like Bram Dennis."

"Meacham told me that as well. He must have questioned the same man. You can't use that information without getting confirmation from a reliable source. The person he saw could have been anyone."

William shook his head. "This is so *weird*."

Then it hit him. "Do you suppose this has anything to do with Braithwaite's side project to cure erectile dysfunction? He could have planned to market the chip to his friends."

"Not likely. Remember, Braithwaite was an engineer, not a surgeon. Without FDA approval, his buddies would have to go somewhere like Latin America or Southeast Asia to find a doctor who'd perform the implants. There aren't a lot of guys dumb enough to trust their manhood to some foreign quack."

"So, what would *you* do with this information?"

"Nothing, William. It sounds preposterous. I wouldn't touch it. People get sued for less."

William thought for a moment. "Wow. If this ever got out, think what it would do to Dennis' Senate campaign." He glanced at the time on his phone. "Thanks, Pops, I need to head home."

"You won't find your mom there. Brandy took her and your Aunt Kathy out for lunch at the Old Vinings Inn."

"Sounds expensive."

"Yeah. Brandy's been wanting to get together with them for some time."

"Good. Mom needs to get out more often."

William's next call went to Harmon.

"Hey, Grandpa."

"How's my young reporter?"

"Good. But school's kicking my butt. I just dropped Misty off to visit her grandma. She's coming home from the hospital tomorrow. Misty's dad has hired nurses to take care of her."

"I'm glad she's on the mend. I heard on the news they caught the man who killed Dr. Braithwaite?"

"That's what they say."

"You sound skeptical."

"Well, it seems too . . . convenient."

"What do you mean?"

William hesitated, debating the journalistic ethics of divulging hearsay to his grandfather. "I heard some pretty credible rumors about Dr. Braithwaite having orgies with a bunch of teenage girls. The burglar may have gone there to steal his home movies."

Harmon's voice grew softer. "William, that's some pretty disturbing stuff."

"We got this from one of the Atlanta cops investigating the case. He even said Bram Dennis, one of our Senate candidates was a regular guest of Braithwaite's."

"Yeah . . . Well, I don't think I'd repeat those stories until you can verify them . . . especially as an aspiring reporter. By the way, I wanted to give you a heads up on something. A few weeks ago, the Chinese government reported a viral outbreak in the city of Wuhan. Tomorrow the World Health Organization will make an announcement calling it *pneumonia*, but it's a lot bigger than that. The White House will play it down to avoid getting people stirred up, but this thing is highly contagious and deadly. So far, our government has no plans to shut down travel to and from China."

"Wow! That sounds scary. I'll check that out."

"You do that. And take care of yourself."

"Will do."

* * *

Harmon wasted no time following up on William's story. As crazy as the rumor sounded, he knew a lie could outrun the truth every time, *especially* on social media. He reached for his phone.

"Hey, Homer. I'm afraid I've reconsidered my support for your boy, Bram."

"What? Why would you do that, Harmon?"

"Let's just say I'm revisiting my options."

"Your options!"

As the man began to wheedle, Harmon quietly disconnected.

His thoughts drifted back, as they often did, to Christmas. What had started as a joyous reunion quickly degenerated into bitterness and recrimination. As angry as he had been with William at the time, he now realized that much of that night's events had been his own fault. He thought about Henry, alone at Wellington. *There are few things in life you can undo or make up for, but I know of one.*

His next call went to an old friend with the Georgetown University pre-college summer program.

"I'd like to tell you about a remarkable young lady. Her name is Lisa Chu."

* * *

Marie Wakefield arrived late for her lunch date with her sister and their dad's girlfriend. She ordered a white wine, while Brandy sipped a Bloody Mary and Kathleen an unsweetened tea.

"This was a wonderful idea, Brandy. My office is just down the street. Thank you very much."

Brandy raised her glass in a toast. "I've been wanting to get together with you girls for a long time. And I appreciate you taking time away from your busy careers."

"No. No." Marie paused and set down her drink. "We're the ones who should have reached out to you. After our mom passed away, Kathy and I were at wits end as to what we should do about Dad. Every time we turned around, he was running off somewhere, doing Heaven knows what. You have been an absolute Godsend."

Kathleen nodded in agreement.

Brandy ran a finger through the condensation on her glass. "Actually, I was hoping you could help me with that. Lately, Tom seems to have slowed down a lot. He gets exhausted easily and he's having balance problems. When we were up at Biltmore, he took a spill. He claimed he just tripped over something, but I know better."

Kathleen said, "Let me talk to him. Maybe it's nothing serious, but I'm sure he's overdue for a checkup."

Brandy sighed and clasped her hands. "Please don't mention that I told you."

* * *

Sean O'Meara closed his eyes and laid his head on his desk. The last of his staff and colleagues had left at 4:30, and the vacant halls and offices echoed his profound emptiness.

Over the past four months his project had faced one setback after another. First, Braithwaite's murder, then Chu's sudden deportation and now Foster's arrest. The call this morning from his sponsors telling him they'd frozen his funding came as no surprise. They cited the project's numerous delays . . . and yet they'd been so patient before.

There's something more to this. In a moment it came to him. Not a paranoid man by nature, Sean distrusted coincidences. He pictured the invisible hand of Harmon Wakefield in all this. *How far would he go to undermine my research? Could he have sanctioned Garth's murder?* He shook off the thought as delusional.

Braithwaite hired Foster for reasons Sean never understood. Sean had heard rumors of the man's gambling addiction but dismissed them and defaulted to Braithwaite's judgement on the matter. In retrospect, he realized that Foster lacked the basic skills needed to design the chip and had no commitment to acquiring them. From what he'd seen, Foster relied heavily on the work of doctoral students and spent most of his time examining drawings made by others. Clearly, he had another agenda. *How could I have missed so many clues? Hell, I'm a college professor, not a counterespionage agent.* He stood and walked over to his window. *Where do I go from here? Another grant proposal will take time I don't have, and my prospects for success are slim, at best.*

Progress on the chip had come to a halt. Interviews with other research professors had yet to produce a replacement for Chu. Sean would *never* find new funding without a partner, and no engineer would commit to a job without funding. The university didn't offer salaries commensurate to those in the private sector. *And besides, I too have a family to support.*

Last Gleaming

He picked up his phone. The screen displayed a newsfeed from the World Health Organization, which he ignored. He thought of calling his old boss at Emory but decided it could wait. First, he'd break the news to his family.

Chapter Twenty-One

Contagion

Smyrna/Cherokee County/Atlanta
January 4, 2020

Still ruminating over David Meacham's statements about Garth Braithwaite and Bram Dennis, Tom Williams poured a second cup of coffee and called him. He put his phone on speaker, so Brandy could listen in. The voice that answered startled him.

"White."

It took Tom a moment to recall Meacham's partner. "Oh. Officer White. This is Tom Williams. I was trying to reach David Meacham."

The policeman let out a deep sigh. "Mr. Williams, I'm at Piedmont Hospital in Conyers. David's in ICU. His wife, Diane, called me last night. She said he'd been coughing, sneezing and running a fever since yesterday, and he couldn't smell anything. I live nearby, so I went over there and got him here as fast as I could. By the time we arrived, he was hacking up blood. He didn't look good . . . He didn't look good at all."

White sounded haggard and distressed. "Sorry. I've been here all night."

He stopped, and Tom heard him mutter to someone, followed by the echo of an intercom.

Tom instinctively reached for a notebook. "I'm sorry to hear that. Any idea where he caught this?"

"Only thing I can think of is when we answered that call over in Virginia Highlands a couple of days ago, an Asian woman found dead on the floor of her bedroom. The medical examiner said she had pneumonia."

"Was David wearing a mask or any other protection?"

"He had a little paper one he carried in his car."

"What did you do when you got there?"

"We followed all the protocols. We had no idea what we'd find. We knocked, and nobody answered, so I breached the door and cleared the house."

Tom could hear him hyperventilating.

"I tell you, it's the craziest thing I've ever seen. It was just day before yesterday. Now David's sick, and I'm not feeling too good myself. I don't know what to do."

"Did the lady have any family you know of?"

"I found a picture of a young man who might have been her son. But we didn't see any contact information for him."

"Had she travelled anywhere recently?"

"No idea. The neighbors said she walked her dog every day. Then suddenly she stopped."

"Did they see anyone coming or going?"

"Nope. Far as we can tell, she was a loner."

"Did you find anything suspicious in the house?"

White stopped as if remembering something. "I came across some of those disposable phones in her closet. I bagged them and took them downtown, and an FBI agent was there waiting for me. He said they were part of some investigation."

"Did he tell you anything about the investigation?"

"No. But I found out later the woman was a spy, working with that Delbert Foster guy they arrested."

"I understand you guys wrapped up the Braithwaite murder."

White spoke closer to his phone in a conspiratorial tone. "Well, that's what our boss wants people to think. Somebody hired this Saldano guy to steal Braithwaite's phone and laptop. When we got it we found some home movies of old men having sex with teenage girls. Turns out you can't recognize any of the men on there, but we're still looking for a young lady we believe was among them. We have to do it on the down low to keep the brass from coming down on us. Looks like somebody got to them."

"Is it okay if I follow up with you on that?"

"Sure, only please don't mention my name to anybody."

"I won't, and I'm sorry to hear about Officer Meacham. He's a good man. He let my grandson interview him for his school paper. Send him my best. I hope he gets well in a hurry . . . and you too."

* * *

William and Misty spent the morning cleaning Esther's house. She arranged cut flowers in every room, hoping their fragrance would mask the odor of Pine Sol.

The lift van arrived, followed by Jeff. He and Misty supervised the home healthcare worker as he lowered Esther's wheelchair and pushed it up a hastily constructed ramp. Despite their gentle efforts, Esther winced in pain.

"Be careful," Misty yelled. She clutched William's arm, digging her fingers in so hard it hurt.

When they'd gotten Esther safely into her specially equipped rental bed, Jeff stepped into the den and leaned against a wall to catch his breath. To William it seemed that the man had aged several years in the past few days.

"Mr. Sax," he asked, "how long will you be able to stay?"

"After all you've done for us, William, please call me Jeff." He gazed down the hallway at Esther's bedroom. "I'll be leaving tomorrow," he said apologetically. "Barbara has things I need to take care of on Monday. Why don't you guys go out somewhere, get away for a while. I'll handle things here."

* * *

William backed his Jeep into the last available parking spot on Virginia Avenue near Murphy's Restaurant.

"Wow," said Misty. "When my dad said we should get away somewhere, I don't think he meant this far."

"I haven't been here in years. I thought it would be a nice break."

"Yeah. And I suppose this trip has nothing to do with the death of that Chinese woman down the street, the spy."

"I thought we might take a stroll past there, then come back here for lunch."

"Fine. But we're not going in there posing as homebuyers."

The trip proved underwhelming. The tiny brick home had little to recommend itself, besides perhaps the large padlock on the door. Plywood coverings on the windows prevented them from seeing inside.

Misty wrinkled her nose. "I understand she and her dog were in there for weeks, putrefying. Talk about a massive cleanup. They'll have to completely sterilize the place."

William surveyed the picturesque neighborhood. "It kinda creeps you out doesn't it. Thinking that an enemy agent could take up residence right here under our noses. Who knows how much confidential stuff she sent back to Beijing? All of Uncle Sean's research has gone to shit, at least for now."

"Maybe he'll end up working for your Grandpa Harmon after all."

William stopped, struck by an epiphany. "Maybe he will. It's his best option at the moment. I think I know who can talk him into it."

Chapter Twenty-Two

The Investment

Kennesaw / Cherokee County
February 17, 2020

Sean O'Meara stepped into his darkened classroom and flipped a switch, bathing its empty theater-style seating in harsh fluorescence. Despite reports of a new flu epidemic, the university still retained its in-person instruction, with no antiviral precautions. *Insanity is continuing to do the same thing and expecting different results.* He squirted a blob of clear, foul-smelling disinfectant into his palm and rubbed his hands together, wondering if it did any good.

Following his loss of funding, Sean returned to teaching with a profound sense of disappointment. Finding a less invasive means of detecting and destroying tumors had been a passion he shared with his wife, Kathleen, ever since she lost her mother to cancer.

He remembered his call, months earlier, from Harmon Wakefield wanting him to come work for MedChip fighting infectious diseases. An oncologist by training, Sean had but a passing interest in virology. *The world needs more doctors. It also needs better medicine. I can't do both.*

He placed his hands on his podium and leaned on it for support as he stared at his lecture notes.

A voice startled him. "Good morning Dr. O'Meara."

"Good morning."

* * *

Kathleen collapsed into a chair, exhausted. Her patient load had continued to grow, exacerbated by the loss of ICU beds to an outbreak of flu and pneumonia.

Day and night she sat vigil with cancer-stricken children crying for the comfort of parents who waited in the lobby for good news that seldom came. Try as she may, she couldn't bring herself to imagine *their* anguish. Her one hope for a long-term solution had been Sean's work at Georgia Tech.

Years earlier, she'd read of a biochip research grant, while at the bedside of her mother, Colleen Williams.

Inside her scrubs, she felt her phone shudder.

Sean had bought Mary Frances a new iPad and stand for Christmas, so she could record her dance rehearsals. Kathy beamed at the video of her younger daughter.

"Hi, Mom," the tiny voice said as she practiced her moves. "I thought you might need a break. I wanted to show you what I've been learning online."

The girl took up dance at age five, when Kathy decided she needed to get her away from the television. When neither she nor Sean could drive her to lessons, they called Grandpa Tom who saw the task as a labor of love.

Tears welled in Kathleen's eyes as she watched the tentative yet graceful rendition of *Swan Lake*, her daughter's commitment evidenced in her every move. Never had she seen a child obsess so much. Her thin arms and legs moved with the grace of a swallow in flight. *She seems so fragile, like a crystal sculpture. My God, what would she do if she ever discovered she couldn't make it as a professional dancer?*

After showering and changing at the hospital, Kathy arrived home to find her older daughter, Lauren, setting the dining room table.

Mary Frances ran to her mom and threw her arms around her. "You won't believe this. Hari cooked us an authentic Indian dinner, and he let me help." She kissed Kathy on the cheek.

"We thought we'd come over and surprise you guys," added Lauren.

Kathy found her daughter's boyfriend in the den deep in discussion with Sean about healthcare and global economics. She kissed her husband and hugged Hari. "You two are the biggest *nerds* I've ever known."

"Mom," said Lauren, "You need to take a seat . . ." She waited until Kathy settled in and Sean had given her his full attention. "Mary Frances," she shouted, "come here. I don't want to have to repeat myself . . . Hari and I are getting married."

"Cool," said Mary Frances. "Now you can stop pretending you're sleeping in your *dorm room*."

When Lauren and Hari left, Mary Frances retreated to her room to finish her homework.

Kathy curled up beside her husband, placed her head on his shoulder and said, "Tell me about your day," lacking the emotional energy to talk about her own.

"The teaching's fine *for now*," he shrugged. "But I'm not giving up on my research. I *am* going to find another grant." He paused, as though searching for words. "I feel like it's more important than academics, especially with this damned pandemic."

"No one's calling it a pandemic yet."

"That's because the doctors at the WHO have become spineless bureaucrats. You see what's happening at the hospital. You tell me."

She leaned back and studied him. "What are you thinking, Sean?"

"Well, if it's the only thing open to me, I might as well go to work for those friends of Harmon's." He bit his lip.

Kathleen despised Harmon but saw this as Sean's only chance at resuming his work. "Well, it *would* give you a chance to develop new biochip applications. And eventually, when you return to oncology, you will have published your biochip research in virology. You'll be a rock star."

He sighed. "Okay. I'll call him tomorrow."

Kathy permitted herself a smile. Ever since her call earlier from William, she'd wondered how she could make her husband think he'd made this decision on his own.

* * *

Dismissing her cook with a grateful smile, Evelyn Wakefield bowed her head and gave thanks for the feast before her. Tonight, she added a special mention of her grandson's weekend visit.

That afternoon, Harmon had made the journey, three hours round-trip, to pick Henry up at Wellington. "So," he said, "tell your grandmother about school."

"It's great."

"Henry made the wrestling team," Harmon added.

"I'm also running cross-country."

Evelyn beamed at him. "We're very proud of you, Henry."

"Tell her about your other surprise."

Henry blushed. "I got a call last night from Lisa Chu. She's been invited to a two-week pre-college program at Georgetown this summer."

Evelyn turned her astonished gaze toward Harmon, who smiled, shrugged and put a fork full of food in his mouth.

When his cell phone rang, Evelyn gave him an icy stare.

"I'll make it quick," he said. The caller ID read *Abigail Martin*.

"Harmon, I hope I didn't interrupt your supper, but I have some great news for you. I've found the funding you need for your MedChip project."

"Darling, you have just made my day. We're about to bring on a premiere researcher and can use the cash."

"Glad to hear it. I'll let you get back to your family. Just let me know when we can get together over here in the District to work out the details."

Chapter Twenty-Three

Lockdown

Kennesaw / Cherokee County
March 12, 2020

Emerging from the Social Science Building, William received an email from one of his professors. "By tomorrow," it read "you'll receive an official notification that the university system is closing all its campuses due to COVID-19. Our class will meet online for the rest of the semester. I will email you a link . . ."

William stopped and gazed across the campus. *My God. It's like the world's coming to an end.* He stared at his phone dumbstruck, uncomprehending, then dialed Misty.

"Have you heard?," he asked. The school's going to virtual classes for the foreseeable future."

"Yeah. I got similar messages."

"How are your lab classes going to meet?" he asked.

"I don't know."

"Is it okay if I come over?"

"I'm not sure that's a good idea, William. They're telling us to stay at home as much as possible and cover our faces when we go out. I just got back from Home Depot with a box full of painter's masks. I'm not taking any chances with this shit. I have my grandma to think of."

"We could stand out in your front yard. I just want to see you. That's all."

She took a moment to respond. "Okay, but I'll have to listen out for Grandma, and we won't be able to . . . you know . . . get close to each other."

Twenty minutes later they met in front of Esther's home like duelers at twenty paces.

William forced a wry smile. "Wow! This sucks!"

"Welcome to the new normal, Baby. It's not like we couldn't see this coming."

"Yeah. Well, I hope it goes away soon."

"Don't bet on it. Experts have been telling us for years to expect a major worldwide outbreak, like the Spanish Flu a century ago. This is not your common cold, no matter what some would have us believe. It'll take months at least. And it'll probably keep coming back for a long time."

"What'll we do. How will people get to work and shop for the things we need?"

"We'll *adapt*, William. Forget about the way things used to be. We're starting over. It's what people have always done. It's called evolution." She gazed down the street at the horizon. "The problem is that viruses adapt faster than we do."

"But how will we see each other?" The whine in his voice sickened him.

"*Until* this thing goes away, we'll just have to Facetime each other or meet online. *I can't put my grandma at risk.*"

"Okay. I'm just having trouble processing this whole pandemic thing. It's like something out of the Middle Ages."

As she shook her head, an auburn lock fell across her face. "I don't know why everyone's so surprised. We have epidemics every few years, SARS, MERS, Legionnaire's Disease. But this one . . . This one's going to be a lot worse. I spoke to my biology professor. He's *already* calling it a pandemic."

"Have you talked to your parents? Are they coming?"

"They wanted to, but I told them to stay away. Who knows what they've been exposed to in Charleston? *I* can't risk infecting *them*. Shit, I even had to let the nurse go." Her lips trembled. "I'm scared, William. I'm alone in charge of my grandmother. She isn't well, as it is, and I don't know what to do."

In her face William read the weary look of someone twice her age. Instinctively, he moved toward her, arms outstretched.

"No, William. Stop."

He felt the ground shift beneath his feet.

"I'm going back inside now, William. And *you're* going home to take care of your mom."

Numb with grief, he watched her retreat into the house, never glancing back.

Unable to recall driving home, he thanked God he made it there alive. In the living room he found Marie sitting on the couch, face buried in her hands. A spent cigarette smoldered on a plate beside her. William picked up her phone where she'd dropped it, knelt and put his arms around her.

"What's the matter?"

"It's your brother," she choked. "They've shut down his school, and he refuses to come home."

"Where's he going?"

"Harmon and Evelyn are on their way to pick him up. He'll live with them for now. I can't believe they're doing this at their age." She reached for another cigarette.

"Nope," said William, as grabbed the pack.

A rabid look came over her. For a moment he expected her to lunge at him.

As she settled back into her seat, he asked, "Have you talked to Dad?"

She pulled back and regarded him as one might an idiot. "What do *you* think?"

"Well?"

"I called his office. They told me he was in a meeting. I left a message. Fat lot of good that'll do."

"What are *you* going to do? You can't go into the office. You don't know who might have this shit, a client, a staff member, another attorney."

"I'll work from home. I'm awaiting word on trial postponements. Right now, I'm more worried about your brother."

Her hands shook as she spoke. In all his years, William had never seen her like this. Without her face-to-face interactions at the office and in the courtroom she would find herself adrift at sea.

"Mom, Mom . . . I'll call Henry later and find out what's going on. Right now, I just want you to sit there. *I'll* clean up the kitchen and make us supper."

"*No*. I'll take care of that. Let me get you a list of things to pick up at Publix."

For a moment he weighed the wisdom of having her cook in her state, then decided it might provide a needed diversion. "Okay. But there's one thing you're going to do first."

"What?"

"Get rid of those *goddamned cigarettes. Throw away the whole fucking pack!*"

She stared at him in shock.

Before she could recover, he added, "I want you to order a refill for Chantix. I'll pick it up while I'm out."

As he entered the store, he passed a woman wearing a makeshift mask fashioned from a scarf. Shoppers rushed about, frantically grabbing toilet tissue, paper towels and disinfectants. A man passing with a basket full of fresh produce and canned goods swerved as far from William as the narrow aisle would permit.

Growing up in Virginia, William had seen more snowstorms and grocery store stampedes than he could remember. He'd seen people on television rushing to markets and liquor stores ahead of hurricanes. But today he caught something different in the faces of the shoppers and clerks . . . a growing fear of the unknown.

As he left, he noticed that the parking lot had filled in the short time he'd been inside. A driver waited for him to pull out of his space.

* * *

William and Marie dined in silence as gloom descended on their modest home. Unable to take it anymore, he suggested they walk over to Tom and Brandy's. By the time they arrived the sun hung low above the village of Smyrna.

He rang the doorbell and retreated ten feet. Brandy answered but left the storm door closed. She called out to Tom, and they convened on the back patio. Marie went to hug him, then stopped, gave him an awkward wave and backed away.

Tom looked more careworn than William had seen him since his wife had passed. Tom's dog, Bogie, bounded over and jumped on everyone. Apparently, no one had explained to him about social distancing.

When Tom inquired about school, William told them about the shutdown at KSU and his inability to visit Misty. Marie explained that she'd arranged to practice law remotely. "We're not leaving the house, except for grocery runs and doctor appointments, and we're wearing masks just to be safe," she said.

"Well," Tom sighed, "the beauty of being retired is that we don't have to go anywhere. And when the weather's nice, we can entertain guests out here."

"Provided they mask up," Brandy added, "which reminds me. I still haven't used the bar out here. Your grandfather installed it before Christmas. William, Marie, what'll you have?" Wearing latex gloves, she made Marie a whisky sour and opened an IPA for William.

"Thank you," he said. "I'm afraid I took the last of the painter's masks from Home Depot. I'll bring some with me next time. By the way, have you heard any more about Officer Meacham?"

"Not since he went into the hospital." Tom filled in Marie on the rumors of Garth Braithwaite's orgies with Bram Dennis and underage women.

"I'm not surprised," Brandy said. "I'm already sick of Dennis' campaign ads. He has *creep* written all over him."

William glanced at Marie. "Maybe I could interview Officer Meacham again when he gets out of the hospital."

"*Maybe you and your grandfather should mind your own damned business and stop acting like amateur cops*," Marie snapped. "You need to concentrate on your schoolwork, William."

* * *

Later, on his evening walk, William called Henry at his grandparents' home in Virginia. When he answered, they talked for a long time about school closings, COVID-19, and what it might mean to them.

"How do you like staying with Grandpa Harmon and Grandma Evelyn?" William asked.

"What's not to like? The cooking's great, and I get to ride horseback, go fishing, skeet shooting, whatever . . . whenever I have the time. It's like summer camp, only better."

"Have you heard anything else from Lisa?"

"Yeah. She called me last night. She wasn't supposed to. Her parents had just given her back her phone."

"Why?"

"Well . . . you know how you suggested I Facetime her?"

"Yeah."

"That was going great, then one night her mom came in and caught us. She got mad and started yelling at her in Mandarin."

"Just because you were Facetiming?"

"Well . . . she wasn't completely dressed."

"Wow, Henry! Have I mentioned lately how proud I am that you're my brother."

Henry laughed. "Look, I have to study for a test." He paused. "Tell Mom hello . . . and tell her I'm okay."

"I will. Good night."

William smiled, unable to remember a time when his brother had sounded so happy.

Chapter Twenty-Four

The Toll

Smyrna/ Cherokee County
March 19, 2020

As Tom turned on the evening news, his phone rang. He didn't recognize the number and debated answering it.

"Hello."

"Mr. Williams, this is Mark White." The policeman sounded hoarse. His voice cracked as he spoke. "I wanted to let you know we lost David this afternoon. He never left the hospital. He slipped back into a coma over the weekend . . . I just left from visiting his wife, Darlene, and their kids."

"Mark, I am *so* sorry. I can't even imagine what you're going through. And please . . . call me Tom."

"David was my partner for twenty years. We went through some tough times together."

"I'm sure you did. Could you tell me more about him?"

White took a few seconds.

"That's okay," Tom said, reaching for his notebook. "Take your time."

"David was a good man, a good husband, and a good father. Most folks on the police force don't know this, but he was a deacon in his church. Before we met, the last service I'd gone to was my mama's funeral. David took me to lunch one day, a week or so after my wife left me. He shared his faith with me and talked me into joining him and Diane on Sunday morning."

He started sobbing. "Them people brought me back to life, Tom. I don't know what would've become of me. He made a better cop out of me. He stood up for me when I made stupid mistakes. Now he's gone, and I think I might have caught what he had."

They spoke for another fifteen minutes. When they'd finished, Tom said, "Mark, I can't tell you how much I appreciate your opening up like this."

"And I appreciate you. I don't know who else I could've talked to."

"Anytime you feel like it, call me back. You have my number."

He went silent for a moment, then said, "Sure. I'd like that."

* * *

Beth Long unpacked her meager belongings, with help from Nancy. She and Grafton would stay with her while she sorted out what to do about the specter of a worldwide plague. Perhaps getting out of the city would make social distancing easier.

Sid called, his third time in as many weeks. He extended his condolences on the death of David Meacham. "He was a good man. I know you relied on him."

"Thanks. I'll miss him a lot. Mark's been a big help."

"Still no word on Mandy," Sid said. "I just hope Balboa's killers haven't gotten to her."

"Or COVID-19."

"That occurred to me. We put out discrete notices at area hospitals in case she shows up."

He let out a deep sigh. "Beth, I'm afraid we're at a dead end, without Mandy. The texts we found on Steven Saldano's phone prove that he and Scarborough knew each other, but that doesn't help us with Scarborough already in jail for receiving stolen goods. Whatever he knows about Braithwaite's parties, he certainly won't tell us now. Hell, without Mandy I don't even have a victim."

Long hung her head. All her efforts had come to nothing. "Isn't there something we could offer Scarborough?"

"Nothing *I* can think of. With good behavior he'll be out in a few months anyway. If he sticks to his story, he could end up going back to work for whoever hired him. After all, he took one for the team."

"There has to be something that'll put a fire under him to get out of there sooner."

"Well, if you come up with anything, let me know."

As Long hung up, Brandon Markham texted her, wanting to come by.

Nope, she replied. *Besides the obvious health concerns, that wouldn't be fair to Grafton.*

Her next call came from Mark White.

"Beth?" he croaked.

Ever since calling to tell her David Meacham had died, he'd begun using her first name.

"Hey, Mark."

"I wanted to let you know I called in sick for tonight's shift. I didn't want you finding out at roll call . . . I'm afraid, Beth. I think I caught what David had." A violent coughing fit interrupted him.

"I'm sorry to hear that, Mark. Have you been to the doctor?"

"Yeah. He gave me some kind of test and said all I had was a cold."

"Did he give you something for it?"

"He said to drink Nyquil."

"Then do what the doctor says. Treat it like a bad cold. Stay at home as long as you need. I can pull in someone else if I have to. Right now, I'm just riding my desk and wearing a mask, like a stagecoach robber."

"I still can't believe David's gone."

"Me either. Do you feel like talking about it?"

As she listened, Long glanced at the national news on Nancy's television. It led with the World Health Organization's declaration of a pandemic.

"Well, it's about damned time," Long said.

"What?" White asked.

She explained the WHO announcement. "How many months has it been now? How many people had to die for these bureaucrats to wake up?" She imagined the disease decimating the force, as criminals rampaged through the city. *How am I going to do my job?*

When the broadcast broke for a commercial, up popped a campaign ad for Bram Dennis. Long's thoughts returned to Braithwaite's videos of young women being raped by middle-aged men. In an instant, she recalled why she had become a cop.

"Listen, Mark. Why don't we get together as soon as you feel better? I'll come by your place. We can sit outside and talk."

As she hung up, she stared in disgust at Dennis' smug, triumphant smile. *Bram, old boy, come what may, I will make it my life's mission to see that you never go to Washington.*

She texted Brandon to tell him that, after carefully considering his generous offer to provide for her and Grafton, she'd pass.

* * *

Meanwhile, at the Fulton County Jail, Dean Scarborough lay shivering on his cot, soaked in sweat. He hadn't slept in three nights. His cellmate coughed repeatedly, as did inmates throughout the block.

He pictured himself in a prison ward, surrounded by contagion. His lawyer, Marcelle LaCroix, offered him no hope for an early release and had stopped returning his calls. In his most paranoid moments,

Last Gleaming

Scarborough imagined Homer Starke waiting for him to die here. *I need to talk to that cop, Beth Long, see if she can get me out.*

Chapter Twenty-Five

Esther

Smyrna/ Cherokee County
April 15, 2020

Marie closed her laptop. She'd spent three hours reviewing discovery notes for a long-delayed criminal trial. Working from home gave her the luxury of wearing pajamas all day. She sniffed them. *When did I wash these last?*

She turned on the television and scanned the soap operas. *Is this what I've come to?*

The doorbell startled her. She peered out the picture window and saw her sister standing on the lawn. Her straight black hair had gone mostly gray and frown lines bracketed the pale blue mask with its Emory Midtown logo.

"Kathy!" she said. "I thought you were under house arrest at the hospital." She started to hug her but refrained.

"I'm burning out, Sis. I finally got them to give me an eight-hour parole."

"And you came to see *me*? You could have called, you know, given me a chance to get dressed."

"I spoke to Dad this morning. He tells me you and William have cloistered yourselves, that you've stopped bathing, and now you aren't even returning his calls."

"That's not true. I spoke to him the other day . . . and I bathed . . . uh . . . last week."

"Get yourself cleaned up, and let's go for a walk. I'll wait out here."

"I don't know . . ."

"If you don't get in that shower right now, I will throw you in there and scrub you myself."

Fifteen minutes later, Marie returned, suitably clothed, her hair still damp. "Okay. Are you happy?"

"Is William here?"

"No. He went out for another run."

As they strolled through the neighborhood, keeping their distance, Kathleen asked, "So tell me, how are things at work?"

"Scary. We've lost *so* many key people to COVID. One of our investigators quit on us recently. Apparently, her mom's care giver stopped coming in. I don't know how we'll replace her."

"How are William and Henry?"

Kathy listened as Marie complained about her ungrateful sons.

"You mean Henry hasn't called you?"

"We spoke last week. The whole conversation lasted about two minutes. I'm sure his grandmother put him up to it."

Marie applied mosquito repellant. "Here. Take this. You'll need it."

Kathleen choked as she sprayed her bare arms and legs. "What about William?"

"He spends all his time out walking or running or locked up in his room talking to that girlfriend of his. The other day, for some reason, he asked me for Brandy's number. Maybe he's talking to her. He barely speaks two words to me."

"Girl, you need to get a life and stop blaming all your issues on Bill and the boys."

Marie sighed. "I know. I've been busy with work."

"Don't give me that crap. You're just making excuses so you can feel sorry for yourself. Why don't you and William come by the house

Saturday evening. Sean can fire up the barbeque, and we'll eat on the patio . . . six feet apart, of course."

"Okay. Okay. I'll be there."

* * *

Bored with his Zoom classes and late-night studies and unwilling to watch another news story on the rising death toll, William had begun running every day and working out with his old weights. As he wended his way through Argyle Estates and west on Campbell to Atlanta Road, the realization hit him that no matter how far he ran he could not escape the COVID malaise.

A scrap of paper rode the warm breeze across a deserted street, reminding William of a cheesy apocalypse movie. He glanced at the empty sidewalks, cast in the shadows of adjacent buildings, half expecting to see zombies crawl out of the storm drains. Eyes tearing, he ran harder, thinking he might awaken from this nightmare. *Misty says we have to adapt. I'm fucking tired of adapting.*

Slowly his endorphins kicked in. As he returned to his neighborhood, he noticed signs of life, trees budding, homeowners standing in their driveways, chatting with neighbors across the street. Work crews shouted at each other in Spanish above the roar of chain saws and chippers as they cleared the damage left by a passing storm.

A bleary-eyed fox, rousted from its den, gave William a wary glance as he passed. William wondered if COVID-19 might prove as deadly to trees and wildlife as to humans.

Bounding into the kitchen, he nearly ran into Marie brewing a cup of hot tea. She gave him a passable "Good morning" as he kissed her on the cheek and retreated to the shower.

Drying off, he reached for his phone and noticed he'd missed a call from Misty. Rather than playing her message, he hit redial.

"Oh, my God, William!" she screamed. "It's my grandma. I couldn't wake her this morning. She's . . . She's wheezing and running a fever. I think she has COVID."

"Have you called an ambulance?"

"Yes. They're on their way. Oh my God! What am I going to do?"

"Stay where you are. I'll get there as quickly as I can." Ending the call, he threw on fresh clothes and grabbed a mask as he sprinted past a startled Marie.

"Hey," she cried, "Where do you think . . ."

The door slammed behind him, cutting her off.

* * *

By the time he got to Esther's house, the ambulance had arrived. William said a silent prayer of gratitude that the cops hadn't stopped him for speeding. Glancing at his phone, he found he'd missed three calls from Marie. He shoved it back into his pocket.

Helpless, Misty stood in the driveway, tears staining her mask. The EMTs refused to let her ride with them and told her she wouldn't be able to get into the hospital. One of them gave her a number she could call for updates on Esther's condition.

Oblivious to the threat of infection, William took her into his arms and let her cry onto his chest. They sat on the steps, and she explained that she'd called her parents, that they should get there by nightfall. Meanwhile, she had to disinfect the house, as best she could, and launder all the linens.

"I'll run over to Publix and see if they have any wipes and Lysol spray," he said. "And I'll get as many bottles of hand sanitizer as I can. How are you set for masks?"

On his way to the store, he returned Marie's call.

"Where the hell are you?" she screamed.

"Misty's grandmother went to the hospital. Her parents are on their way over from Charleston. I'm helping her clean up."

"William are you out of your fucking mind?"

He disconnected the call.

Returning from the store, grocery bags in hand, he found Misty seated on the couch, speaking to an ICU nurse, berating her for not putting her through to a doctor. Frustrated, she hung up and threw the phone across the room.

William kneeled and took her hands in his. "What did they say?"

"They said he's busy with other patients and will call back as soon as he's available."

"Look, I know this is awful, but the hospitals are swamped with patients and short-handed. My Aunt Kathy can't even come home at night. She has to sleep on a cot. This morning, they finally gave her a short break." He reached into a bag. "Meanwhile, I got the last two containers of wipes from Publix. They're running out of everything. Why don't I help you clean up?"

"Sure, but don't touch my grandma's bedroom. In fact, leave the door closed. Start with the kitchen and the hall bath. You'll find latex gloves under the sink."

Hours later, overcome with exhaustion, they shared a chaise lounge on the deck. William commented on Misty's newly planted garden.

"Yeah," she sighed. "I put all that work into it. If anything happens . . . I'll have to leave it behind." She began to sob.

From out front came the sound of car doors slamming. Jeff and Barbara met them in the kitchen. Barbara ran to Misty and embraced her. Jeff shot William a glance of surprise mixed with a hint of annoyance.

"Mom, Dad, William's been helping me clean up and disinfect this place. You'll need to stay in the third bedroom."

"I'll help you bring in your bags," said William.

"No. That won't be necessary," Jeff said. "Look, we appreciate all you've done, but you shouldn't be here. You have your mom to think of."

William stared at Misty for a moment before realizing Jeff was right. "Okay," he said. "Please keep me posted."

As he left, she started to follow, then stopped, her bloodshot eyes proffering an unspoken goodbye.

* * *

Marie met him at the door. "I can't believe you went over there to that infested house, with no regard for your own health or mine. We're in a *quarantine*, William, or have you forgotten?"

He nodded as he headed to his room.

"Take another shower," she shouted, "and *burn those clothes.*"

William spent the remainder of the day in a futile effort to focus on his studies. His thoughts returned to images of Esther, mortally ill and spending what could be her final hours hooked up to monitors and life support in ICU.

What will Misty do now? She told me she only came back here to take care of Esther. Her parents won't let her stay by herself. She can just as easily complete the semester online from Charleston.

The call came at a quarter to midnight. William, still awake, answered it lying in bed.

"She's gone, William," Misty whispered. "The doctors confirmed it was COVID. Her weakened condition left her vulnerable."

"Oh my God, Baby! I'm so sorry. This is horrible."

She remained silent, but for sniffling and heavy breathing.

"What . . . what about you," he stammered. "You haven't been coughing or running a fever, have you?"

"No."

"Can I come over and see you in the morning?"

"*No*. Are you crazy? You can't continue to expose yourself. Besides, we're packing tomorrow. I'm following my parents back to Charleston. My dad's putting this house on the market."

"But . . . how will we see each other?"

"I don't know, William. I want you so much. But what we can do?"

"Will you call me before you leave?"

"Sure."

He ran to the bathroom and lost his supper.

* * *

The next morning, after a fitful night, William rose and put on a pot of coffee before his mom got up, measuring out enough for three extra cups.

When Marie finally stumbled into the kitchen, he told her about Esther's death and Misty moving back to Charleston. She held him for a long time, then suggested he go for a walk to clear his head.

On the way, he texted Misty asking if he could call.

"Not right now," she replied. "*I'll* call *you* when we're ready to leave."

Not wanting to return home, he went over to Bad Daddy's Restaurant and found it closed. He sat on the curb and called Tom.

"Hey, William. Are you guys okay?"

"No."

"What happened?"

He told him about Esther and about Misty's return to Charleston.

"I'm sorry to hear that. You want to come over? We can sit out front and talk. But we have to stay six feet apart."

William arrived to find Tom sitting on his porch in a folding chair wearing a Florida Gators mask in honor of his alma mater. "Where did you get that?"

"Brandy ordered it for me on Amazon."

"Cool."

A second chair sat in the walkway about six feet away with a mask lying on the canvas seat. It reeked of Lysol. Bogie ambled up and lay at William's feet.

"So, tell me how you plan to get this girl back," Tom asked.

"I don't know, Pops. Her dad's selling the house, and Misty has no reason to come back here. She can take her online classes anywhere."

"Okay. So, what's keeping you here? You're taking online classes too, as I recall."

William's breath caught. "You mean . . ."

"Well? You tell me. I've heard the way you talk about her. Sounds to me like she's the one."

"But I . . . Where would I stay? I don't know anybody in Charleston."

"What have you been studying this semester, William?"

"Writing, photography, web development . . ."

"Yep. I've seen your portfolio. It's pretty impressive. What are you planning to do with all that?"

"Find a job when I get out of school."

"Why wait 'til then? You could get a job now. Might not be what you want, but with your internet skills and this pandemic lockdown, there ought to be plenty of opportunities out there."

"I guess."

"You guess? Boy, things are changing fast. You better catch up."

"I see what you mean."

"People aren't just taking classes remotely. They're *working* remotely. You can do your schoolwork in the time you'd otherwise spend commuting. With a little ingenuity, you can even find stories to publish on your blog site."

"You mean I should move to . . . Charleston?"

"Of course. Work out the details when you get there. When you and Misty graduate, you can always come back here."

"Where will I stay?"

"Sleep in your Jeep if you have to. Park outside a Starbucks and work on your phone until you find a place."

"Wow! Thanks, Pops."

Tom leaned forward and, in a conspiratorial tone, added, "One more thing . . . For God's sake don't tell your mom where you got this idea."

William laughed for what felt like the first time in years. "Believe me, I won't."

Chapter Twenty-Six

Bram Dennis

Atlanta/Cartersville, GA
April 23, 2020

As Beth Long took a bite from her Big Mac, her phone rang. "You're interrupting my lunch, Mark. This better be good news."

Following a brief illness, White had returned to work, just in time. Atlanta's homicide rate had climbed, blamed on a proliferation of guns, pandemic stress and a diminished trust in the government's ability to do anything about it.

He sounded out of breath. "Beth, I just got a call from the owner of that house where Steven Saldano holed up. Actually, the guy was calling David, but I had David's phone forwarded to mine. . ."

"What did he call you about?"

"His new tenant texted him, saying his heat had gone out. When the HVAC man opened up the furnace he found a cell phone. Looks like Saldano stashed it there. Anyway, the landlord said he'd hold it for us."

Following David Meacham's death, Long had noticed a change in White's demeanor. Meacham had always been the straight man of the comedy duo, White the jovial wisecracker. The older policeman's departure had deprived White of a mentor.

"Give me the landlord's number," Long said.

An hour later, they met at the small rental home in Cabbage Town.

Weighing the nondescript phone in her hand, Long pondered what she should do with it.

"Since it ties to the Braithwaite murder," asked White, "are you going to have to turn it over to the FBI?"

She smirked. "Who says it has anything to do with Braithwaite? Besides, that's a closed case. And Agent Prillaman has everything he needs to prosecute Delbert Foster as a spy. I think I'll let Sid handle this. I'm not even sure we need to let Darnell know."

As if on cue, her phone rang.

"Hey, Sid. What you got?"

"Mandy Carter. She showed up at Grady a few days ago, almost dead from COVID. I just found out. She's been in ICU on fluids and a respirator, but now that she's recovering, the hospital has moved her to a regular bed. I'm waiting for permission to interview her. I still have to wear a mask and stand six feet away."

"Mind if Amy Springer and I join you?"

"Not at all."

Long arrived to find Sid and Amy standing outside Mandy's door, masked and engaged in conversation with her physician. As the doctor left, Sid said, "Okay. She's still weak. The hospital gave us only a few minutes. Let's go easy on her."

The girl had undergone a marked transformation in the months since Long last saw her. Her face had healed, leaving no trace of bruises, but she'd lost weight and grown her hair longer. Her gaunt features and pale complexion made her seem much older than her thirteen years.

Springer knelt beside her. "Hey, Mandy. I don't know if you remember me. I visited you the last time you were here."

"Yeah," she muttered.

"I'm so sorry to hear about your illness. You gave us quite a scare."

The girl said nothing.

Springer offered her a sip of water from her bedside table. "Where have you been living?"

Mandy took a deep breath and mustered her strength. "With a friend."

"We worried about you after Franco . . ."

A single tear streaked the girl's face. "Franco," she mumbled.

"Listen. You remember Sergeants Long and Cosgrove."

Mandy flinched.

"They're here to help you. *I'm* here to help you. When you get well, I'll find a place where no one can hurt you again."

She shook her head violently.

"Mandy, we're not talking about Child Protective Services. I can get you into a place of your own, where no one can find you. You'd like that wouldn't you?"

She rolled over and stared at the window. "Go away."

"Mandy," said Long, "Whoever murdered Franco Balboa won't stop until they find you. With what you know, they *cannot* afford to let you live. Given their resources, it's a miracle they haven't gotten you already."

The girl's shoulders shook as she surrendered to her grief.

"We need your help finding the man who beat you up. That's the only way we can keep him from coming back."

Slowly, the girl turned her head, eyes filled with tears, and examined Long's face as though searching for signs of deception.

Springer gave her another sip, and she licked her lips.

Taking a deep breath, she said, "Dan."

"Yes. Dan," Long said. "Who is he?" She held out a photo. "I want you to think hard. Is this him?"

Mandy shrank back as though Long had tried to hand her a snake. "Yeah," she whispered.

"Can you tell us why he beat you up?"

Something steeled in the girl's eyes as she forced herself to speak. "I met him several times, over at that professor's house. He never gave me his real name. Later, he started picking me up over on Howell Mill and taking me to an apartment."

"Can you tell us where this apartment was?"

"Somewhere off Chattahoochee Avenue."

"Okay. What led to him slapping you and throwing you out of his car?"

"One day, I saw him on television, and I found out who he was. I needed money real bad. I told him I was pregnant with his baby and needed an abortion. He called me a lying whore, and I told him I knew who he was. I said I'd call the cops. That's when he tried to kill me."

"Who is he, Mandy?"

"That politician, Bram Dennis."

Long's jaw tightened. "Mandy, you will never have to worry about him again. That creep will spend the rest of his life as some inmate's *bitch*."

"Thank you, Mandy," said Springer. "We have to go now and let you get some rest. But I'll be back to check on you. Don't leave the hospital without us. We won't be able to protect you if you run away again."

When they got to the lobby, Sid turned to Long. "I just hope she'll sit tight and stick to her story."

"Something tells me she will. This should be enough for an arrest warrant."

"Alright, let's go see the judge."

Long hugged Springer. "Amy, I can't thank you enough for all you've done."

"Don't mention it. Go get that bastard. I am *so* looking forward to testifying against him."

* * *

Elaine Dennis bustled from kitchen to dining room and back, giving last minute instructions to her caterers. She'd spent all day with the cleaning and yard crews and the florist, preparing her country club estate for tonight's dinner party honoring several of Bram's major contributors.

A crystal punch bowl in the foyer held plastic-wrapped masks in case anyone forgot theirs. Specially printed for the occasion, they read "Bram for Senate" in white lettering on a red background.

Stopping in the living room, Elaine admired her image in the gilded mirror and touched up her lipstick. The conservative outfit she'd chosen fit the picture of a senator's wife perfectly. The straight, black dress also helped hide the weight she'd put on since the pandemic began.

Gazing out her picture window, she saw a man and a woman coming up the long drive. Given their appearance, she knew they weren't early arrivals. *Probably selling something.*

Answering the door before the bell rang, she said, "Yes. May I help you?"

"Mrs. Dennis?" the man asked.

"Yes."

"I'm Sergeant Cosgrove and this is Sergeant Long." In unison, they displayed their badges. "We're with the Atlanta Police Department, and we'd like to speak with your husband."

Taken aback, Elaine asked, "Why? Whatever for?"

"I'm afraid we'll need to discuss that with him."

"Well . . . he's not here."

"Any idea when he'll be home."

In desperation, she lied. "No. He often works late."

Cosgrove glanced at Long. "That's okay. We'll wait out front. Meanwhile, here are our cards with our cell numbers."

Retreating to an upstairs bedroom, Elaine closed the door and dialed her husband's law office.

"Bram, when are you coming home?"

"I'm finishing up a few things. I'll be right there."

"Our guests are about to arrive, and there are two Atlanta police officers outside. They say they need to talk to you."

"About what?"

"They didn't say." She perused their business cards. "One's a Sergeant Sid Cosgrove with Special Victims, and the other's Sergeant Elizabeth Long with Homicide."

Elaine thought she heard her husband gasp.

"Is this Sergeant Long a young woman with dark brown hair?" he asked.

"Yes."

There followed a long pause before he said, voice trembling, "I need to make some calls. When everyone gets there, let them in quickly. If the cops try to speak to them, phone me immediately."

"What do I say to our guests?"

"Tell them I've been tied up unexpectedly on an urgent matter and will be home as soon as possible. Keep them entertained as long as you can."

* * *

Cosgrove waited in his car, while Long went to a nearby MacDonald's for cheeseburgers and coffee. At the end of the tree-lined street resplendently dressed men and women, young and old, arrived in luxury automobiles. Sid smiled to himself. *This should prove an interesting night. One we'll talk about for years to come.*

When Long returned, she asked, "Any sign of our boy?"

"Nope. Just a bunch of stretch limos."

A Bartow County Sheriff's Department vehicle rolled up. The passenger side window came down with a soft whir. Behind the wheel sat a thin young man with close-cropped red hair. Long recognized Deputy Ty Butler from a homicide scene they'd worked two years earlier.

"Good evening, folks," he said. "Just thought I'd come by and check on you. Have you had a chance to speak with our would-be senator?"

"Nope," said Sid. "We spoke to his wife. Seems he's been . . . detained."

Butler stared at the cars lining the circular drive as though counting them. "You suppose the wife called him and warned him off?"

"Could be," said Cosgrove.

"Want me to go by and check his office?"

"We'd appreciate that very much."

Twenty minutes later, Long's phone rang. She put it on speaker.

Butler sounded out of breath. "You guys need to get over here right away. When I arrived, I heard a shot. I kicked in the door and found Dennis on the floor with a bullet wound to the temple. He left a sealed envelope addressed to his wife. EMTs are coming, but he's well on his way to room temperature."

Long pounded the dashboard. *"That fucking asshole."*

Fighting to compose herself, she said. "That envelope is evidence, Ty. We need to see what it says. *Dennis did not act alone.*"

Butler took a moment to reply, "I'm afraid you'll need a search warrant, Beth."

"But we have an *arrest* warrant."

"I understand," he said, "but that doesn't change anything. Meanwhile, we've locked this place down. Any evidence you need will still be here in the morning."

"Beth," said Sid. "I know you're frustrated, but we still have to do this by the book. There's nothing else you can do tonight. Go home to Nancy and Grafton. I'll wrap it up and call you in the morning."

* * *

That night, after putting Grafton to bed, Long sank into her dad's old recliner. She closed her eyes, unable to clear from her mind the image of Mandy Carter lying in a hospital bed. She couldn't let Bram Dennis escape justice by taking the coward's way out. His family, his enablers, needed to know his true character.

Seeking relief, she reached for the remote, catching the tail end of a breaking news announcement. A reporter stood outside a lakefront mansion surrounded by dense woods and a high security fence. The banner at the bottom of the screen read "Hartwell, Georgia." In the distance a man appeared in a large picture window and quickly stepped away as he came into focus.

"Arlene," the reporter said, "I'm here outside the residence of Homer Starke, a major force in Georgia politics for decades. Mr. Starke has not answered our calls, and his security detail has refused to allow us onto his property. Until today, Starke has been the principal backer of State Legislator Bram Dennis in his special election bid for the U.S. Senate seat vacated by . . ."

Long hit the mute button and opened her laptop. She spent the next three hours researching everything she could find on Starke. A picture formed in her mind. *This has to be the creep who hired Scarborough and paid him to take the fall. It was all about protecting his candidate. I just need the thread that connects them.*

Chapter Twenty-Seven

Moving Out

Atlanta
May 5, 2020

Up before the sun, William paced his bedroom floor, afraid he might hyperventilate. He'd spoken with Misty last night, seeking news on Jeff's promise to find him a job in Charleston.

When she finally called back, he nearly dropped the phone. Misty said hello and handed him off to Jeff.

"William, I have an opportunity for you. Simonton Duval, the private equity firm that bought out my company a few years ago, has acquired a small cybersecurity outfit here in town. They need someone to help their marketing department with web development and press releases. Are you still interested?"

"Yes... Yes, sir."

"It won't pay much at first, but you'll get your foot in the door. They want an online interview with you tomorrow. They sounded like they might make you an offer on the spot."

"Thank you *so much*, Mr. Sax. I can't tell you how much I appreciate this." He thought for a moment. "I was wondering if you knew where I might get an apartment in Charleston."

"You won't find anything you can afford in a decent neighborhood. So, I've spoken to Barbara, and you can stay here on our boat, at least until you save up some money. We haven't used it in a while, and it's just sitting here. You and Misty still need to meet outdoors and *social distance*."

"Oh my God, sir! You can't imagine what this means to me."

"Just remember, when you talk to them tomorrow, I want you to knock their socks off. And be ready to send them samples of your stuff."

"Yes sir."

Since his earlier conversations with Tom, William had spent night and day polishing his portfolio, often to the neglect of his schoolwork. *Wow! I've got this. I'm going to be living on the Sax's yacht, right there in front of their house, working remotely. Sweet!*

The next day, following a heated argument with Marie, William packed his Jeep and hit the road. On the way out, he stopped to say goodbye to Tom and Brandy. They set up chairs on the walkway. William shifted from one foot to the other as Bogie circled him, vying for attention.

"What did your mom say when you told her?" Brandy asked.

"First, she tried to tell me I couldn't go. When I reminded her I'm eighteen, she said I couldn't take the Jeep. Then I replied that Dad signed it over to me, *not her*. I thought her head would explode."

"She'll get over it . . . in time," Tom said. "Meanwhile, you're a free man. Before you go, though, there are some things I want you to have."

Easing from his chair, he winced as he stood and went inside.

"I'm worried about your grandpa," Brandy said in a low tone. "Please don't say anything to him about this, but the other day he fell again and bruised his shoulder. It was all I could do to get him to go to the doctor's office."

"What did they say?"

"That he's getting old and needs to take it easy. You and I both know that won't happen. They gave him some pills for dizziness and sent him home. They also put him on blood pressure medicine."

"Is this anything new?"

"No. He's been unsteady on his feet for a while now."

The conversation stopped abruptly as Tom returned with a stack of CDs.

William shuffled through them. "Oh my God . . . the travel songs we listened to on our trip out west."

Tom reached into his pocket and pulled out a thick envelope "Oh, and you'll need this as well."

William peeped inside and nearly fainted. "You don't have to do this."

"Take it, William," Brandy said, her eyes moist, "and go chase your dreams."

* * *

As he passed the Wheeler Road exit outside Augusta, William popped in another of Tom's CDs. Billy Joel's *Movin' Out* reverberated inside the small vehicle. He glanced at his gas gauge, reminding himself that he needed to stop soon and fill up.

Despite William's protests, Tom had insisted on loaning him two hundred dollars in cash. The thought of leaving him behind brought with it a wave of guilt. William pictured him again, getting up slowly from his chair. Every scintilla of his career he owed to that man. When he got to Charleston, he would call and check on him.

His phone interrupted his reverie. He pressed the Bluetooth button on his console. "Hey, Grandpa."

"William," Harmon asked, "What's this I hear about you running away from home?"

"Misty's grandma died, and she had to move back to Charleston with her parents. They're going to let me stay on their yacht."

"Their yacht! If her parents have that kind of money, you'd better marry that girl right away, before she wises up."

William smiled at the thought. "Yeah. I'm only staying on the boat until I can save up enough for my own place."

"How do you plan to make a living?"

"Jeff . . . Mr. Sax got me a digital marketing job with a cybersecurity company. I'll be able to work remotely."

"That sounds like a good deal, son. I'm damned proud of you."

"Thanks. I can't even believe it."

"Tell me more about this company you're working for."

"It's called Shaheen Cybernetics."

"I've never heard of it."

"It's a startup founded by a guy named Mac Shaheen. Simonton Duval, the private equity firm that bought out Jeff's fleet tracking company is now a major partner."

"What do they do?"

"They're developing firmware that detects unauthorized access and tracks it back to the source. That's all I know so far."

He could almost hear Harmon processing this. "I'm proud of you, William. That's very important work."

"Well, I wanted a career writing about technology."

"Exactly. And the technology that matters most right now is the technology that helps protect our country. Without it, the rest will all go to waste. Keep me posted on Shaheen."

"Sure. That'll be my job, letting the world know about them."

"Meanwhile, what are you going to do about school?"

"I don't know. Kennesaw extended their withdrawal deadline. I dropped all my classes this morning."

"When do you plan to go back?"

"I don't know. Right now, I have a great job."

"Does this new job provide benefits?"

"Not yet. Fortunately, I'm still on Dad's insurance."

"Well, if they don't treat you right down there in Charleston, let me know. You can always come work for one of my companies."

* * *

As the call ended, Harmon dialed the president of his holding company. "Get me everything you can find about a company called Shaheen Cybernetics, founded by a Mac Shaheen and now controlled by the private equity firm, Simonton Duvall."

Taking a break, Harmon went to the bar and poured himself a tall bourbon over ice. He'd spent all day calling in favors, pressing friends, associates and total strangers for campaign contributions. His stable of candidates now included five Republicans and four Democrats. Since reading of Bram Dennis' suicide, he'd stopped taking Homer Starke's calls.

Staring out at a spectacular sunset, he admired the green pastures and rolling hills of his estate. A lone thunderhead threatened to spoil the view.

Soft footsteps echoed in the hall, interrupting his reverie. Evelyn gave him a sly smile, wrapped her arms around him and laid her head on his chest. "I thought we might have dinner by the pool."

"That's a splendid idea, my dear."

Henry joined them on the veranda.

"There's our handsome young man," said Harmon. "How's the packing coming?"

"I'm done."

Bill had invited Henry to Georgetown for the following week.

As he settled into an Adirondack chair, Harmon placed a hand on his shoulder, "Henry, I can't begin to tell you how proud you've made your grandmother and me. I know these last few years have been tough, with your parents splitting up, you moving away from your friends, having the pandemic interrupt your school year. We want you to know you can stay here as long as you want."

Henry shifted uncomfortably. "Thanks."

"You're the most focused young man I've ever known."

"Much like your grandfather when I first met him," added Evelyn.

Paloma arrived with glasses of iced tea on a serving tray.

Harmon continued, "You're in great shape. You're making straight As. If you follow through on your plans for a military career, you'll have a bright future. And when you get out, I just might have an opportunity you." He stole a glance at Evelyn.

Chapter Twenty-Eight

The Great Resign

Atlanta
June 12, 2020

Strolling along a lakeside path with her daughter, Beth Long replayed in her mind her conversation with Lieutenant Art Darnell . . . the conversation that led to her suspension. She could almost laugh about it in retrospect, picturing his red face, veins pulsating around his temples.

"I've had it, Sergeant," he shouted. "You work for *me*! And yet you've continued to pursue this Braithwaite investigation in direct violation of my orders. It's a *closed case*. Instead, I'm putting you on administrative leave. You are not to go anywhere near Bram Dennis' family *or* Dean Scarborough."

She started to throw her badge at him but caught herself, determined to finish what she'd started. *I'm not gonna let a weasel like Darnell have the last word.* Instead, she took Grafton to a neighborhood park while she plotted her next move. She would unearth the events leading to Braithwaite's death and make them public, *then* she could tell Darnell to go fuck himself.

Her thoughts returned to the demise of Bram Dennis and his political career. Under intense pressure from child advocacy groups, the Fulton County DA had obtained a search warrant for Dennis' law office. Sid called to say that his team had executed it under the supervision of a defense attorney appointed to protect any confidential files.

They scoured Dennis' home, his car and the dumpster outside his office building, finding nothing that would incriminate him. Dennis had been alone the night he shot himself, as far as anyone knew. None of the surrounding tenants had seen any visitors in the short span between Elaine's call and Ty Butler's discovery of his body.

Long kept coming back to Darnell. A political animal, he never cared what she did as long as she cleared homicides and didn't cause trouble. *Did Homer Starke get to him? One way or another, I'll find out. Homer has no idea who he's screwing with.*

Dennis' suicide note said an Atlanta cop tipped him off about his impending arrest. *Could it have been Darnell?* Long discarded the idea as a paranoid fantasy brought on by her frustration with the man.

The letter also dismissed the accusations against him as a character assassination orchestrated by his political enemies and the liberal media. It went on to say that his attorney had assured him that he had nothing to worry about. *So, why did he choose to take his life. What happened after his wife called to warn him?*

Maybe he feared the damage an arrest would bring. As a trial lawyer, Dennis surely knew the differences between *not guilty* and *innocent.* Rumors, fake news and innuendos would hound him for the rest of his life, branding him a pedophile and an accomplice to murder.

As Long closed her eyes, she could almost hear Dennis' Montblanc pen scratching his final missive across the surface of his embossed stationery, a frantic plea that none of this had been his fault, that *he* was the victim.

She stopped at a small pond to let Grafton feed the ducks.

Dennis *had* to have had a burner. He must have ditched it somewhere before he shot himself. But where?

Studying Grafton's intent expressions as she watched a flock of geese glide onto the smooth water, Long marveled that voters could fall for the pretensions of hypocrites like Dennis. Would his exposure have made any difference in the election?

Even if he'd withdrawn from the race, there would still be those who admired his Dorian Gray image, oblivious to the corruption that lay beneath. *How long will it take Homer Starke and his minions to produce another Bram Dennis?*

Long's research into Scarborough's possible connections to Starke proved fruitless, leaving her with nothing to justify a search of Starke's office or his home on Lake Hartwell. *Even if I could find something, Sid would have to investigate it.*

Returning to her car, she dialed him.

"Hey," he said. "I heard the boss gave you some time off."

"If you want to put it that way."

"Beth, I'm sorry."

"It's not your fault."

"You just need to lay low for a while. Let me see what I can do from here. I can't tell you how much I appreciate your sticking your neck out the way you have. Without you, we never would have gotten Dennis."

She shook her head. "Dennis is a dead end . . . literally. He wouldn't have had the balls to hire Scarborough anyway. It was Homer Starke. I can feel it."

"Beth, I know that. You know that. But without evidence we're stuck . . . Sometimes you just have to let one go."

"*Not a chance.*"

As she strapped Grafton into her car seat, an idea came to her.

"Let's go see Scarborough. Even if we can't tie him to Starke or Dennis, the least we can do is put some heat on him. If we accuse him of getting in bed with a bunch of pedophiles, literally, word will spread through that prison by nightfall. We'll give him a little time to think about that. Perhaps, then, he'll tell us who paid him to hire Steven Saldano."

"Nope. *You're* on leave, remember? *I'll* go see him and let you know what happens."

* * *

Long's mandatory vacation lasted less than two weeks. The rising homicide rate and the demonstrations following the murder of George Floyd left the department short-handed.

Long picked up a case involving the daylight shooting of a known drug dealer at Little Five Points, two blocks from the Zone 6 Mini Precinct. This finally gave her a chance to sit down with Mark White over a cup of coffee at a nearby Dunkin Donuts.

"So," she asked, trying to think of something to say, "catch me up on everything I missed during my . . . sabbatical."

As White walked her through his case load for the past two weeks, Long gazed into his eyes. They'd taken on a dark, hollow look. Broken blood vessels on his nose and an incipient pudginess around his jowls testified to late nights spent drinking alone in his one-bedroom apartment.

She leaned across the table and, in her most soothing voice, said, "Mark, you and I are a *team*. We depend on each other for our work and our lives. I want you to know that if there's anything you need to talk about, I'm here for you."

His gave her a curt nod, pursed his lips and gazed out the window.

She thought about Brandon Markham and wondered how he got his patients to open up to him. *He sure did a fine job on me.* When they rose to go, she embraced White, in what *had* to be a breach of protocol.

On her way back to the office, she got a call from Sid.

"Hey," she said. "Have you been by to talk with Dean Scarborough?"

"Yes. He *could* be ready to flip on Homer Starke."

She caught something in his voice. "And now you're about to give me the *bad* news."

"I've been told to drop the whole thing. The excuse I got was that this is no longer a *priority* item, and I've wasted too many hours on it already."

Long wanted to scream. "Sid, this reeks of a fix."

"It sure seems that way. Like somebody's shutting us down at every turn."

"What do we do?"

"*I'm* not doing anything, and neither are you. We both have too much to lose. Time to move on."

"Sid, *you* have too much to lose. You're closing in on retirement. I'm young enough to start over."

"Don't do it, Beth."

Long felt heat rushing to her face. "Sid, if I can't protect children like Mandy Carter from predators simply because of their political connections, then I don't want this job."

"Think about it before you do anything rash. Give it twenty-four hours at least."

Reluctantly, she agreed. She hung up and stared at the paperwork piled on her desk. She texted Darnell saying she didn't feel well and needed to go home.

* * *

Two days later, Sid got a call from the prison. Another inmate had attacked Scarborough, leaving him hospitalized. When Sid and Long arrived, Scarborough had a new attorney, a public defender. In exchange for immunity from further charges, he admitted contracting the Braithwaite burglary and gave up Homer Starke.

"Starke hired Marcelle LaCroix to represent me and told me to keep quiet."

Sid referred the information to the district attorney, who said he'd take it under advisement. Meanwhile, Long got a copy of Scarbrough's confession.

Long and Sid rendezvoused at a QT on MLK to discuss what came next. As she sipped her coffee, her eyes lit on a young woman standing on the opposite corner, maybe fourteen years old. Her outfit, a tight blouse and black leather miniskirt, said it all.

"Sid, do you ever wonder why we even bother?"

He pursed his lips and stirred in more cream. "I'd say about once an hour."

"And?"

"And then I tell myself that things would be a *lot* worse if we weren't here. We don't get paid to wonder *why*, Beth. We get paid to do our job."

She watched as his eyes strayed to the young woman, now climbing into a nondescript sedan driven by a white man, middle-aged in appearance.

"So, what's next with Mr. Starke."

"I don't know. It's all up to the DA. I'm not sure how much good the word of a convicted felon will be in implicating someone as powerful as Homer." He gave an exasperated sigh.

* * *

On the following morning, Long heard the heartrending news of the Rayshard Brooks shooting. Brooks, unarmed and apparently drunk, stole an officer's taser and ran. The officer shot him in the back. Long called Darnell to let him know she still felt under the weather.

With the neighborhood pool still closed, she'd bought an inflatable at Walmart. She and Nancy chatted on the patio as Grafton splashed and squealed.

"Mom, I'm thinking about quitting the force and going into another line of work."

Nancy gazed skyward, crossed herself and mouthed the words, "*Thank you, Lord*." Turning to face her daughter, she said, "Dare I ask what brought this on?"

"I don't think I'm doing any good under this current regime, and I don't see things changing anytime soon. I've reached a point where I can't deal with all the politics. I don't want to end up like so many cops, burned out and waiting for retirement."

"Or worse," said Nancy.

Long watched as Grafton splashed water out of the pool forming a puddle on Nancy's lawn. She thought about her dad, Sergeant Leonard Long, gunned down by a violent drunk, all those years ago. That had been her impetus for joining the force . . . that, and perhaps to spite Nancy. Now that decision no longer made sense.

"What would you do?" Nancy asked. "All you've ever been is a cop . . . and a mom."

"I don't know." Long chewed her lower lip.

"You could always go back to Georgia State. It's never too late. You could move home. I could take care of Grafton while you're in school."

Long's jaw set, but she said nothing.

Nancy rose without a word and went inside, returning with two wine glasses filled to the brim.

"I need to take Grafton home tomorrow."

"Beth, this *is* your home. You and Grafton have spent more nights here, lately, than you have in that *damned* apartment. You have everything you need right here." She smiled at her granddaughter and asked, "What would it take for you to break your lease?"

"I'm not going to do that. Besides, when I move, it'll be to a place of my own."

As hours passed and the sun sank behind the trees, Long pulled Grafton from the pool, dried her off and dressed her. Nancy, meanwhile, smothered pork chops in cream of mushroom soup and turned on Fox News.

Long retreated to the guest room, where she read to Grafton from a stack of old children's books Nancy kept. Overstimulated by all the excitement, Grafton sat up squealing, "Mamaw house. Mamaw house."

Long had finally gotten her to sleep when her phone buzzed.

"Mark, what is it?"

"I know you called in sick, Sergeant, but you gotta get down here. We need you."

"Where are you?"

"I'm down on University Avenue, and all hell's breaking loose."

"What?"

"They're smashing car windows and . . . Oh shit! They set the Wendy's on fire."

"Mark, I *can't* come down there. For God's sake, get yourself out of there." She pictured his helpless situation and the very real likelihood of other shootings. "Go home, Mark. *Now*. It's not worth it. There's nothing you can do."

She heard a police siren, and the phone went dead. After lying awake all night, she rose quietly and slipped into the kitchen to start a pot of coffee.

As it brewed. she picked up her phone and scanned a seemingly endless list of texts, stopping at one from her lieutenant wanting to know if she would make it into work.

Retreating to the living room window, she stared out at people working in their yards, taking long walks, oblivious to the previous night's mayhem. She texted White, asking, "Are you okay?"

No reply.

She turned on the radio in the kitchen and poured herself a cup. Then a news announcer broke in with a report that sent her to her knees.

"Dick, I'm outside the Conyers townhome of Atlanta Police Officer Mark White, found dead this morning of an apparent self-inflicted gunshot wound."

Long doubled over, wracked by heaving sobs. *Oh my God! I could have stopped him.* Fifteen minutes later, she replied to Darnell's message. She'd made her decision.

Chapter Twenty-Nine

The Boyfriend

Charleston, South Carolina
June 15, 2020

Relishing the air-conditioned comfort of the forward cabin, William poured himself into his work. Before him, illumined by the fading sunset, lay a proposal for an online training site he'd prepared for his employer. The boat swayed in the passing ripples of a smaller craft. *Man, this is the life. If only Misty and I could share it.*

Bare feet hit the deck above. Without a word, Misty swept in, landed on him, took him into her arms and kissed him as she removed his shirt.

"I can't stay long," she said. "My mom and dad went for a bike ride. *Let's rock this barge.*"

Later, as he recovered from the pleasant diversion, William asked, "How long did you say they'd be gone?"

"Are you angling for another round?"

He gave her a wolfish look. "Perhaps."

"It'll take them a while to circumnavigate the resort, especially if my mom stops to window shop for a new tennis outfit."

"Have you heard back from UGA?"

"Yes," she squealed, bouncing up and down. "I just got my fall acceptance an hour ago and had to come celebrate with you. Have they contacted you?"

"Not yet, but I applied the same time you did. I should hear from them soon." He paused, recalling his grade average. "If I don't get in,

I can still take my online classes at KSU. And I can work remotely from Athens as easily as I can from here. Let's drive over there next week and start looking for a place."

"Have you talked to your mom?"

"Not yet. I figure I'll wait until I get accepted."

Misty began tickling him. "Oh my God! Marie's going to have a fit. What I'd give to be a fly on that wall!"

"She'll get used to it." Suddenly he sat up in bed. "Oh, I meant to tell you. I spoke to Pops this morning. You won't believe this."

"What?"

"My mom has a boyfriend."

Misty laughed hysterically.

"Aunt Kathy fixed them up. She invited Mom over for a family barbeque and ambushed her. Mom acts like it's nothing serious, but Pops tells me they have another date this weekend."

"William, two dates don't make him her boyfriend. Not unless they're sleeping together."

"Please! I don't want to think about that."

Misty wrapped the sheets tightly around her and sat up. "So, tell me, what does this mystery man do?"

"He's a biomedical researcher, a friend of Uncle Sean's."

"What's he working on?"

"It's *so* dope. He's testing fabrics that are supposed to absorb and analyze your sweat, measure your body temperature and notify you if you have something bad, like cancer."

"How will that work?"

William nearly choked from laughing. "They're going to make undergarments out of this stuff."

"You mean like . . . Captain Underpants?" she howled.

"More like Doctor Draws."

As Misty rolled on top of him and ran her hands down his chest and stomach, Barbara's voice rang out up top.

"Melissa!"

"Oh shit!" Misty whispered as she gathered her clothes and ran to the rear compartment.

* * *

Alone in his bunk, William thought about the family he'd left behind. He considered calling his mom or dad but couldn't think of what he wanted to say. He glanced at the clock and wondered if it was too late to call Tom. On a whim, he texted Lauren O'Meara instead.

"Hey, William," she replied, "Let me Facetime you."

Seconds later she popped up on his screen with Hari seated beside her in what appeared to be his apartment. "You won't believe what a day we've had."

"Really?"

"We went to Decatur to participate in a Black Lives Matter rally at the courthouse, and the police starting telling us we all had to leave. They ignored me, but when they got up in Hari's face, I let them have it."

"Oh shit."

"Yeah. Oh shit. My dad had to come bail us out of the Dekalb County Jail. Needless to say, he wasn't happy."

"I can imagine."

"He said he agreed with what we were doing, but that we should have left when the cops told us to."

"I can see how he would say that."

"Well, we had to do something."

"We do. But don't get arrested again. I'm pretty sure public schools won't hire you if you have a record. Misty and I can afford to take risks like that."

"Don't tell your mom that. Listen. Hari and I have to go. You and Misty take care of yourselves."

"I'm proud of you guys."

William lay awake most of the night, thinking about what Lauren and Hari had done. *How far would I be willing to stick my neck out for things that matter, to speak out against injustice? When do I stop being a reporter and become a participant in life?*

* * *

On the following morning, Tom and Brandy returned from their visit with Marie and her new boyfriend, Kofi Osinbajo. A native of Ghana, Osinbajo had recently renewed his visa, in hopes of remaining in the United States to complete post-doctorate at Georgia Tech.

"I don't think Marie could have found anyone more different from her," said Brandy.

Tom shook his head. "He's so laid back. Maybe that'll rub off on her. I worry about her."

Brandy wrapped her slender arms around Tom's waist and kissed him on the lips. "Of course, you do. She may be William and Henry's mom, but she's still your little girl."

"Yep."

She stood back and gazed at his waistline. "Tom, have you lost weight?"

"Maybe. We've been getting a lot of exercise lately, with all these long walks."

His phone rang, and the caller ID read *Beth Long*.

"Hey, Sergeant," he said.

"You can just call me Beth now."

Tom took a moment to catch her meaning. "Don't tell me you quit."

"Yes, I did. Do you have a moment?"

He rummaged through a drawer for a notebook and pen. Cradling his phone on his shoulder, he said. "Beth, I am *so* sorry. I just heard the news about Mark White."

"Yeah. That was the final straw."

"Tell me about it."

She filled in the details of the Bram Dennis investigation, leading up to his suicide.

Tom scribbled furiously. "I heard about that, but I didn't know you'd connected him to Garth Braithwaite's murder."

"That's the problem. We never managed to prove Dennis' connection to the burglary *or* the murder. Every time we got close, someone body-checked us. I could almost feel an invisible hand, playing us like chess pieces, always two moves ahead."

"So, you think Dennis contracted the burglary?"

"No. I think it was someone with a huge stake in Dennis' campaign and the ability to make career-ending scandals disappear."

"That sounds like a stretch. Who did you have in mind?"

"Dennis' primary backer, according to our sources, was a Homer Starke."

"I've heard of him. What evidence do you have?"

"We got a confession from Dean Scarborough, but we're not sure the DA will do anything with it. Meanwhile, Sid's lieutenant squelched any further investigation."

Tom paused to catch up on his notes. "I'd say this reeks of a coverup."

"It does, but what can I do? Besides, after last night, I'm out."

"I'm afraid I can't do anything with this until there's more evidence."

He thought for a moment. "What I'd like to do is get your perspective on the Rayshard Brooks shooting and the deterioration of morale at the cop shop. I'll find out who's covering this for the paper, and maybe we can work together on a larger story."

"That'll be great." She took a deep breath. "Let's do this. Where do you want to start?"

"What drove your decision to resign?"

"A lot of things. Mainly the realization that politics is more important to my bosses than protecting young women like Mandy Carter, but this has been a long time coming. The city puts us out on the street like paper targets. They don't give us the tools we need to do our jobs. We have to handle situations we aren't trained for, like homelessness and mental illness. We put our lives in danger every day, and we sure as *hell* don't do it for the money. The turnover has only made matters worse. Mark took his life because his career, the one thing in his life that mattered most, no longer made sense to him. I know that feeling. I've reached that point myself. Unlike Mark, I can *find* something else."

"Have you made any plans?"

"Not yet. I have a friend, Amy Springer, who counsels runaways and sex workers. I'd like to help her as a volunteer, but I'm a single mom."

"I know somebody you could speak to. My daughter Marie's firm needs a new investigator. It won't pay much, but you'll have benefits."

"Sounds interesting. I know Marie. Yeah. I'd like to talk to her. Thanks."

"No worries. By the way, there is a favor I'd like to ask."

As the conversation ended, Tom texted William.

Last Gleaming

* * *

William parked his Jeep and removed a stack of protest posters from the back. Misty kicked off her sneakers and rubbed her tired, aching feet.

Jeff glared at them from the porch. "Where have you two been?"

"Dad, William and I went down to Market Street to show our support for Black Lives Matter."

"There's still a pandemic on, or have you forgotten?"

William stood beside the Jeep and stared at the ground. Barbara glared out at them from her living room window. William made eye contact with her and thought he caught a triumphant smile.

"Dad, we wore masks and stood at least twenty feet from the other people," Misty pleaded.

"That's not good enough. Our hospitals are still full of the sick and dying."

Her face reddened and her eyes seemed to bulge from her head. William had never seen her like this. "Yeah. And Black people are dying in the streets, innocent, unarmed people, like George Floyd and Breonna Taylor, gunned down by cops who continue to get away with murder. *Do you expect us to stand by and do nothing?"*

William gazed at a pleasure craft making its way out of Morgan Creek, wishing he and Misty were on it, going somewhere, anywhere but here.

"Misty, go inside," Jeff said.

He wheeled on William. "So, this is how you repay my hospitality. Son, I did *not* help you find a job in Charleston and invite you to stay on our boat so you could sleep with my daughter and put her life in danger."

"Dad," Misty screamed. "It wasn't even William's idea."

"*Go inside,*" he yelled back.

In the short time he'd known the man, William had never seen Jeff get angry over anything. Recalling Misty's story of him kneecapping a boy who tried to molest her, William made a futile effort at placating him. "Mr. Sax, I . . ."

"William, I want you out of here by tomorrow. You are *not* to see Misty again."

"That is *not* your choice," she bellowed. "If he leaves, I leave."

"Then the car we bought you stays here."

"*Fine.*"

Chapter Thirty

South of Broad

Charleston, South Carolina
June 15, 2020

A warm, moist breeze swept through the carriage house, redolent of salt air and bougainvillea. At Misty's insistence, William opened the windows and French doors while they cleaned. Standing on a ladder, he dusted the ceiling fan and cornices, while she removed furniture covers and swept the tile floors. From her small stereo came the sounds of Charleston's own Hootie and the Blowfish. The place belonged to William's boss, Mac Shaheen.

"How long did Mac say we could stay here?" she asked.

"Until the fall semester starts."

"I can't believe he would do this."

"He puts up out-of-town guests here. He hasn't used it since March. Who knows how long it'll sit empty."

"Well, he sounds like a great boss."

"That he is."

"We need to find a place near Athens."

William climbed down and gave her a long kiss. "Sure. Why don't you get on Zillow and find us something? I can take off early on Friday and we can drive over there. Meanwhile, I have a call with Beth Long."

Together they moved a couch, so Misty could sweep behind it. "Isn't she the one investigating the Braithwaite murder?"

"She was. The APD shut it down just as she was about to bust the person who hired the burglar. She got pissed and quit. She's going to work for my mom as an investigator. Isn't that crazy."

"Is it okay if I listen in?"

"Of course."

William opened the Zoom meeting, and in a few minutes a face appeared on the screen. It took him a moment to recognize her in her Georgia State sweatshirt and jeans with her hair down. Smiling, she seemed to have lost the worry lines he'd seen in her press announcement about the closing of the Braithwaite murder.

"Good morning, Sergeant."

She smiled. "You can call me Beth."

"Beth, I appreciate your joining the call this morning. If you don't mind, I'm going to record this. It'll make it easier for me to remember our discussion."

She pursed her lips. "Sure. What harm could it do me now?"

"So, how does it feel to be a civilian again?" The recorder allowed him to study her facial expressions rather than scribbling down her responses.

She spoke in a soft, almost undetectable Southern accent. "As disappointed as I am with the Atlanta Police Department, I feel a profound sense of relief." She turned her gaze, apparently toward a window, revealing a classic profile. "It'll give me more time to spend with my daughter."

In an effort to build further trust, he asked. "When did you decide you wanted to be a cop?"

"As far back as I can remember, I guess. My dad was a cop. All his friends were cops. They'd come over to the house, and I'd bug them with questions about their work."

"I understand you've landed a job as a legal investigator."

"Yep. I have your mom and grandfather to thank for that."

"So, tell me, what do you think Steven Saldano was looking for in Garth Braithwaite's house."

This brought her up short, perhaps her investigator instincts kicking in. As she eased up, she gave him a crisp response. "Dean Scarborough, a resident of Grant Park, has admitted to paying a fence named Simon Wilhoite to get him some video and equipment from Braithwaite's residence. Wilhoite subcontracted the job to Saldano."

"And what exactly did Saldano steal?" William imagined the questions Marie would ask if she had Long on the witness stand.

"We believe he wanted some videos that Braithwaite had. Braithwaite walked in on him. Saldano shot Braithwaite with his own gun. He grabbed Braithwaite's laptop and phone and ran."

"Why do you suppose Scarborough wanted the videos?"

"When we found Braithwaite's laptop at Saldano's hideout, we searched it and discovered videos of men having sex with underage women. Initially we thought Scarborough might have wanted them because he was in the videos. He later admitted that someone had hired him to steal them."

William leaned closer to the screen. "Did he give you the name of that person?"

"He claims now that Homer Starke, a political operative in Hart County, hired him. Starke was the primary backer for Senate candidate Bram Dennis. We took a statement from a young woman who claims that Dennis paid her for sex and then assaulted her. As my associate and I closed in to arrest him, Dennis took his own life."

"It would seem that Starke, at the very least, was an accomplice to the murder of Bram Dennis. What criminal recourse might the Atlanta Police take against him?"

Long gave him a look of utter disgust. "Apparently they're not willing to pursue it."

William made a note to research Starke and asked, "Wouldn't Braithwaite's family have grounds for a wrongful death lawsuit?"

She paused, as though contemplating the question, then gave him the briefest of smiles. "I suppose we'll have to ask Marie."

"What was the final impetus for your resignation?"

Her lower lip trembled as she told him about Mark White's tireless service to the City of Atlanta, how he returned from an apparent bout with COVID and his bravery during the riots following the George Floyd murder. "I had already decided to quit, even before Mark's suicide. I could no longer be part of a profession that defended people like Derek Chauvin and apparently cared nothing for the young women in those videos.'

When the call ended, William sat for a long time, staring at the empty screen. At length, he started scribbling a list of points he wanted to make on his blog site, backed by selected quotes from his recording.

He stood, stretched and invited Misty for a walk.

As they passed a row of churches on their way up to Broad, William said, "By the way, Grandma Evelyn has a surprise planned for Henry. Today's his birthday, and I set up a Zoom call for her, so my mom, Pops and Brandy could attend."

"When?"

"One o'clock"

"That sounds like a *wonderful* idea. How did Tom and Brandy meet."

"He picked her up in a bar."

"No. Seriously."

"Seriously. Pops took Bogie and me on a road trip out west in a Winnebago. It was the summer before my junior year. When it came time for me to go home, he bought me a ticket at LAX and took the long way back to Atlanta. He showed up a month later with Brandy."

They returned to the carriage house, and Misty collapsed onto a couch, exhausted from the walk. She sighed as she took in her new surroundings. "Baby, how can we to afford live on our own?"

"I have a job, remember? Mac's okay with me working from Georgia. It's no different from what I'm doing now."

"What about when things go back to normal?"

"*If* things go back to normal, I imagine we'll still be able to work online. If I need to come back here for an occasional meeting, I will."

She stopped, as though suddenly remembering something. "Oh my God! I don't know if my parents will pay for my tuition. They're pretty pissed at me."

He shrugged. "You're on your own now. You can apply for a Pell grant. You'll need to emancipate yourself."

She went to the window and stared out toward Fort Sumter. "I'm not sure I'm ready to secede yet," she said, giving it her best Scarlet O'Hara. She gave William look of resignation. "I guess I'll call them."

She hit speed dial and put it on speaker. Barbara's voice came on.

"Who is this?"

"It's Misty, Mom."

"Misty who?"

"Mom!"

"So now you think to call me. Did it occur to you I might be worried about you, living downtown in some crime-ridden neighborhood with *that boy*?"

"Mom, William and I are living south of Broad. It doesn't get better than this."

"Okay . . . so, what do you want?"

Misty took a deep breath. "We're planning our move to Athens." She paused and bit her lip. "I'm already registered for the fall. William can pay the rent, wherever we stay. But I need your help with my tuition."

"And why should I do that, when you can go to school here?"

"Mom, we've been over that. My lab classes will be in person, starting this semester."

"Sorry, kiddo. You created this situation. You figure it out for yourself." With that she hung up.

Misty collapsed into a chair and let loose a torrent of tears. As William took her in his arms, her phone rang. Wiping her eyes, she read the caller ID and pressed Receive. "Hey, Dad."

She nodded. "I will. Don't worry."

William waited patiently until she hung up. "What did he say?"

"He said he'll pay my tuition and all, as long as I take online classes. He still doesn't want me going back into a classroom until we have a vaccine. Oh . . . and they won't let me take my car."

"What?"

"The car's still in my dad's name. My mom's just being a bitch. We'll have to get by with the Jeep for a while."

William stared into her eyes. "You seem more relieved than happy."

"Yeah. I hate bumming money off my parents."

"Look, it's only for a little while. Before long we'll have enough that we won't depend on anyone's help." He squinted at her. "And what's your mom's problem? Why wouldn't she pay your tuition?"

"My mom's a lot like yours, William. Since the day I was born, she's had plans for me. And those plans don't include you. She still thinks my agronomy major is a passing thing, that I'll grow out it, that

I'll transfer to some posh school up north, so she can brag about it to all her friends."

"Don't worry, Baby. We'll figure it out somehow. Let's take a walk down to the Battery. When we come back, I'll cook us up a low country boil."

* * *

Gusting winds, driven by an offshore storm, tore at the palmettos and flowering trees along Charleston's Rainbow Row as William and Misty made their way toward the tip of the peninsula. The city had survived killer hurricanes and an earthquake.

It now showed signs of emerging from a devastating lockdown. Shops and restaurants struggled to reopen. Others remained shuttered, awaiting new owners. All along the harbor tourists strolled with their cameras, mothers with young children, many clad in rain slickers, defying the elements.

As they reached White Point Garden, Misty hooked her arm inside William's. "This all seems so . . . sudden."

"It's what we've wanted all along," he said. "you getting into Georgia, me starting my writing career."

"But it's the first time I've ever been out on my own."

"Misty, you're *not* out on your own. We have each other."

"I mean away from my family."

"We *are* a family."

"But what if we have another wave of infection and can't travel? What if, God forbid, one of us gets sick?" she pleaded.

"Nothing comes without, risk, Baby. Think about our ancestors who sailed across that ocean out there to an unknown land. Look around you. The whole world is coming back to life." He raised his right hand in a universally recognized salute. "And we're all giving COVID the finger."

"I know. But I *just* moved back here. Now I'm leaving again." She wrapped her arms around him and laid her head on his shoulder. "It'll take me a while to adjust."

* * *

William hooked up his laptop to Misty's television and brought up the virtual birthday. In seconds, the faces of Tom, Brandy, Marie and Kofi appeared. "Hey, everybody. We're waiting for everyone else to come on. Remember, this is supposed to be a surprise."

"William," said Marie. "This was a wonderful idea. I only hope your brother appreciates it."

"If not, we'll at least have the pleasure of embarrassing him."

Another face materialized on the screen. Staring back with a boyish grin, a handsome, middle-aged man said, "Hey everybody." Behind him a sliding glass door provided a clear view of London's Tower Bridge, brightly lit against the night sky. "As you can see, it's nine p.m. over here."

"Hey, Dad. I want you to meet Misty. Misty, this is my dad."

Misty waved at the screen. "Hey, Mr. Wakefield. I've heard so much about you."

"Don't believe half of it." He paused. "Hello, Marie. Hey, Tom."

Marie smiled. "Hey, Bill. I also have someone I want you to meet." She turned to the large African man seated beside her. His bald scalp shone in the overhead light. "This is Kofi Osinbajo. I met him through Sean and Kathy. He's a researcher at Georgia Tech."

"Nice to meet you Kofi."

Harmon's face suddenly appeared, so close to the camera that William could see his nose hairs. He stepped back revealing an elegant dining room table with Evelyn and Henry on either side.

Henry favored his family with a rare smile. "Hey, everybody. Misty, I hear you've moved in with my brother. What could you possibly see in him?"

She glanced at William and shook her head. "I have no idea. But I guess I'm stuck with him now."

Beside Henry sat a beautiful young Asian woman. "Guys," he said, "I want you to meet Lisa Chu. She's here in the District attending a pre-college program at Georgetown. She had the day off and I invited her out."

Everyone's eyes shifted as they focused on each other's images. But Bill's never wavered, transfixed by his own face. As he spoke, he tucked a lock of hair behind his right ear. For William it brought back memories of a Braves game and the late Bram Dennis on the jumbotron making that same gesture.

As inane conversations overran each other, William scanned their faces, light patterns dancing across a flat screen, imitating flesh and blood people, his family. They reached out to each other in desperation as they drifted in different directions.

Chapter Thirty-One

The Farm

Barrow County, Georgia
August 29, 2020

The old sharecropper's shack stared back at William with a mix of sadness and gratitude. Its porch sagged on decaying piers, and the tin roof leaked like a colander. Its owner had added electricity, a pump and a septic tank, hoping to rent it out until he could sell the land to a developer.

He promised additional repairs, but William and Misty offered to do the work themselves if he would lower their payments. They chose the place more for its fertile soil than its accommodations. Tom and Brandy had driven over from Smyrna to see how the work was coming.

"Well, William," said Tom, as he settled into a battered but comfortable chair on the lawn, "Looks like you've got your work cut out for you. How are you going to fix all this, work *and* go to school?"

William knelt for a closer look at the structure's underside, snapping several pictures. "I'll figure it out."

He stood and got a quick shot of Misty laying out a plot for her fall garden. Looking back, she flashed him a smile.

"Pops," he said. "I can't tell you how much I appreciate your helping us with this place. You didn't have to do that."

Tom shrugged. "Brandy and I don't mind. It's not like we need the money."

"Well, it means a lot to Misty and me, not having to ask our parents."

Last Gleaming

Tom surveyed the old homestead, with its twenty acres rolling back to a stand of pines. "You know, this reminds me of *my* grandaddy's tobacco farm. I spent some of the happiest days of my life there."

"Yeah. I'm afraid it won't be here much longer." William raised his camera for a panoramic scan. "Now that they're able to work and study remotely, people are fleeing the cities for the dream of living in the country. Another couple of years and this'll be just another neighborhood of two-story brick colonials and three-car garages."

"You're right about that."

"I wish there were something we could do to stop it."

"Maybe you should try getting this house on the National Register. Who knows? Eventually, with enough money, you could buy it and restore it to its original condition. You could pick up some extra money by subdividing the land and end up with the kind of neighbors you want. I'll be glad to help."

William shook his head. "Look, you've done more than enough already. You guys need to take care of yourselves."

"Thank you," said Brandy. "If I let him, he'd be over here every weekend. It's all I can do to get him to let me hire a cleaning service for our condo."

Wiping her face with an old scarf, Misty winced and rubbed her back.

"Are you okay, baby?" William called out.

"I'll be fine," she said. "I'm done for today, anyhow. Give me your car keys. I'll run over to CVS and get some ibuprofen. Can I get you guys anything."

"No thank you," said Brandy. "We need to leave soon."

Watching the Jeep pull out, she commented, "You and Misty have been working on this place like field hands."

"Yeah. She's anxious to get it ready for winter."

"Sounds to me like she's nesting."

As Brandy and Tom shared a laugh, William caught her meaning. "No, no, no," he said, eyes widening. "We're not planning anything like that."

* * *

Squinting in the light of a kerosene lantern, William gave the steeple jack a final turn. He levelled the main beam beneath the farmhouse and prayed the concrete footings had cured enough to hold the structure in place. Exhausted to the point of delirium and aching all over, he slid out from the crawl space, stepped up onto the back porch and shucked out of his reeking, mud-caked clothes.

Thinking Misty had gone to bed, he tiptoed in. A dull yellow glow bled out beneath the door. He found her seated at a small table in the corner, a look of incomprehension on her face.

"Hey . . . what's the matter?" he asked.

Before she could answer, he noticed the spent EPT kit . . . the strip . . . and the blue line. He rushed over to her, fearing he would faint. "Oh my God!"

"*Yep.*"

Stammering, he asked "When . . ."

She shook her head. "I don't know. I've missed periods before. I thought it was nothing. Then I began to feel tired, and my back hurt this morning."

"Oh my God. We've gotta get you to a doctor."

"Calm down, William. I'm not having the baby tonight. I'll call the clinic in the morning and set up an appointment."

"Is . . . is there something I can do for you?"

"Yeah. I'm going to lie down, and you're going to give me a back rub."

He studied her as she undressed.

"Don't look at me like that. "I'm not showing yet."

"What are we going to do?"

"You're going to massage this spot right here. Yeah. That's it." She let out a long sigh. "A little lower . . . Yes, there . . . Now, let's not get ahead of ourselves. Okay? First, we'll see what the doctor says. Right now, I need some rest."

"How are we going to tell our parents?"

"*I'll* tell my parents, then *you* can tell yours. I need time to think about what I'm going to say."

"Maybe, you can text your mom. Give her a chance to calm down, then call her."

She nodded in agreement. "That might work."

* * *

He lay awake for a long time listening to Misty's breathing, then woke the next morning to the sounds of her yelling. He came straight up out of bed and onto his feet before realizing she'd gone out onto the front porch.

She sat her with her back to him, shouting into her phone.

"But I'm *not* asking you for money, *Mother!*"

He stepped behind the door, hoping she wouldn't see him.

"*No*. I'm not leaving William and moving home. This *is* my home."

She paced back and forth several times before stepping down into the yard.

"This not an *it, mother*. This is your GRANDCHILD."

William jumped as her phone hit the other side of the wall and shattered.

Storming into the living room, she ran headlong into his arms. He held her as she cried out her rage.

"I love you so much," he managed. "And I will do whatever it takes to provide for you and our child." How he would do that, he had no idea.

Chapter Thirty-Two

Lockdown 2.0

Barrow County
October 23, 2020

Working late by a dim table lamp, William completed his latest press release and emailed it to leading trade publications.

Two months of home renovation by day and sweating over a computer at night had drained him to the point of collapse. Misty still showed no evidence of a baby bump, but he insisted she rest as much as possible.

A light cough came from the bedroom. He went to check and found her dozing restively.

In the morning he would weed the garden and cook breakfast from their stock of summer vegetables, then make his weekly run to the store. Not wanting to wake Misty, he grabbed a blanket from the closet and curled up on the couch.

He sustained himself through all this, knowing that he and Misty were building a family without financial assistance besides the money Tom provided and Jeff's help with Misty's tuition and books. Despite her own exhaustion and her morning sickness, Misty doggedly pursued her remote studies.

Aroused by the morning sun creeping through his window, he rose and started a large pot of coffee. As he stepped onto the porch, there came a loud hacking from the bedroom, followed by wheezing sounds. Running to Misty's side, he placed his hand on her forehead and jerked it away, as though scalded.

"Let's get you up and dressed," he said, struggling to remain calm.

Enroute to the hospital, he dialed 911. Emergency technicians met him as he pulled the Jeep under the canopy. Once inside, he presented Misty's insurance card and prayed Jeff's plan still covered her.

Too weak to talk, Misty could barely breathe through her mask as orderlies lifted her onto a gurney and wheeled her away. Her baleful look as she stared back at him broke his heart.

"Sir," said an elderly ER nurse, "you'll need to go home, we'll take it from here."

"*You* need to know that she's pregnant."

"How far along?"

"About three months."

Concern clouded the nurse's face. "I'll let the doctor know."

"Can I wait here to see how she's doing?"

"I'm afraid not. We have more patients coming in behind you, and we need to take care of them too."

She gave him a number he could call to check on Misty.

Seated outside on a bench, William fought back tears. He stared at the impressive edifice, wondering if any empty beds remained. *Oh God, what have I done?*

He dialed Jeff's cell and spoke to him for the first time since the man kicked him off his property.

"Mr. Sax, this is William. It's Misty. She's sick." He struggled to hide the fear in his voice.

"What?"

"She has a cough and is running a fever . . ."

"Where is she?"

"I took her straight to the hospital. A doctor's seeing her now."

"What hospital?"

"Northeast Georgia Medical Center. In Winder."

"Winder!" he screamed.

"It was the closest."

"Let me speak to the doctor."

"They ran me out of the emergency room. Something to do with COVID protocols."

Sax took a deep breath, and, in a cold, calm voice said. "I want to speak to a doctor, and I want to speak to him now."

"You'll have to call him then," said William. He read to him the hospital's switchboard number and started to say something else, but Sax had hung up.

Five minutes later, when he hadn't called back, William dialed the number himself. He got a recording asking him to leave a message. Frustrated, he wandered around the parking lot.

For lack of a better idea, he called Tom and explained the situation.

"Have you spoken with her dad?" he asked.

"Yeah. He freaked out. I gave him the hospital number, and he hung up. I tried calling back, but I can't get anyone."

"Did you call your boss?"

"Yes."

"Then you've done all you can for now. You need to go home. You gave them your contact information. They'll call as soon as they know something. Hopefully, you'll be hearing from Misty soon."

"But I can't just go home and wait."

"That's *exactly* what you're going to do. Trust the doctors and nurses. Misty will be okay. She's a strong, healthy girl."

William grabbed his hair as though to pull it out. "Ah shit!" he screamed.

"William, this is *not* your fault. You have to learn to accept situations you cannot control. Go home. Do something to relieve your stress.

Go for a run. Tend to your garden. Wait and pray." He paused. "And while you're at it, pray you don't get sick yourself."

"Okay. Thanks."

"Keep your phone on you. Whatever happens, call me back.

William rubbed his eyes. A car honked at him, and he realized he had stopped in front of the ER entrance. He waved, without looking, and stepped out of the way.

Sitting in his Jeep, it occurred to him that, given his exposure, he could easily have caught the virus himself. *Who will take me to the hospital if I get sick? Who will take care of Misty if I'm no longer here?*

* * *

That night, bundled inside his old ski jacket, William shivered on the porch. He stared up at a cloudless sky as though counting the stars. A meteor blazed across the horizon. A coyote howled nearby, and floorboards creaked as he stood and paced. *Oh my God! Oh my God! You can't do this. You can't do this. She's all I have.*

At long last, his phone rang. He pulled it out and answered without looking at the caller ID.

"Hello, Mr. Wakefield. This is Dr. Sanjay Patel at Northeast Georgia Medical Center." The man sounded as exhausted as William felt.

"How's she doing?"

"Ms. Sax is resting well. We have her sedated and have administered a strong steroidal anti-inflammatory." He paused, giving William time to anticipate what came next. "I'm afraid we could not save the baby."

William folded into his porch swing. Dissolving in tears, he couldn't speak as the doctor's voice called out, "Mr. Wakefield? Mr. Wakefield?"

Last Gleaming

* * *

Following Tom's advice, William lost himself in the home renovations, preparing for the day when Misty returned. He scrubbed and painted every room in the house. Whenever his patience ran out, he called the hospital. Whenever he heard from a doctor or nurse, he would relay Misty's progress to his family and to Jeff and Barbara. On the third day, his phone rang.

So weak he could barely hear her, Misty whispered, "William?"

"Yes, Baby."

"William?" she sobbed.

"I'm right here."

"William, I'm so sorry."

"Baby, you have *nothing* to be sorry for. I love you so much."

"I so much wanted this . . ."

"No. No. Don't say it. We can talk about that some other time. Right now, all I want is to hear your voice. When can I come see you?"

"I don't know. I doubt they'll let you in. I just want to get the hell out of here, so I can come home and let you hold me."

"Me too. I'm getting this place ready for you, Baby. When you get here, you won't have to do anything but rest and get well."

They talked until she finally said. "Look, I . . . I need to speak with my parents."

"I know. Call me back when you're done."

Chapter Thirty-Three

The Recovery

Barrow County/Virginia
November 3, 2020

The hospital discharged Misty a week later, with strict instructions, including round-the-clock bedrest. William met Jeff and Barbara outside the main entrance.

Barbara wanted Misty to ride with them, but she declined, saying she'd be more comfortable in the passenger seat of the Jeep. As they wound their way through rural Barrow County, Misty entertained William by speculating on the conversation in the car behind them, imitating Barbara's nasal voice to perfection. William laughed so hard he nearly missed a turn.

As Jeff and Barbara arrived, with dust settling on their new Mercedes, they gaped at the farmhouse. Barbara appeared ready to faint. William half-expected her to kidnap her daughter and take her back to Charleston.

Instead, Jeff helped Misty up the steps and back to the tiny bedroom. Catching the aroma of fresh paint, Misty said, "My God, William. Did you do the whole house while I was gone?"

"Yep. And I'm glad to know you can smell again. Welcome home."

He tucked her into bed, kissed her cool forehead and went to fetch some chicken soup. From the kitchen he could barely make out the sound of Barbara trying to coax Misty into leaving him. Misty gave no audible reply.

As he returned, she said to them. "I appreciate you guys coming to get me, but you should leave now. I don't want you getting sick."

"What about William?" Barbara asked.

"Mom, if William were going to catch this, he would have already."

William sat next to the bed and gave her a sip of water. "She's right. You guys need to understand that taking care of your daughter is my *only* concern. Besides, if I don't, I'm sure Jeff will kill me." He glanced at the man and caught a nod of agreement.

"No, he won't," Misty yawned, closing her eyes. "He'll just knee-cap you."

As the Saxes rose to leave, William stepped outside with them. Fighting back tears, he said, "Jeff, Barbara, I love your daughter more than life itself. As long as I live, I will never let any harm come to her."

Jeff stared into the distance and said, "Okay. I'm going to hold you to that."

Trembling, Barbara ran to William and embraced him, squeezing him tightly until Jeff finally said, "Come on, Honey. We have a long ride back to the Isle of Palms."

William returned to the bedroom to find Misty fast asleep.

Exhausted, he stepped outside and sat on the stoop, wondering what to do next. He reached into his pocket and dialed Tom.

For supper, he prepared a soup from the butternut squash he'd harvested and stored weeks earlier, before the first frost. He added a minimum of spice and served it with a dollop of sour cream, the way Misty liked it. Its aroma filled their tiny home.

Looking in on her, he found her awake, staring at the ceiling. "Thank God," she said. "I thought this paint smell would make me puke."

"No, no. We can't have that. Here, let me prop you up. While you eat, I'll bring in the TV, and we can watch the election coverage."

"Election coverage? Oh my God! We forgot to vote."

"I believe we had other, more pressing matters." Sick of all the propaganda-laced punditry, William switched to C-SPAN. "Whoever wins, I hope they can do something about this fucking pandemic."

"I wouldn't bet on that. I lost interest in politics a long time ago. At least Bram Dennis is out of the race. What a scumbag!"

"So, you think he was the only pedophile politician?" William laughed.

Misty's phone rang on her bedside table, and William answered it.

"Let me speak to Misty," Jeff said.

As William handed it to her, she said, "Put it on speaker."

"Hey, sport," Jeff said. "We just got home. How are you feeling?"

"Better now that I'm sleeping in my own bed."

His tone softened. "Is William taking care of you?"

"Spectacularly."

"He'd better, or I'll come over there and kick his ass. Listen, on the way home, I called an old friend. I mentioned to him that you're majoring in agronomy at UGA. He's starting a company in Athens, designing hydroponic farms, and he's looking to hire an intern. It's called Magnoponics. I told him you're sick at the moment. He said there's no rush. You can call him when you feel better."

"Dad, that's wonderful."

"I'll text you his number."

When the call ended, William cleared away the dishes. "That sounds like a great opportunity. You'll have to hurry up and get well."

"Yeah. I've always wanted to learn hydroponics."

"That could be your career."

Misty gave him a sharp glance. "If you think I'm giving up my dreams of working on a kibbutz when I graduate, you'd better think again."

He shrugged and arched an eyebrow. "Whither thou goest, I will go, and where thou lodgest, I will lodge, and thy people shall be my people."

"Oy. So, now I'm as old as Naomi. I didn't think I'd aged that much."

Eyes glistening, she laid her hand on his. "William, I just can't seem to shake you."

"Till death do us part."

She rolled over and dozed off.

William finished cleaning the house and stepped out onto the porch to watch the sunset. On impulse, he called his brother. They hadn't spoken since the birthday call.

"Hey. How's school going?"

"Great. I have *way* better teachers here than I had at Campbell. I'm learning advanced calculus and physics. I'll need them for my engineering classes at the Naval Academy."

"Dude, you are amazing. You got all the academic genes. I sure didn't. I can hardly stay awake in those classes. When you make your first million, can I borrow some? Maybe you can go work for one of Grandpa Harmon's companies and get some stock options."

"Oh. About that. A few months ago, I overheard him talking to someone about buying out your employer . . . Shaheen."

William let out a sharp breath. "What did he say?"

"I shouldn't be telling you this. One of his companies is developing a top secret communications system for the Defense Department. They need a device that Shaheen is developing."

"Portcullis?"

Henry laughed. "What a dumb name! It sounds like the Dungeons and Dragons game Dad gave us for Christmas that time."

"Yeah. It's just a code name for the project."

"What can you tell me about it?"

"Nothing. Not until we're ready to release it."

"Well good luck with it." Henry imitated Harmon's voice. "Son, the survival of our nation depends on it."

William laughed. "I'm sure it does."

When he'd hung up, he checked in on Misty. Finding her still asleep, he donned an old sweatshirt and went out to check his crop of sweet onions and autumn squash.

His mind drifted back over the past two years to a more innocent time, before pestilence had robbed the world of so many lives. He recalled something Misty told him one night as they lay in bed. *"Everything tends toward entropy. Things fall apart, mountains erode, everything dies. That's why each moment is so precious."*

* * *

Harmon pushed back his recliner and pulled a blanket across his legs to stave off the chill. Evelyn settled in beside him with a mug of hot cocoa as he tuned in to the news.

"Well," she asked, "How are your horses running as they approach the finish line?"

"I'm liking our chances, dear," he said, reaching for a tally sheet he'd printed. "No matter who wins, maybe both parties will finally realize who our friends and enemies are. Let's just hope it's not too late."

Picking up his phone, he dialed a number from memory and said, "Congratulations, Mr. President."

"Don't congratulate me yet. They're still counting, and I'm afraid my opponent may have something up his sleeve."

"I wouldn't worry about that, sir. We can deal with him."

As the call ended, his phone rang in his hand. He looked at the ID and started to shut it off. Giving his wife an evil grin, he said, "You know what. I believe I *will* take this."

Putting it on speaker, so Evelyn could hear, he said "Homer, tell me you're not still soliciting donations at this late hour."

"Not at the moment, but we might be raising money for a lawsuit by tomorrow. I'm seeing things here in Georgia I hoped I'd never witness again in my lifetime."

"Sounds to me like *you* have a problem, Homer."

Starke ignored the jab. "We need your help, Harmon. We've got rumors flying around about ballot box stuffing in Fulton County."

"Yep. And I can just guess where those rumors are coming from. Maybe you should save your money for your cronies. They'll need them for their legal defense funds."

Starke started to say something else, but Harmon cut him off. "Have a nice evening, Homer. And try to get some sleep. This drama will go on for days."

Evelyn shook her head in resignation.

Chapter Thirty-Four

Insurrection

Barrow County
January 6, 2021

William touched up his latest web page. From out front came the crunch of tires on gravel. Misty had borrowed the Jeep for her first day at Magnoponics. She rushed in and threw her arms around him, nearly knocking his laptop off the desk.

"So how was it?" he asked.

"You would not believe. This is so exciting. We're installing demo units for two local churches. They'll be able to produce fresh food for low-income people year-round. It'll be cheaper and more nutritious than anything they get at the store. Once they get going, they'll begin supplying local restaurants. It's all a proof of concept for the broader markets."

"Cool."

"So, how has *your* day been?"

He sighed. "I still like what I'm doing, I guess. But ever since Grandpa Harmon's company took over Shaheen they want to micromanage everything I do. Next week they want me to come over to Charleston for a day-long class they're having on social media usage. Working for Mac was great. He told me what he wanted and trusted me to do it. Now we have this asshole who doesn't even understand our business."

"Have you thought about calling Harmon?"

"I don't want to play the grandaddy card. If it comes to it, I'll start looking for something else."

"Okay, but in the meantime, I need to do my homework. Can you take a break and make us some lunch?"

"Sure."

William warmed a pot of soup and pulled out bread, cheese and sandwich meat. Reaching for the remote, he found C-SPAN, hoping to catch the certification of the presidential election. Instead, he saw a tight image of the outgoing president on a podium outside the White House addressing what he *claimed* were "hundreds of thousands of people."

Bundled against freezing temperatures, he asked that the "fake news media' turn their cameras around so viewers could see his throngs of supporters, people "from all over the world" whom he said, "are not going to take it any longer." The camera remained fixed on him.

As he continued his rant against news outlets and "big tech," the same media he'd employed for four years, William's response shifted from curious to amused to disgusted. This man, elected to the highest office in the land spun unsupported claims that his opponents had "rigged" the election. "No one knows what the hell is going on. There's never been anything like this."

He then called upon his vice president to "do the right thing" so that he would win reelection. "The states," he said, "want to revote." He ended by saying, "So, we're going to . . . *we're going to walk down Pennsylvania Avenue . . . and we're going to the Capitol, and we're going to try and give . . . our party members in Congress . . . the boldness they need to take back our country.*"

"Hey, Babe," William called out, "you need to come see this."

From the bedroom she replied, "No. I have homework to do."

"It can wait. Something crazy is happening in Washington."

He changed the channel to CNN, which showed a chanting, sign-waving mob marching on the seat of American democracy. It seemed to extend all the way back to the White House. They broke through barricades, boosted each other up to balconies and crashed into the building where Congress had gathered for the ceremonial task of certifying electoral votes.

Misty cried, "Oh my God! What's happening to our country?"

William grabbed his phone and dialed Harmon. "Are you seeing what I'm seeing?"

His reply came back tired and overwhelmed. "Son, these are our worst nightmares come true. We have a *former* president who's coming unhinged. *Every one* of his predecessors has surrendered office graciously. This man wants to be president for life."

"Did you see this coming?"

"No. I spoke a while back with a friend who tried to warn me about him. But I brushed her off."

"But he can't get away with it. His cabinet members have the power to remove him."

"Authority is not the same thing as power. They don't have the intestinal fortitude, William. Most of them, by now, have snuck out the back door. All he has left is a bunch of yes men who will do whatever he says."

"Why can't they call out the National Guard or the military?"

"*They who?* The man with the power to do that just sent his *personal militia* to the Capitol to overthrow our democracy. Look at the ones in tactical gear. These *are* our military personnel. I'm getting reports that some of these guys are special forces. They call themselves the "Proud Boys" and "The Oath Keepers." When they enlisted, they took an oath to defend America. Now they're *breaking* that oath, and apparently they're proud of it. They've been planning this for months."

"But why are they doing this?"

"Because *their* president told them they won't have a country left if they don't. He's been spewing this shit for months, lies originating from conspiracy groups like QAnon. From what I've heard, all this is coming from the Kremlin. Vladimir Putin wants to create a fascist dictatorship, under an American Mussolini who will abandon NATO and allow him to rebuild the Warsaw Pact. Even the liberal media are afraid to say that."

"This is crazy."

Ashen-faced, Misty asked "What can we do to stop him?"

Quietly, Harmon answered, "All we can do right now is pray that our vice president has the guts to do his job." The line went dead.

Suddenly, William's issues with his boss seemed trivial.

For the next two hours, he and Misty watched history unfold. "How will we explain this to our children?" she asked.

Exhausted and numb, William shut off the television. "Baby," he said, "let's make sure we vote next time."

As he set the dinner table and served their plates, William turned on the local news, hoping to catch an update on the events in Washington. Instead, the anchor woman said, "We go now to Armando Price in Hart County."

An earnest-looking young reporter appeared, standing at a wrought iron fence. Beyond it lay a palatial residence backing up to a large lake. William moved closer. *Where have I seen this place?*

"Amelia," the announcer said, "I'm standing outside the Hartwell estate of powerful political figure Homer Starke."

"Oh my God . . ." Before William could finish, the shot pulled back to show three women.

"Just moments ago, officials served Mr. Starke with a summons for not one, but three lawsuits related to the murder of Georgia Tech professor Garth Braithwaite last September. I have here with me Atlanta attorney Marie Williams Wakefield. Ms. Wakefield represents plaintiffs in all three cases. Counsellor, could you explain for us the nature of these suits and what role an influential figure, such as Mr. Starke, would've played in a killing that took place months ago in West Midtown?"

Misty squealed in delight as William motioned her to be quiet.

Marie gazed into the camera and gave her most confident lawyerly smile. "Thank you, Armando. We came here today seeking justice for Garth Braithwaite and Franco Balboa's families and for dozens of young women sexually exploited with Mr. Starke's knowledge and consent. We will produce sworn statements that Mr. Starke, acting on behalf of a now-deceased senate candidate, paid for the break-in at Mr. Braithwaite's home and that the intruder he hired killed Mr. Braithwaite when he returned home unexpectedly. The object of the burglary was to locate evidence that might incriminate various protégés of Mr. Starke."

William had seen that look only once, when his mother allowed him and Henry to accompany her as she delivered closing arguments in a multi-million dollar malpractice case, one that she ultimately won.

"And how did you come upon this information?" the reporter asked.

Marie turned to a well-dressed younger woman standing beside her. "My colleague, Ms. Long, formerly of the Atlanta Police Department, led the homicide investigation and teamed up with the department's Special Victims Unit tracking down a child trafficking ring operating in West Midtown. She and Amy Springer, an advocate for abused women, have counselled our youngest client, a thirteen-year-old girl we believe was repeatedly raped and abused by Mr. Starke's late senate candidate. Ms. Springer, acting as the young woman's court-appointed guardian, is suing on her behalf."

The reporter gave Long a confused look. "Ms. Long, can you explain why you weren't able to make an arrest in this case?"

"Mr. Braithwaite's killer, Stephen Saldano, died in a shootout with Grant Park resident Dean Scarborough. We discovered later that Mr. Scarborough, who now resides at the Atlanta Prison Farm, paid for the break-in. We have his signed confession implicating Mr. Starke in the scheme."

"But . . ."

"But the Atlanta Police Department chose not to make an arrest, we believe under political pressure brought by Mr. Starke."

William stared at Misty, dumbfounded. "Can you please explain to me why my own mother would choose to give someone else this exclusive?"

Misty poked him in the ribs. "Perhaps because you don't have a live audience spanning all of North Georgia."

Chapter Thirty-Five

The Road Trip

Smyrna
January 8, 2021

    William loaded suitcases into the Jeep as Misty packed a cooler with snacks for the road. They'd taken Friday off and completed their school assignments for the week. Tired from being housebound, they looked forward to a weekend visit with his family in Smyrna. Marie had received her vaccines, as had Tom and Brandy.

    William and Marie had spoken several times in recent months, but he hadn't seen her in person since the day he set out for Charleston. Her boyfriend, Kofi, had not received his shot yet, so William and Misty would have to remain outside when visiting them. Tom and Brandy graciously offered to put them up in their guest room.

    During the lockdown, Marie had hired a contractor to install a flagstone patio and fire pit in her back yard. She also had a tree removed and cut up for firewood. Kofi stacked the logs and kindled a blaze using leaves, sticks and twigs he'd gathered beneath the spreading oaks.

    "I have still not acclimated to such freezing weather," he said.

    William and Misty took an instant liking to the man, his precise diction, gentle baritone and hearty laugh.

    "This is nothing," Misty explained. "You should go up north this time of year, say . . . Minnesota."

    His expression became more serious. "What is this . . ." He seemed to search for the right word. ". . . insurrection? Such things are quite common in most countries, but I never thought to see them in the

United States. I came here to get away from corrupt presidents and political violence. Why would anyone want to overturn a democracy?"

"We don't," said William. "They're just a bunch of toothless hillbillies rioting because their candidate convinced them that folks here in Atlanta stole the election. They're idiots to believe anything he says."

Tom's expression told him he'd overstepped. "Son, if you ever hope to be a journalist, you need to learn to understand people better than that. How about you and I take a road trip tomorrow?"

"That would be wonderful," Brandy intervened. "Misty and I can go shopping."

"Nope," Marie butted in. "You are not driving all over North Georgia at your age. We could have snow tomorrow."

"Then we'll take William's Jeep. He can drive, and I'll direct him."

Marie started to object again, but Tom raised his hand. "William and I will be fine. That's all there is to it."

* * *

Tom woke William before sunup. The aroma of coffee, bacon and eggs filled the condo. Tom wore a flannel shirt, faded blue jeans and an old, stained cap advertising a John Deere dealership in Mississippi. He handed William a similar one. "Here. You're overdressed."

Ten minutes later they merged onto I-75 North.

"I want you to know I understand how you feel, son. Seeing that mob trying to overturn a free election sickened me as much as anybody. But you can't understand people until you sit down and look them in the eye. You don't have to agree with them. You only need to listen. I'd have thought our trip out west would've taught you that."

Shamed, William could only nod.

"One thing we all have in common is that we're broken human beings. We're just broken in different places. These people you're disparaging may be less educated than you and me, but they love this country every bit as much. Politicians and the media have ridiculed them for generations as a bunch of gun-toting, Bible-thumping ignoramuses, and now they're sick of it."

Turning onto I-575, they travelled on in silence until they reached the Ball Ground exit. "Let's get off here," Tom said. A few miles down the road, he had William pull into a roadside diner. "This oughta be as good a spot as any."

"How do you know about this place?" William asked.

"A buddy of mine and I like to fish the lakes around here. We always stop in here for breakfast. This is God's country, William, and these people here are God's children, just like the rest of us. Don't you ever forget it."

"Do you think we should where masks?"

"You do that, and you'll stand out like an evangelist in a whorehouse. Just try not to get too close to anybody. You'll be fine."

As they crossed the gravel parking lot, Tom stopped him. "Now, I don't want you to say anything unless somebody asks you a question, then give them a short, simple answer."

"You mean like Henry would do?"

"Exactly. But take in everything you hear and see. Most of these folks are regulars. The food's great, and they all know each other. If you're still hungry, let me know and I'll get you something."

Inside they found a surprisingly large crowd, as though no one had heard about the pandemic. None of them wore masks. Tom found them two empty stools at the counter. To the left sat a heavyset man in coveralls. He wore a red cap with a familiar message in white lettering. On the other sat a middle-aged woman with a man William guessed to be her husband. She wore a simple flower print dress.

Scanning the place, William saw people, young and old, most of them looking as though they'd just rolled out of bed. A group of men packed into a corner booth chattered and joked with each other in Spanish. A man at an adjacent table cut them a sideways glance. He leaned closer to his companion, muttered something to him and cocked his head at the Latino laborers. They didn't seem to notice him. William figured they'd arrived on the landscaping truck he'd seen parked out front.

At another table sat a couple who appeared no older than William and Misty from the way they dressed. Their faces, though, had about fifteen more years on them. The girl, overweight and acne-ravaged, had dyed her hair blue with purple streaks. Her boyfriend wore a mullet. They had more piercings than William could count, and tattoo sleeves up both arms. He looked away as the young man glowered at him and demanded, "What are you looking at?"

Tom smiled at the waitress behind the counter. She pulled a pad from her apron and a pencil from behind her ear. "What can I getcha, sugar?"

"We'll have two black coffees," Tom said in a drawl William would never have recognized.

"You're not from around here. What brings you boys to Ball Ground?"

"I thought I'd let my grandson see what paradise looks like."

She snorted. "Well, you better take a picture, Hon, while you still can." She stepped away and returned with two steaming mugs.

Tom turned to the man seated next to him and said, "How y'all doing?"

"Fine, and you?"

"Couldn't be better."

"Where'd you say you're from?"

"Cobb County. Name's Tom Williams. I moved up there a while back to be near my daughter and her boys. This one here's William." He made no mention of being from Atlanta.

"Pleased to meet you," the man said as he reached across Tom to shake hands with William. He turned back to Tom and introduced himself as Wallace K. "The K's for Korzeniowski. People around here can't pronounce it, so I thought I'd make it easier for them."

Tom laughed. "So how did the K family come to live in Ball Ground?"

The man leaned toward him and, in a conspiratorial tone said, "Don't tell anybody, but my great-great-grandaddy was a *carpet bagger*. They ran him out of Atlanta, and this was as far as he got."

William tried not to look at the man's cap, but before long the conversation ventured into recent events. A couple of seats down, a man lit a Marlboro. Afraid he'd gag, William leaned away from it.

"What do you think about what happened Wednesday?" Tom asked.

"Well, I don't think they should have tore up the capitol like they did," said Wallace, "but there ain't no doubt in my mind them folks in Atlanta stole the election. I heard on the radio they was bussing in boxes full of ballots all the way from San Francisco."

William bit his tongue.

"This has been a long time coming," said a man seated at the end of the counter. He appeared to be nursing a hangover. "They oughta string up all them bastards."

Tom ignored him. William stared into his coffee mug half-expecting somebody to pull out a noose.

"Where do you think all this came from?" asked Tom, looking at Wallace.

"For me it started when them folks in Washington and Hollywood began making fun of us, talking about how we cling to our guns and our religion."

"Damn right we do," said the man at the end of the counter, ignoring the fact that no one had spoken to him.

"For us," said the lady seated beside William, "it started with Billie here losing his job. His company started making their tires in China, and we had to move back here from Dayton."

Her husband nodded and looked away as though pained by the memory.

"Billie had a good job, a union job," the woman said. "Do you think they did anything about it. Hell no. They're all in the pockets of the politicians and them Wall Street bankers."

William listened as comments poured in from all direction, everything from the heartbreaking to the inane. When, at last, Tom paid his check, they returned to the car.

"Do you think they really believe that crap?" William asked.

Gravel crunched beneath their feet.

"Of course, they do. They don't trust legitimate news sources. Instead, they listen to right-wing politicians, talk radio hosts and bloggers who tell them what they want to hear."

As they pulled away, Tom glanced back at the café. "These folks are *scared,* William. They watch the nightly news on the Atlanta stations and all they see are stories of murders, rapes, drug busts, burglaries and drive-by shootings, *replete with mug shots of Black men.* People here believe that's all that happens in Atlanta. They never see anything good coming out of there. They think MARTA's gonna come all the way up to Cherokee County, bringing with it gang violence and slum housing.

"These folks have relied on unskilled and semiskilled jobs all their lives, and now they're losing them to immigrants who work harder for less pay. Without a college or vocational education, there's not much they can do. They blame that on previous administrations, but the truth is, it's been a long time in the making. Their lives as they know it are coming to an end. The young people who can escape this place are deserting it in droves. Those who can't are turning to Crystal Meth and Oxycontin. It's no wonder they'd vote for a scam artist who promises to make America great again."

When they got back to I-575, Tom told William to keep going. They continued through the town of Waleska and took a right. "I want to show you something these people fear most," Tom said.

They arrived at the sales office for Paradise Lake, a private real estate development. "Coming from suburban Washington, you've probably never heard the expression *Yankees with U-Hauls*, but you're about to see some."

They cruised past stately mansions fronting onto the picturesque lake. On both sides of the road, workers swarmed over building sites like so many ants.

"These places," Tom said, "cost well into the millions. Before long, they'll be in the tens of millions. *This* is the future of North Georgia, resorts and retirement centers that will crowd out affordable housing."

"But won't all this construction bring new jobs?"

"I doubt it. These contractors come from out of town and bring in their own crews, mostly from south of the border. This may be a boon to real estate investors but it's an existential threat to surrounding communities. They'll either get forced out by rising land prices and property taxes or by an influx of low-income residents drawn in by service jobs. Are you beginning to see how they might think differently from you and me?"

"Why don't we here about this on cable news?"

Tom cackled so hard he choked. "All the networks want to do is sell advertising, most of it for prescription drugs to cure the medical conditions brought on by the worry and stress of bad news. They're not interested in solving problems. They'd rather scare the crap out of us with wars, natural disasters and crime stories, most of which happens elsewhere. It's called *Mean World Syndrome*."

William had never heard his grandfather sound so exhausted and disgusted. "What can we do about this?"

"Nothing that I know of, but one thing's for sure. You won't be able to understand people by dismissing them as idiots and . . . what was that you said yesterday . . . oh . . . *toothless hillbillies*."

"Look. I'm sorry."

"I understand. You got caught up in the moment. Just remember, if you're going to be a journalist, you need to be able to respect people. When you interview them, you have to meet them where they are, not where you think they oughta be. You don't have to like them. It's more important for *you* to understand *them* than for them to understand you."

Tom stared at the road ahead and bit his lower lip. "William, I'm not getting any younger. I don't know how much longer I have. Every day's a gift. I'm not sure what kind of world we've left for you guys, but it looks to me like a God-awful mess. I only hope that, with your talent for interviewing and writing, you can showcase those people who *are* making a positive difference."

William stifled his emotions and forced a smile. "You sound like Grandpa Harmon."

"Yeah. Well, he and I agree on *something* then."

"Pops, you know who I've always wanted to write about?"

"Who?"

"You. You promised me once that you'd tell me your life story."

Tom sighed and stared into the distance. "Okay."

William pulled out a pocket recorder and thumbed the button as he drove. "I appreciate your doing this. For starters, what are your earliest memories?"

"I don't know how much of this I actually remember and how much my grandparents told me. It was a hot summer day. I must have been three years old. My mom and I were sitting on a platform listening to my dad give a speech. He had just come home from the war . . ."

Epilogue

The Long Way Home

Atlanta
March 8, 2021

William returned from class to find Misty planting her newly plowed field. She stopped, leaned on her shovel and mopped her brow. As he strode toward her, she shaded her eyes against the afternoon sun and scanned his face. "What's the matter?"

"Mom called me at school. It's Pops. He's in the hospital. They think he had a stroke."

"Oh my God, William." She stopped. "I'll shower and change while you pack." She gave him a hard look. "And *I'm* driving."

They arrived at Atlanta's Northside Hospital to find Kathy struggling to console a grieving Brandy. Marie, Sean, Mary Frances, Lauren and Hari sat nearby in stunned silence. William stared at them, unwilling to accept their mute testimony.

Marie rushed to him and wrapped him in her arms. "He's gone."

In time, William's shock gave way to conversations with his extended family. From Kathy he got what he wanted most, the details of Tom's passing. Somehow, her compassionate explanations helped him detach himself, knowing there would be time and more time for him to process the loss of the one person who, besides Misty, had meant the most to him. Again, and again his thoughts returned to Tom's words on the ride back from Ball Ground . . . to the careful instructions he'd hoped would guide William for the rest of his life.

At some level he must have known he didn't have much longer. He'd wanted to die knowing he'd prepared me for the best future my passions and talents could provide.

A few feet away, Marie and Brandy had begun making funeral arrangements.

* * *

A mild breeze stirred the dense tree canopy as pencils of sunlight outlined names inscribed in marble, names William recognized from stories Tom had told him. A short distance away, fronted by a lush lawn and surrounded by resplendent azaleas, stood a white clapboard structure, its sole adornment, a gunmetal grey steeple, topped by a simple cross, pointing the way home for the saved.

Located just outside the tiny hamlet of Monrovia, Florida, the New Hope Baptist Church, William knew, had been a spiritual home for generations of Tom's family. Though it seemed to him a relic of a distant past, this tableau gave him a sense of his place in the great expanse of time . . . like a map in the mall with a red arrow reading, "You are here."

A black sedan pulled up, and a rear door opened. Kathy and Marie helped Father John O'Malley traverse the treacherous carpet of new-mown grass set in soft, sandy soil. William marveled at the stamina of the ninety-year-old priest.

He stopped long enough to take in the church and the grounds. If denominational differences bothered the good father, he gave no indication. "I understand this is where Thomas received the sacrament of holy baptism," he said in his thick brogue, "though with a bit more water than I'd have used."

As the priest greeted family members, a second car arrived, a small rental. Out stepped Henry Wakefield, late as usual, replete in the dress uniform of Wellington Academy. Gone were the curly, blonde locks. The whitewall haircut, high and tight, made William's brother all but unrecognizable.

As William went to greet him, Marie rushed past in a blur. William would never have guessed she could move so fast. As she threw herself upon her younger son, William stopped and gave him a small wave.

Over Marie's shoulder Henry smiled back. Beside him stood Lisa Chu, taller and even more beautiful than William remembered.

The crowd of mourners grew, joined by an attractive woman with medium length brown hair. Marie called to her, "Beth, so good of you to come. Did you have any trouble finding your way?"

"Not really," Long said. "I flew into Tallahassee last night and stayed at a Holiday Inn near Perry."

"You could have ridden with Kofi and me."

"I didn't want to intrude."

"Nonsense. Come here. I want you to meet everyone. I think you know my son, William. This is his brother, Henry. Everyone, this is my investigator, Beth Long."

Beth favored William with an ironic smile. "It's good to finally meet in person. I just wish it were under happier circumstances."

Glancing back, William saw Father John standing beside the open grave. "Mom," he said, "it's time."

"For those of you who happen to be Catholic," the priest announced, "I'll start by saying that I'm not here in any official capacity. The family has asked that I say a few words today on behalf of a man whom I've had the pleasure of calling my friend for many years."

He said a prayer, which William found mercifully brief. When he'd finished, Lauren held for him a gold-laminated Bible. "The family has asked that I read from St. Paul's Second Letter to Timothy."

For I am already being poured out like a libation, and the time of my departure is at hand. I have competed well. I have finished the race. I have kept the faith.

"I seriously doubt that Thomas Spivey Williams, born here in this lovely community, would ever have compared himself to St. Paul. Over the years there were times when I saw in him more of the saint for whom his parents named him. And yet, as I scan the faces here present, I see people for whom this passionate man gave his last ounce, borne out of a bottomless well of faith.

"I met Thomas when his late wife, Colleen Gentry Williams, first brought him and their daughters to the Shrine of the Immaculate Conception. He would sit in the back, as though unsure of his welcome . . ."

William could hardly imagine a more appropriate sendoff. Father John had been Tom's unofficial confessor in his darkest hours. Wishing to avoid conversation as he regathered his composure, he strolled among the graves of complete strangers.

A soft voice called to him, "William?"

He turned to find a woman who might have been a bit younger than his mom. Straight, blonde hair, cut just below her ears framed a careworn face that might have been beautiful once.

"My name is Dawn Sawyer," she said.

The name echoed from one of Tom's many stories. *The woman who shot her boyfriend on the steps of the Cobb County Courthouse.* "Dina Savage?"

"Please don't call me that. Dina Savage was someone I pretended to be a long time ago. Along the way, I did things that cost the lives of people whose only mistake was that they loved me. In the end, when others had abandoned me, your grandfather visited me in prison. A couple of years ago he stopped by again. He told me he had taken you on a cross-country trip and was returning to Atlanta. I can't tell you what he meant to me. I never knew my own father, but your grandfather was as close to one as I could imagine. I promised I'd come see him when I got out. They paroled me three days ago."

* * *

As the interment concluded, the family gathered under a canopy erected beside the church. Kathy again thanked those who had come so far to celebrate Tom's life. With Marie beside her, she described him as a man of many moods, but always a loving husband, father and grandfather.

Later, as William and Misty chatted with Marie and Brandy, filling them in on their latest work at the farm, Marie turned to Brandy and said in a tone William could barely discern, "Brandy, I meant to tell you this earlier. Dad named me executor of his estate. He left the condominium for your use for the rest of your life."

Taken aback, Brandy struggled for words. "Oh my! I don't know what to say. I had planned to move to Apopka to live with my sister."

"Well, think about it. We'd love to have you stay in Smyrna."

"I will. This is all so . . . unexpected."

"Brandy, will you need help caring for Bogie?" William asked.

"To be honest, I hadn't given it any thought. I have a neighbor taking care of him right now." She paused and studied William as though reading tea leaves. "William, your grandpa would have wanted *you* to have that dog, I just know it."

Unable to speak, William turned to Misty.

Smiling through tears, she said, "Brandy, Bogie will have a loving home with us on the farm."

"Then that settles it," said Brandy. "Why don't you stop by the condo on your way home?"

A voice called out. A middle-aged man, medium height with a round, pleasant face extended his hand. "William, I don't know if you remember me. I'm Mitch Danner."

"Yes. Hey, Mr. Danner."

"I was talking with your grandpa a few months ago, and he told me you were coming along with your journalism degree. I found out from a buddy of mine that there's an opening at the *Atlanta Business Chronicle*. I didn't know if you'd be interested . . ."

"I appreciate your thinking about me, Mr. Danner, and that would be a dream assignment, but I . . . uhm . . . have a long-term commitment in Barrow County."

He turned to Misty, who held out her left hand to reveal a large engagement ring.

Kathy turned to Marie.

"Did you know this?" she asked.

"Yep," Marie said, tears painting her cheeks. "You recognize it?"

"Oh my God! You gave him Mom's . . ."

"Yep."

* * *

Standing on the back stoop of the old farmhouse, William gave the new Frisbee a spin. Bogie chased after it as well as his arthritic joints would permit.

"You need to put him on some medication," Misty said.

"First thing in the morning."

William studied the dog as he sniffed and pawed at a mound of newly tilled earth. "I'll need to put up a new fence around the garden, with chicken wire beneath."

"He seems to like it here."

"He makes our little family complete."

As he gazed out upon the small homestead, William remembered something he'd wanted to say what seemed like ages ago. He turned to Misty and stared into her eyes. "Someday, hopefully decades hence, when I draw my last breath, I want the memory of this day to be my last thought. Then I'll know I've had a happy life."

The End

About the Author

A writer, lecturer and consultant, Ray Dan Parker lives in suburban Atlanta with his wife of more than forty years. When not writing, he spends his time working outdoors, teaching and serving in his community.

As a student at the University of Georgia, Mr. Parker studied literature and history and wrote for several campus publications. It was there he developed his love of writing.

Mr. Parker's first novel, *Unfinished Business*, is the story of Tom Williams, a young newspaper writer who returns to his hometown in 1968 to investigate the deaths of his parents and the lynching of a friend for a murder he didn't commit. In his second novel, *Fly Away*, of the Tom Williams saga, Tom and his wife, Colleen, meet the lovely Dina Savage and her date, artist Liam Sanstrom. When Dina files assault charges against Liam, Tom discovers that she has no apparent past. In time, he traces her back to a tiny hamlet in Mississippi and a twenty-year-old unsolved murder.

Now Available!

RAY DAN PARKER

The Tom Williams Saga
Books 1 - 4

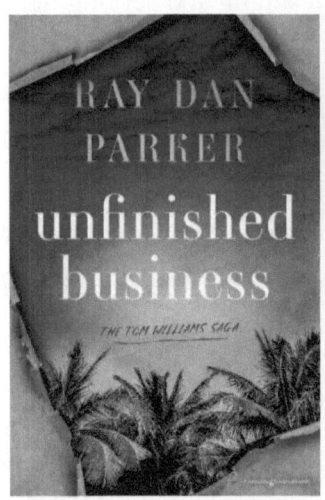

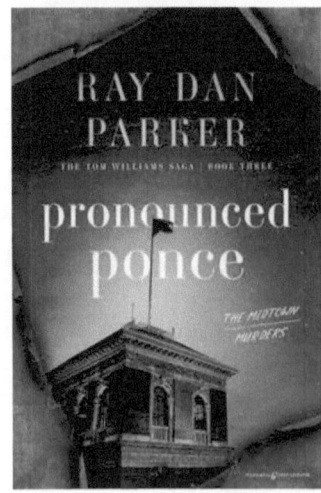
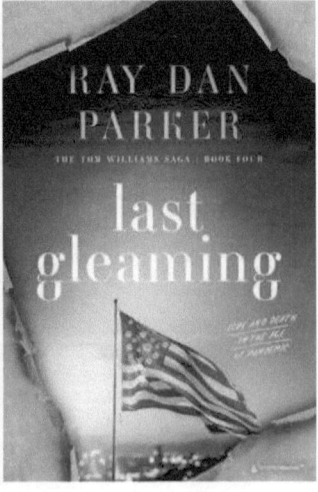

**For more information
visit: www.SpeakingVolumes.us**

Now Available!
CHARLENE WEXLER

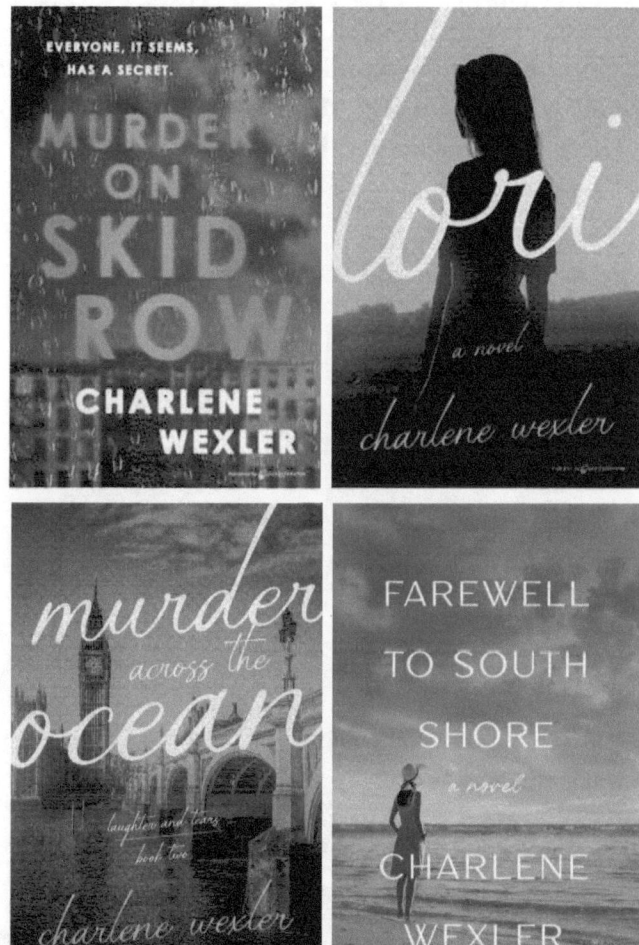

For more information visit: www.SpeakingVolumes.us

Now Available!

JAMES V. IRVING

JOTH PROCTOR FIXER MYSTERIES

"Irving's writing is relaxed and authentic and takes readers inside a compelling world of legal and social issues…"
—Bruce Kluger, columnist, USA Today

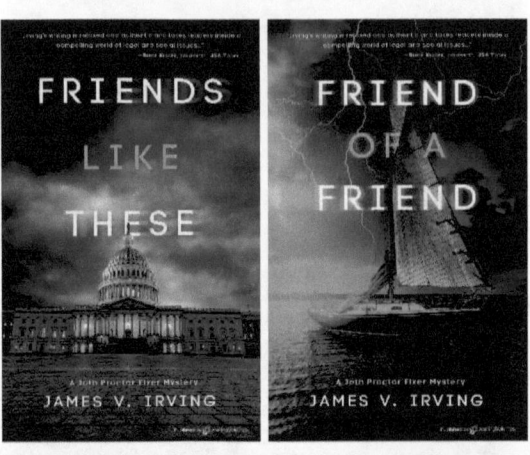

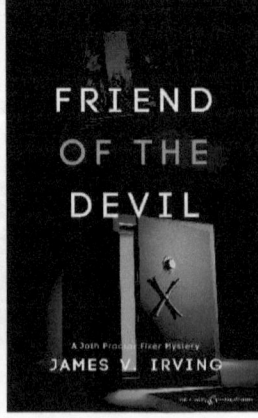

**For more information
visit:** www.SpeakingVolumes.us

www.ingramcontent.com/pod-product-compliance
Lightning Source LLC
LaVergne TN
LVHW041657060526
838201LV00043B/469